SINFUL LONGING

BY LAUREN BLAKELY

ALSO BY LAUREN BLAKELY

The Caught Up in Love Series (Each book in this series follows a different couple so each book can be read separately, or enjoyed as a series since characters crossover)

Caught Up in Her (A short prequel novella to
  Caught Up in Us)
Caught Up In Us
Pretending He's Mine
Trophy Husband
Stars in Their Eyes

Standalone Novels

BIG ROCK (Early 2016)
Mister Orgasm (2016)
Far Too Tempting
21 Stolen Kisses

The No Regrets Series

The Thrill of It
The Start of Us
Every Second With You

The Seductive Nights Series

First Night (Julia and Clay, prequel novella)
Night After Night (Julia and Clay, book one)
After This Night (Julia and Clay, book two)
One More Night (Julia and Clay, book three)
Nights With Him (A standalone novel about Michelle
  and Jack)

Forbidden Nights (A standalone novel about Nate and Casey)

Playing With Her Heart (A standalone novel about Jill and Davis)

The Sinful Nights Series

Sweet Sinful Nights
Sinful Desire
Sinful Longing
Sinful Love (2016)

The Fighting Fire Series

Burn For Me (Smith and Jamie)
Melt for Him (Megan and Becker)
Consumed By You (Travis and Cara)

The Sapphire Affair
A two-book series releasing Summer 2016

ABOUT

He's the inked brother. The one you're wondering about. The bad boy of the family.

Colin Sloan has a past. He's done things he's not proud of, but he's living differently now. Making changes in his life. Working hard, working out harder, and trying to win over one woman. He's utterly crazy about Elle Mariano, and though the sex is epic, their friends-with-benefits arrangement just isn't cutting it anymore. He wants all of her, and is determined to prove he's what she needs in her life.

Elle is fiery, loyal, and in major lust with Colin Sloan. He's everything she craves in a man—smart, sexy, kind—and a rock star between the sheets. But his past hits too close to home for her, and the people she has to protect. There isn't room in her life for a relationship with Colin. Especially when she's forced to keep a secret that could tear his family apart...

DEDICATION

This book is dedicated to Jen, for going
the distance on this series, and, as always,
to my dear friend Cynthia.

CHAPTER ONE

The Night of the Community Center Beethoven Benefit...

The sparrows were a treasure map, weaving a path from her right shoulder blade, along her sexy, elegant neck, then curving into her hair. Rich, chestnut hair he longed to have his hands in.

Preferably tonight.

Because... Well, why the hell not?

Especially since he'd learned to read her moods, and she was in *that* kind of a mood. As for him? Every time Colin was near Elle he was in *that* kind of mood.

This very second more so than usual, because her arms were wrapped around him in a triumphant hug, and she was exhaling big sighs of relief, and laughing, too, a buoyant sound, like bells. "I can't believe this happened," she said, breathless. "It feels like a dream."

"I didn't doubt it for a second. We're all behind you," he said, stealing a quick inhalation of the utterly enticing vanilla-honey scent of her shampoo.

She broke the embrace, but not the contact. She parked her hands on his shoulders, her fingers curling on his suit jacket. Her hazel eyes shone with happiness and a hint of joyful tears. "I know, and I'm so grateful," she said, her voice threatening to break. "But you just don't know 'til it happens if you're going to raise enough money, and I've been working on this for two years. Two solid years to finally get the funds to expand the center. It needs it so badly. I felt like I was holding my breath for the last month, hoping we'd make it. I have so many plans."

"And now you can take a breath because you made it happen," he said, beaming. She'd been driven in her mission to rebuild the broken-down community center, and he was damn pleased to be one of the donors supporting it. His venture capital firm had contributed significantly to the haul.

She wiped her fingertip under an eye, erasing the evidence of that tear. She shook her head in disbelief. Her eyes seemed to light up with the spark of an idea. "Colin," she whispered, as if they had a secret. And admittedly, they did. "We have to celebrate tonight."

He could think of a few ways.

Unknotting that hair.

Roping his fingers through it.

Kissing her neck 'til she fell apart in his arms.

"Do you want to? After the event?" she added in that conspiratorial tone. "I don't have much time, but we can manage something."

He scoffed. "What kind of question is that? Do you take me for a man who doesn't want to celebrate with you?" He was ready to rattle off a litany of suggestions. Anything to prolong the evening with her, especially since she'd changed her tune from earlier, when she'd called him incorrigible and told him to stop all this flirting. Now, her hands were on him again.

Elle was a seesaw when it came to him, and he'd learned to both deal with it and try to catch her on the upswings in his friend and now-and-again lover. Colin Sloan was a man who knew how to sniff out opportunity. He wasn't letting the opportunity in this giddy exuberance of hers slip away from him tonight.

"Not at all. You look like a man who wants to play poker with me tonight," she said, with a sexy arch of her eyebrow.

"The chips are on me," he said, glad that she wanted to cozy up to the tables, since they were like oysters for Elle— a bit of an aphrodisiac. By no means was Elle a high roller; the *baby tables*, as she called them, were her idea of a good time. Besides, the last time he'd had his hands on her was after she won a round of poker. She was a Vegas girl at heart, and winning amped up her adrenaline.

"I believe you just convinced me," she said in a flirty voice. God, he loved that tone. He fucking ate it up.

"A little poker. A little buffet. Maybe if you're lucky, I'll take you for some late-night roller rink action, too," he said with a wink, rattling off some of her other favorite things.

She narrowed her eyes. "Okay, that's just not fair. That's like putting steak out for a dog and not letting him have it."

"Did I say you couldn't have it? You know I'll give you everything."

She pursed her lips, as if she was considering his offer. Maybe all of it, from the evening to the *everything*. "Fine. I'll take the steak you're dangling."

He rubbed his hands together. "It's well done. You'll like it."

She laughed then tipped her head to the stage. "After the Beethoven. Obviously, I'm not skipping out early on an event for the center I run."

"You think that might look bad?" he asked, deadpan.

She crinkled her nose. "Just a little."

He held out his hands, playfully relenting. "Fine, we'll be good a little while longer." He brushed a strand of that chestnut hair over her ear, watching her shiver as he touched her. Why did she have to pull him in and then push him away? Let him get close then shove him off? Hot. Cold. On. Off. That was her style.

But he knew why she did it, and there wasn't a damn thing he could do about his past. He was the black sheep, and she didn't date black sheep. She'd made it one hundred percent clear from the get-go that they could never be a real couple, so he'd settled on what she *would* give—her body.

With a hand on her lower back, he guided her through the crowd to the fourth row and gestured to the first two chairs. "Why don't you sit in my lap?"

She rolled her eyes, then tapped his shoulder. She was terrible at sticking to her own rules about not touching him. He loved the lack of restraint in her. "I told you, we need to stop flirting."

"Yeah, you did," he said with a shrug as they took their seats. "But it's impossible. I can't be inside a ten-foot radius and not flirt with you. If you need me to stop, you should kick me out now."

She gathered up the silky material of her dress, adjusting it as she crossed her legs. Tilting her head toward him, she lowered her voice and confessed. "You know kicking you away isn't my strong suit, either."

As the opening notes of Beethoven's Ninth Symphony floated through the ballroom at the Venetian, Colin settled in beside Elle Mariano, the woman he'd wanted for the last year, since the first day he'd met her. The woman he'd been lucky enough to have in his arms a few times. Each encounter stoked the flames for another. Every second with her made him want her more. But she eluded him. For reasons his head understood. For reasons his heart girded to battle.

As the violinists poured forth rich notes, quickly shifting from a slow to a fast tempo, his own advice came to him.

Something he occasionally advised startups to do.

Don't give up.

He'd respected her relationship no-fly zone, but what if he tried a new approach? What if he aimed to win her heart by wooing her body?

She'd held up the stop sign on dating. But don't tell a man who wants to climb Everest that he can't do it. Nothing will motivate him more. Elle was his Everest. Not just having her, but having all of her. He'd keep trying. Keep scaling. Keep climbing.

He'd find a new way up the mountain.

He wasn't going to give up on her. Hell no. He was going to show her the time of her life in bed, and out of it.

Tonight would start with the bedroom.

CHAPTER TWO

His hip.

She was dying to see the new tattoo on his hip. And lord knew, she wasn't a hip woman. But she couldn't stop wondering what it looked like.

Because...*his body.*

His gorgeous inked body was her kryptonite.

All through the evening, as the symphony played, her mind kept returning to what Colin had told her earlier. He'd acquired a new tattoo, and he said it matched her favorite one on him. As she pictured the simple black lotus design on his right pec—the fine lines and details, the interlocking leaves of the lotus flower—a ribbon of heat unfurled in her chest, tracing a dangerous path from her breasts to her belly and down, down, down.

Warming her up.

Turning her on.

She closed her eyes and tried to focus on the music. Surely Beethoven never had these problems. But Elle? No such luck. Elle Mariano had an affliction, one she'd suffered from since she was a teenager. She liked boys too much. Now, she liked men too much. She liked dangerous men. Risky men. Tattooed men.

Like Colin.

She liked him way more than she should.

But she had no room in her life for this kind of longing. No room in her head for thoughts of how he looked when he unbuttoned his crisp white shirt, button by tantalizing button, revealing the body that visited her in all her bedtime fantasies. *His.* She would spread open the shirt, run her hands over his chest, and kiss and lick and nip that lotus tattoo, trace each fine line in it with the tip of her tongue.

She wanted what she couldn't have, and she most definitely couldn't have him, even though her body begged to disagree; it pulsed for this man by her side, just as it had since the day last year when he'd walked into her office at the community center, offering to volunteer.

Instant chemistry.

Desire in a bottle.

It had only grown stronger the more she knew him and talked to him, making it harder and harder to keep him at bay. That was the problem. The *big* problem. She had to draw boundaries with him. She'd made promises—being with him would break them. He was a line she couldn't cross. He was a risk she couldn't let herself take.

He rustled in the seat next to her, inching closer as the music crested. His sexy scent drifted under her nose. He smelled so fucking good. Like sex in an elevator. Like hot kisses on her neck that made her writhe.

"Do you like the music?" he whispered, his lips so close to her skin. Goose bumps rose on her flesh as she blinked open her eyes.

She nodded, trying desperately to let the violins and cellos, the flutes and bassoons, the sophisticated sounds floating from the stage, guide her thoughts to a sweeter, purer shore. To let the music take her away from these primal, base notions traipsing through the dirty meadows in her head. For the last month she'd done a good job resisting him, keeping him at an arm's length after she'd fallen into his arms again one night after a round of poker at the Wynn. Winning had excited her. He had excited her.

She would do better tonight.

Right?

Right.

She sneaked a peek at him, taking in the face she knew well. Strong cheekbones. Lightly stubbled jawline. Dark hair, nearly black, and so damn soft. Brown eyes, like chocolate. Sculpted lips that had kissed her many times. A body built by rock climbing, and hiking, and white water rafting, and Ironman triathlons, and oh God, why did she have to slam into his orbit tonight? She should have come alone to the benefit. She should have brought her sister. Her mother, even.

He raised a hand to adjust his tie—he was always doing that, as if ties weren't his thing—and her gaze settled on his fingers.

Magic fingers, she called them. She knew what they could do to her.

"Yes, I like the music," she said, trying to center herself.

"I do, too," he said softly, then stroked his chin. "It's beautiful. And it reminds me of something."

She raised an eyebrow. "What does it remind you of? Some other piece of music?" She hadn't known him to be a classical fan. He was rock, alternative, and indie music all the way.

He shook his head. "Not music. But something else I enjoy. Trying to remember exactly what."

"Tell me," she whispered, her curiosity now piqued. Her eyes met his. She searched those dark brown irises, as if she could find the answer there.

The sounds from the stage grew louder. "Wait. I think I know."

She widened her eyes, and held out her hands as if to say *tell me now.*

"Turn back to the stage. It helps me think."

She shot him a look, because that made no sense. Shrugging, she returned her focus to the musicians and the victorious sound of the final movement of Beethoven's Ninth.

"Ah, that's it," Colin whispered. "Now I remember. It reminds me of *that thing* you like so much."

That thing.

His fingers gently traveled up her neck. A small gasp escaped her lips. "Your neck. The way you move when I kiss you right here," he said, stopping to trace the outline of one of her birds with the pad of his thumb. She nearly moaned out loud. Elle was convinced every woman had a spot on her body that melted her from head to toe when touched the right way by the right man.

For Elle, it was her neck.

"How you sound when I touch your shoulder," he continued, letting his fingers graze her collarbone. Her bones turned liquid. Any ounce of resolve still left in her evaporated. She could say it was the thrill of the night, that it was the joy of hitting a massively vital professional goal, or perhaps it was the fact that no one had made her feel this way in years.

But none of that was true.

It was *him*. He just did something to her.

A shiver rolled down her spine. "No, it doesn't sound like that at all," she said, trying faintly to deny the way she responded to him.

He nodded vigorously. "Yes, it does. Just listen to that crescendo. It sounds like you when I— "

She grabbed his thigh and dug in her nails. The contact silenced him, but reminded her of how much she *liked* contact with him.

Great job, Elle.

Being so close to him was an injection of lust in her bloodstream, and Elle knew what happened when she was ruled by lust. She knew it well, and she had the lifetime of upended choices to show for it.

Not that she regretted anything in retrospect.

Not one bit.

But she was older and wiser now. Wasn't she?

She must be, because that wisdom was jostling its way to the front of her brain, trying to strike a deal with her body. They'd tangoed, they'd played—they'd done plenty. But she'd only fully had this man a few times. Maybe one more time and she could finally eradicate him from all her thoughts, from the dirty dreams that lasted all night and lingered too long during the day. She could say good-bye to these rampant hormones, and concentrate on her job, her family, and her promises.

There was no reason not to enjoy the final minutes of this evening to the fullest. One last night of passion, then she could move on from this turbulence of longing that engulfed her every time Colin Sloan was near. Let go of the longing, let go of him.

She couldn't have him in her life, but she could have one more night.

The concert ended, and the crowd applauded; their clapping and cheering rang through the ballroom.

Seize the night. She turned to face him. Arched an eyebrow. Took on his challenge.

Forget poker. She had other plans now. "So what's the new tattoo, Colin? You ready to show me?"

His eyes glinted with desire and satisfaction. "I will be after I take care of you first."

CHAPTER THREE

Moonlight bathed the patio at the Venetian. Slivers of silvery light reflected on the turquoise waters as he led her across the terrace to a secluded corner, behind planted palm trees, low stone walls, and hedges that framed the array of small pools.

"Where are we going?" she asked.

He nodded to the farthest corner, which boasted a tented cabana. "The after party for the benefit will be here on the private pool deck. But it doesn't start for a little while, so it's all ours for now."

"Except for the bartender setting up, and the waiters and waitresses," she whispered, gesturing to the bar they'd passed near the front entrance of the deck.

The patio was lush with greenery and fountains, like a New Orleans hotel courtyard. A warm July breeze stirred the foliage as Colin walked past, focused intently on his goal. He'd spotted the cabana only seconds ago, when they'd entered the pool area. He hadn't mapped out a location for an evening tryst. If he had, this would never have happened. With Elle, he had to take things as they came, moment by moment.

Luck and improvisation were his companions when it came to this woman.

That, and privacy. The cabana was all the way on the other side of the deck, away from the set-up crew.

Glancing behind him to make sure the coast was clear, he held open the flap to the cabana, and she walked in, turning in a circle, taking in the dimly lit tent with a handful of lounge chairs centered around a glass table. "Are we allowed to be here as they get ready?"

"No clue," he said with a shrug. "But I'm not afraid to break a few rules."

"You're trouble," she said, shaking her head.

"Yes, but you know that about me. Besides, you like trouble."

"Too much for my own good," she mumbled.

He pressed a finger gently to her lips. "Not tonight. No talk tonight of why we're a bad idea."

She bit her lip then flicked her tongue against his finger. A mischievous look flitted across her eyes.

He nodded, encouraging her to let go. "That's right. Tonight we're a *good* idea. Because tonight I'm going to make you feel things you've never felt before."

She inhaled sharply. Her skin shimmered with the flush of desire. It was a good look on her. "Like what?"

"You've worked hard to make a ton of people happy, and to make an incredible thing possible with the center. The next thirty minutes are all about you, and you're going to feel what it's like to be with someone who is obsessed with your pleasure. Every ounce of it, every inch of it, every second of it." He ran his other hand down her arm, leaving a trail of goose bumps in his wake.

"Colin," she said, as if she were trying to resist him. Trying futilely. "You say these things..." She trailed off as she seemed to collect her thoughts. "You say these things that make it so hard to resist you."

"Nah. That's not what makes it hard for you to resist me. This is." He tugged her body to his, letting her feel his erection through their clothes.

She laughed. "Fine. You win for best innuendo of the night," she said then pressed into him, her voice turning feathery, the way it did when she started to melt for him.

"Excellent. Let's see if I can win at making you want to come more desperately than you've ever wanted to in your life," he said, and her eyes widened, giving him a yes, telling him she wanted all the same things. To come hard in his arms.

God, he fucking loved getting her off. And taking his sweet time doing it.

He brushed his thumb over her top lip, tracing a soft line, and she parted her mouth, closing her eyes. But he didn't kiss her. He had something else planned. He moved his mouth to her ear and whispered, "How sensitive is your neck?"

"This isn't fair," she moaned in a feathery voice as he spun her around and sat her down on the end of a lounge chair. He stepped back a foot, so he could look in her eyes as he stripped off his jacket and tossed it on the back of the chair. The way she watched him sent bolts of lust through him. From the edge of her seat, she stared unabashedly, with hunger in her amber eyes.

"What's unfair about me giving you what you want?"

"Because you know I'll do anything if you touch me there," she said, raising her hand to the back of her neck as he unknotted his tie.

"Anything?" He arched an eyebrow. "Anything at all?"

"Pretty much."

"Anything sounds damn good to me. Besides, if you truly wanted me to do nothing, you wouldn't be here," he said, always ready to give her an out. In whatever capacity she was going to be with him, she had to be with him. To choose him. To want him.

She held out her arms and shrugged. "I want *anything.* Anything and everything with you."

"You can have it all with me."

He unbuttoned the cuff of his right shirtsleeve. His every nerve ending fired for this woman. How he felt for her was physical and so much more. Her passion for her work, her drive to make a difference, her heart that gave and gave and gave—all of it had spurred on his feelings. But then *this*—her body, her desire, her fucking fantastic face—she drove him wild. He was confident he did the same to her. He rolled up his other cuff, each fold of the crisp white shirt revealing the art that adorned his forearm. A sentence in curling script: *Nothing ventured, nothing gained.* It suited his job, but it had little to do with how he made a living. It was his mantra. It was how he lived. It was his mission in life ever since he'd taken the biggest chance years ago and gained so much in return.

"So tell me something," he said, moving closer, dropping his hand behind her to touch her lower back, then tracing a line up her spine with his fingertips. She arched into him, vertebra by vertebra.

"Yes?"

He bent his head closer to her ear, and whispered hotly, "Did you wear your hair up for me?"

She exhaled deeply, as if it cost her something. "Yes."

He dragged his index finger up the back of her neck, as he rested one knee on the lounge chair, positioning himself behind her so he could devote all his attention to her neck. "When you were getting ready at your house, were you thinking this might happen?"

She nodded.

"So you came here tonight already wanting me?" he asked as he stroked her skin.

"More than I should," she murmured.

"You think you shouldn't, but you're giving into it, aren't you? It sure looks that way to me."

"I am. You know I am," she said, and he could hear the fevered desperation in her tone. He was going to reward that wanting.

"Give in," he whispered. "I'll make it worth your while."

Lowering his mouth to her shoulder, he licked the line of birds up her neck and to the edge of her hair. She shuddered.

He smothered her neck in kisses. Up, down, across. Over her shoulder blades and back up her spine.

Every kiss unleashed another moan from her, a sexy gasp, a needy sigh. Noises that were only a prelude of what he wanted to hear from her tonight.

CHAPTER FOUR

Why, oh why, did he have to be off-limits? Why did he have to fall squarely under the heading of *do not pass go*? It was truly fucking unfair because no one had ever made her feel like this. Like she was high on a touch. Like she was deliciously dizzy from a kiss. She wanted him so badly, and not just physically. She wanted more of him, but her emotions had to be cordoned off tonight. She told herself to let go for this one last night, let go of everything but the way he made her feel so alive.

"Close your eyes," he told her firmly, and she let her eyelids drift closed, giving in to sense. Giving in to touch.

Maybe she was selfish. Or maybe she just wanted to feel a little something that was solely for her tonight. Nobody could deliver that better than this man.

He was kneeling behind her. She couldn't even see him. But she was keenly aware of his presence as he dipped his mouth closer to her skin. His lips fluttered over her sensitive neck once more. She ached, pulsing between her legs as he kissed her all over. A snapping sound fell on her ear, and her hair spilled from its clip onto her neck as he undid her twist.

"Oh God," she gasped, because she knew what was next.

His hands dove into her hair.

Fuck me now. Just fuck me now.

He'd discovered all her secrets the very first time he'd kissed her and explored her body. He'd read her responses as if it were his top-secret assignment to know every inch of her skin, then he'd remembered and sought them out, focusing on all the places that drove her wild. The back of her knee. The inside of her arm. Her neck, the gateway to her pleasure.

She was hopeless with him. He'd unlocked the code to all her desires, and he used it masterfully.

He threaded his talented fingers through her curls, gripping, and she moved with him, moaned for him, as if she were the notes he played on a cello. He was the musician; she was the instrument. He played and he played and he played, and her body sang for him, a song of pure desire. Of heat. Of want.

He twisted her hair once around his hand, pulling it to the side, and she tilted her head that way, giving him more room to devour her neck with kisses, like he was starved for her. He lavished pleasure all over her, leaving her drenched in sensation from soft, fluttery whispers along her neck, territorial kisses that claimed her as his, all mixed with the whiskery rub of his stubble. His ever-present scruff was trimmed to mere millimeters but long enough to brush against her skin with every kiss, bringing the intoxicating mix of soft and hard, of rough and tender. He rubbed his chin along her shoulder, and she arched into him.

He snaked an arm over her shoulders, grazing along her breasts as he traveled down her belly, his fingertips dancing against her waist.

"You like what I do to you." It wasn't a question.

"So incredibly much," she said, as he flicked the tip of his tongue across her shoulder. When he kissed her like this, and he touched her like that, she wanted to give herself to him fully. The way he wanted. The way he'd asked for. A voice in the back of her head started to argue with her, to warn her what happened when she made choices in heated moments like this, and she tensed for an instant.

But this was different. This was a moment she was choosing to relish. A night of pleasure.

His hand reached the crest of her hip and her brain went dormant. He traced the top of her panties through the fabric of her dress. "Show me how much you like giving in. Show me how wet you are."

She yanked up her skirt, bunching it near her waist, giving him instant access to the *V* of her legs. Even with her panties on, there was no hiding her arousal.

He groaned huskily. "Look at you, Elle. Look at how wet you get. For me." His fingers glided up the soft flesh of her thighs, and she parted her legs for him. Grazing the wet panel, he whispered, "I want to feel that all over my dick. I want this sweet wetness all the fuck over me. Tell me how much you want me inside you right now. Tell me."

"Oh God," she panted. "Yes, God yes. I want that. I want it so much."

"You want *it*?"

"*You*," she said quickly, correcting her error. "I want you so much."

"I want you to want me even more," he said then took his hand away from her wet heat, returning both to her shoulders, sliding them up her neck to her hairline. He grabbed her hair, wound it all up in his fist and pulled hard, making her shudder. He bit the back of her neck, his teeth rough on her flesh.

She gasped as he soothed away the sting with his lips. She was nothing but cells and atoms, electrons and protons, smashing and colliding into lust and desire, and she could barely track where he was on her body. His lips were on her shoulders, her neck, her throat, then her jaw, her ears, her cheeks. His hands pressed into her breasts. His fingers raced down her arms. His erection rubbed against her spine through his clothes, making her gasp and want to beg for him.

And there, right there between her legs, she was an inferno for him. She arched her hips and said his name like a chant. He'd trapped her and she wanted to be his captive— captive 'til she came. "*Colin*," she said. "I can't take it anymore."

"Tell me what you want most this second. Tell me," he said, his voice hot and demanding.

The answer was easy. There was only one thing she needed. "I need to come, Colin. Please, I need to come so badly."

In a flash he rose, lifted her, and set her on her feet. She turned around and skimmed off her panties. He sank down on the end of the chair.

"Unzip my pants," he told her. With greedy, eager fingers, she bent forward and did as he asked, tugging his pants to his thighs, then his boxer briefs, freeing his cock. Her mouth watered as she stared at his erection—hard, heavy, and so fucking long. So many glorious, gorgeous inches that she loved to take deep inside her.

He pressed a condom into her hand, and she quickly opened it then rolled it on him, stopping only when she spotted the new ink on his hip. A simple black phoenix, akin to a stencil design. It matched the lotus, like he'd said. Matched it in symbolism.

"For new beginnings," she whispered softly, tracing it with her fingertip. It mesmerized her, the art and lines, the placement on his body, but she shook off her reaction because she didn't want to think of beginnings. She wanted to think only of ending this epic ache in her body.

She straddled him. His fingers grasped her hips, and she lowered herself onto his shaft. She was ready to build a shrine, to make holy offerings, because he was divine. Anyone who said size didn't matter had never experienced the unmitigated erotic joy of this kind of cock filling her up. Yeah, the motion of the ocean mattered, but so did the size of the boat. Long, thick, and steely, his dick operated like a precision-timed machine of pleasure.

She moaned, stilling for just a moment to savor that delicious stretch of taking him all the way in, her slippery heat coating his cock. "I almost forgot how good you feel," she said as she started to move on him.

"That would be a damn shame. We shouldn't let that happen," he said, thrusting up into her.

She clenched around him. "No, we shouldn't because this is…"

Words stopped forming as he drove into her. Gripping her hips, he jerked her down harder, filling her deeper.

"This is what, Elle?" he asked, his voice a sexy taunt, urging her on.

"Intense," she said on an exhale, as he filled her so deliriously she nearly screamed. She was vaguely aware that there could be people nearby—workers, waiters, bartenders—and she somehow found the will not to sing and shout her pleasure to the stars. But she felt it. The intensity thrummed in her bones, sizzled across her skin. "Incredible. It's so incredible," she said on a moan, as he thrust into her.

Then, because he was a fucking expert, because he'd studied all the shortcuts to her pleasure, he looped his fingers in her hair and pulled hard, exposing her throat to him. That was like an electric burst of ecstasy.

"Fucking you is the best," he said, layering kisses onto her skin. "You get so wet, and I love how it feels to slide into you over and over."

"Tell me how it makes you feel," she said, losing touch with the earth as he talked to her, his dirty words sending her into a tailspin. The way he spoke to her was such an insane turn on, and she was already aroused beyond her own comprehension. He kissed the hollow of her throat and drove his cock deep into her.

"It's fucking extraordinary. Being inside you is extraordinary. And I love it when you come on me." He slid a finger between her legs, brushed it lightly against her clit, and her lips parted, forming an *O*. A silent, glorious *O*, containing all the pleasure in the universe. He'd flipped that switch, pushing her from chasing an orgasm to falling apart in his arms. She shuddered, pleasure wracking her cells, racing through her to flood every corner.

Helpless to stay quiet, she felt her silent cry turn to an audible moan as she shouted the beginning of his name. He clamped a hand over her mouth, covering her noises as he thrust up into her like a mad man on a frenzied ride, desperate to follow her to the other side. He fucked her as aftershocks rippled through her, the sensation spreading to her fingers and toes.

As her moans subsided, he dropped his hand from her mouth and gripped her waist. She opened her eyes, watching him, loving the way he looked when he came. Nothing was sexier, nothing was hotter than watching the man she wanted lose control.

All for her.

She didn't understand why, but somehow she was his undoing.

And he was hers.

He fucked her into his own release, his eyes squeezed shut and his face contorted in pleasure. He grunted, and groaned her name before biting her collarbone, holding in all his sounds, too, as he came.

"We can't stop," she whispered, voicing the most dangerous words. Words she shouldn't say. But her body had the reins, making decisions for her, seeking more bliss.

"We can't and we shouldn't," he murmured, layering soft kisses on her neck.

Soon, as they came down from their high and her senses reattuned to the world around her, the tinkling of glasses reached her ears. The after party was starting…

Which meant.

She was about to become a pumpkin.

From inside her clutch purse, the alarm sounded on her phone.

"I have to go. My mom has a shift at eleven. I told her I'd be home by ten-thirty."

"I'll walk you to your car," he said.

In the parking garage, he cupped her cheek gently, pressed his lips to hers, and gave her a sweet good-bye kiss that would linger on the whole way home.

He whispered, "Go."

In three minutes, she was on the road, rushing to return home to her son.

CHAPTER FIVE

Her mother's head was bent over the kitchen counter, her fingers swiping in a wild blur across her phone screen.

"Gotcha, flesh-eater!"

"Saving the world, Mom?" Elle asked, as she closed the front door to her apartment.

"Somebody has to fend off the infected," her mom said with a final slide before she looked up and closed the game.

Elle laughed. "I thought you were giving it up. You said it was giving you video game thumb or something."

Her mother shook her head, her bouncy ponytail swinging with her. "I tried. Oh lord, you know I tried. But your son… He plays a mean game of *Dying Light*, and he challenged me. I can't back down."

"You're going to need to work on *State of Decay* next. Alex and his buddies are moving on in the apocalypse gaming world," Elle said, dropping her keys on the counter and giving her mom a peck on the cheek. Her mother wore green scrubs with Snoopys and Woodstocks on them. "How was he tonight?"

"Fine. Just fine. I plied him with pizza and schooled him with my survival skills."

"No easier way to the heart of a fourteen-year-old boy, is there?" While there was plenty of truth in her statement, for her son, video games weren't just the snack-food-and-candy path to winning his teenage heart—they were essential to his emotional survival. They were the difference between him talking and not talking.

Between speech and a complete breakdown.

Some parents might worry that their kids played too many video games, and while Elle set limits, she also knew what they meant for him. Because the time before? It was the end of the world. Black, empty, cold. A true pit of despair. In those dark days, she'd have given anything—a lung, a kidney, a limb—for him to talk to her. He'd shut down after his father died, completely withered, barely able to utter a word except for the essentials—*yes, no, I don't know.*

Understandable, given what he'd witnessed in their home on that night three years ago.

Somehow games, zombies, and post-apocalyptic stories became a portal for him. Elle never would have predicted it, but on the days after school when Alex would come by the center, he was drawn to the gaming room, and to the raucous energy of the boys shouting at the screen. After a year of being so traumatized by what he saw he'd gone nearly mute, video games reconnected the voice inside him to the rest of the world. They unlocked the part of him that he'd kept quiet, and how she loved to hear him shouting with his friends.

God bless the living dead.

And *The Walking Dead,* too. Alex's favorite show had become a key part of Elle's lexicon, since she had to stay up to speed with Sheriff Rick Grimes in order to converse with her son again. *Zombies.* Who would have thought zombies would rescue her son from the near-catatonic state that the death of his father had sent him into?

Her mother tucked the phone into her purse and gathered up her keys. "How was the benefit? Did you meet your goals?" Her mom held up her hand and twisted her index finger around her middle finger. "I had 'em crossed all night for you."

"We did. It was amazing," Elle said, and quickly gave a recap of the night. Well, the pre-pool-deck portion of the night.

Her mom beamed, then pumped a fist in the air and did a victory dance in the kitchen. "I knew it, I knew it, I knew it!"

The woman had amazing energy.

Elle's mom was pretty much the youngest grandma around. Like Elle, she'd started early when it came to baby making. Her mother was only eighteen when Elle was born. Barely fifty now, her mom poured her ample energy into her two grown daughters, her grandkids, her job as a nurse, and even her new boyfriend. She'd put herself through nursing school when Elle and her younger sister were toddlers, shuttling back and forth between day care and class, struggling to make ends meet with two little kids all to herself. She'd wanted different things for her daughters, and she'd achieved that with Camille, who'd wisely waited 'til she was out of college and married before getting knocked up.

Not Elle.

The bun unknowingly went in the oven on the night of high school graduation, when the condom broke with Sam, the guy who became her on-again-off-again boyfriend, then eventually her husband, then her nearly ex-husband, since she'd been separated from him the last few years of his life while he was on-again-and-off-again in all sorts of ways. On drugs. Off drugs. In rehab. Out of rehab. Like a merry-go-round that gave her whiplash and nothing else but heartache.

"I am so proud of you, baby," her mom said, walking around the counter and clasping Elle in a big hug. "You worked so hard for this, and those kids need you. You have done so much for them."

Her throat hitched. "I'm lucky to work with them."

Her mom stiffened and wrenched back, narrowing her eyes. "Young lady, didn't you have your hair up when you left?" She arched an all-knowing eyebrow that somehow had the power to see right through her daughter.

But Elle wasn't eighteen. She was thirty-two, and she didn't have to hide her activities. Elle patted her mussed-up hair, then raised her chin up high. "I did have it up, but someone took it down."

Her mother held up a palm to high-five her then snapped it back. "Say you used protection. Did you use a condom, young lady?"

Elle rolled her eyes. "Yes, Mommy. I used a condom," she said in a sing-song voice. "And I'm on the pill. So don't worry your pretty little head about me."

"As if I could ever not worry about my baby girl," she scoffed. "Wait. Was it good? Will we see him around here?"

Elle shook her head.

"It wasn't good?"

Elle laughed. "Yes. It was amazing, as in out-of-this-world epic, incredible. But no, you won't see him around. He's not the type of guy I can have a relationship with."

"Why not? Is he an asshole?"

"Definitely not."

Her mom parked her hands on her hips. "Then what is it?"

Elle shooed her to the door. "Get out of here. You're going to be late for your shift. You have fifteen minutes to get to the hospital." Her mom fixed her with a stare that said *this conversation isn't over, missy,* and Elle rolled her eyes. "I love you, but you need to skedaddle. Thank you again."

"Anytime," she said and walked out. But in two seconds, she popped the door back open and held up a finger. "And 'anytime' also applies if you want to booty call this epic, incredible, out-of-this-world guy again, and you need a warm body here. You know where to find me. Because I've got some flesh-eaters to destroy with my grandson."

"Your booty call offer is duly noted," Elle said, then shut and locked the door and walked down the hall to check on her son. Alex was sound asleep, curled up under the covers, air conditioning rattling loudly in his pigsty bedroom. His dark hair was a wild mess and would be sticking up in all directions in the morning. She bent down and dropped a quick kiss on his forehead.

"Night, sleepy boy," she said, then left his room and returned to the living room where she sank down on the couch.

And waited.

Waited to feel the regret.

Waited to feel the shame.

Waited to feel the sting of her bad choices.

She sat, watching the clock, then closed her eyes, trying to meditate, aiming to let her mind clear so she would feel all the things she was supposed to feel after sleeping with a man like Colin. All the things that gnawed at her and vexed her. That nagged and twisted away at her heart. The things that would cement her decision to make this the last time with him.

When she opened her eyes, she didn't feel any of those things. Not a one.

Instead, she simply felt...good.

What the hell? She wasn't supposed to feel okay. Being with Colin broke promises. She needed to feel like shit so she wouldn't go there again with that man.

Maybe a distraction would let the feeling sneak up on her. Leaning forward, she grabbed the game controller from the coffee table and turned on the TV. Lowering the volume so as not to wake her son, she proceeded to blast through a town of the infected, quickly clearing several blocks of zombies as night fell in video-game land. When a flesh-eater appeared out of nowhere, she panicked.

"You need to run away."

Pausing the game, Elle leaned her head back and looked up at her son. "I do?"

With his rumpled hair, basketball shorts, and gray T-shirt, he walked around the couch, and parked himself next to her. "Yeah, you don't have to fight the super zombies every time. If you successfully run away from them, you can level up your agility skills."

"My agility skills suck," Elle admitted, then added, "Why are you up?"

"Had to pee. Is that a crime?"

"Not that I'm aware of. I'll let you know if that changes though."

Alex laughed and grabbed the controller. "I'll show you how to run away from the zombies."

"Run! Run! C'mon you can do it," she said in a rah-rah voice to the big screen.

He swiveled his head to stare at her, then rolled his eyes. Typical fourteen-year-old. "No cheering, Mom. Anyway, here's how it's done," he said, turning the game back on and demonstrating his speed and skill in evading the enemy. "Now, we just need to get back to the safe house."

"So does this count if you're playing for me?"

He nodded. "Of course. I'm like your pinch hitter."

"When we enter the Xbox tournament, can you just fill in for me when I get in a pickle?"

"If there's a tournament and you're holding out on letting me play in it, you're in big trouble," he said, his voice deepening on the final words as he attacked bad guys on the screen.

"Hey! Your voice just went all crazy low there," she said, in her own imitation of a baritone. Alex had been hovering in voice-changing limbo for so long she was sure he was going to set some kind of record. While his friends paraded in and out of the home with Al Greene-esque vocal stylings as they sailed over that cusp of adolescence, Alex was still swinging in between the higher-pitched boy's voice and the deeper notes of an older teen.

"Mom, my voice is fine," he said then thrust the controller into her hand, his way of saying any conversation that dared to touch on the horrific topic of puberty was so over they'd need a new word for it.

"Fine, fine," she said, holding up her hands in surrender. "Forget I said a word about your voice."

"It's forgotten." He yawned. "Try not to get killed before you get back to the safe house."

"I'll do my best. See you in the morning, sleepyhead."

"See you in the morning," he echoed, and returned to his room.

A few minutes later, she flicked off the game. Late-night encounters like that—random, casual, exceedingly normal —had a way of settling her nerves and calming her heart. Things were back to business as usual with Alex, and she was so damn grateful for that.

The question remained, though—what the hell was she going to do about Colin? Tonight was supposed to rid her dirty dreams of him. But who was she kidding? What woman in her rightful mind would want to ditch *that*? She made her way to her bedroom, stripping out of her evening dress and completely useless panties. She tossed them in the hamper on top of her roller derby uniform from last night's game, laughing to herself over the number of pairs of panties he'd melted right off her.

One time at the center, he'd stopped by her office to chit-chat after his volunteer shift and somehow his hands had wound up on her shoulders, and he'd given her one of the best massages she'd ever had, undoing the knots of tension in her shoulders, all while turning her on. Yup, a pair melted that afternoon. A few weeks later, her first kiss with him had pretty much scorched her body and fried all her brain cells. After a movie for the kids in the rec room, he'd stayed behind to help her straighten up, and when they were through disposing of bags of microwave popcorn and washing their hands, she'd turned around to find him behind her at the sink, a hungry look in his dark eyes.

There were no questions. They'd smashed into each other, all sizzle and heat and pent-up desire.

She pulled on a fresh, clean pair of undies, and a soft, faded cotton tee. She headed to her bathroom and scrubbed off all her makeup, staring at the calligraphy *T* tattooed on her wrist. T for her roller derby name. She dried her face and brushed out her hair.

Okay, the evidence of her evening was gone. She was ready to shed Colin, too. Just molt him off, like a snake's skin.

And yet, she couldn't stop thinking about him.

Elle had wanted Colin since the day she'd met him. The initial reaction had been purely chemical. It had been instant and intense, and so damn easy to write off as lust. From his broody eyes, to his dark hair, to the body that was everything she'd dreamt up late at night when spending time with her toys—because she had a drawer full, and the dirty books to go along with them. Fuck romance novels; Elle went straight for the hard stuff. Dirty, filthy short stories that took the edge off her days, helping her sleep peacefully at night, so different from the time when she used to twist and turn under the covers, haunted by memories, by broken vows, and fights. By *this time will be different* pleas. Then she discovered she could self-medicate with erotica to relieve the tension in her brain and body and send herself to the land of nod, courtesy of a naughty fireman ménage story or a horny, hot professor tale paired with her battery-operated Joy Delivered rabbit.

But soon her late-night fantasies zeroed in on one man. Colin Sloan—tall, tatted, tempting, witty, and forthright.

The more she got to know him, the more she liked him, and once they touched…it was a pure rush.

He wasn't an asshole. He was a very good guy.

Maybe sex with him tonight hadn't been the worst idea in the world.

As she flopped down on her bed, shoving a hand through her hair, she found herself wondering if she could have it both ways.

After years of nothing but broken promises from Alex's father, she'd vowed never to put her son in a situation where they might face the demons of addiction again. True, Colin was a recovering addict, but he was still an addict. And an addict was an addict was an addict.

No two ways about it.

Hell, Alex's father had been in and out of rehab so many times you'd think he'd invented the revolving door. He'd sober up, then he'd relapse. Lather, rinse, repeat. That was the pattern with people like him. Before she joined the center as director, she ran several addiction recovery groups as a social worker, and she was well aware of the stark reality of the disease—half of recovering addicts would relapse at some point.

Half.

It could happen with anyone. It could happen with Colin. He had a hell of a history trailing behind him. Sure, the art on his body symbolized his struggle and his sobriety, but while she admired that sobriety deeply, she didn't trust it.

Because she couldn't trust anyone's sobriety one hundred percent, not when it involved the person she loved most in the world—her boy. She had the scars on her heart, the countless nights of lost sleep, the never-ending battles, and bargains, and empty pleas from Alex's dad to prove sobriety didn't always stick.

She'd taken ten thousand chances with the father of her child, and they'd nearly destroyed her and her son. All those chances had ripped her life to shreds, and she'd finally put the pieces back together. How could she take even one with a man she was simply hot for?

Even for someone who seemed together. Even for someone who lived a life of recovery.

But as she tugged the sheets over her body—her body that still hummed with leftover bliss from earlier—she asked *what if.* What if she didn't let Colin into her life or her home? What if she kept him neatly in an after-hours box like she'd done tonight? Hell, she'd managed an orgiastic frenzy of mind-blowing kissing and epic fucking, and it hadn't spilled into her life with her son, who'd been busy warring with zombies and gobbling pizza with his grandma —the same woman who was willing to aid and abet another "booty call." And her own run-in with Alex in the living room had been as normal as they came. Nothing bad had happened from her choice tonight.

Maybe, just maybe, she could manage something with Colin that never got serious. That never crossed the line. That remained below the belt. She could separate the emotions from the sex. The connection from the hotness. She could be with him out of the house and still come home to her son.

She'd maintain her boundaries. Only sex. Only contact. No strings allowed.

Crazy idea?

Perhaps.

Or perhaps it was brilliant.

She picked up her phone and texted Colin.

I still want you.

His reply arrived two minutes later, and they quickly bantered.

Colin: You can have me anytime.

Elle: Anytime, anywhere?

Colin: I believe we established the anywhere tonight. But there was also the time on the hiking path and on the stair-well at the library. If you needed a reminder of our ingenu-ity in finding places.

Elle smiled wickedly at the memory of the day he'd given her a ride home after his volunteer shift and stopped at the library so she could pick up a book she'd reserved. He'd gone in with her, hunting for a new paperback, and when she found him in the stacks, he'd proceeded to kiss the hell out of her, turning her so hot and molten that she'd decided she had to have him right then and there. In the stairwell at the public library. God, she was reckless with him. It had been amazing. A few weeks later, he'd in-vited her to go hiking when Alex was away with friends for the weekend, so they'd hiked high in the hills, under the sun, and gotten hot and sweaty. Then hotter and sweatier in a secluded patch of woods shielded by a boulder, when he'd shown her precisely how magic his fingers were as he fucked her with them, standing up against a tree, next to a stream.

Mother nature rocked.

So did automobiles. They'd screwed in his car after she'd won at poker a few weeks ago.

Elle: The stream was good, too. Everything with you has been.

Colin: Good or excellent?

Elle: Excellent. Most excellent. So excellent I want more. I think Wednesday night could work?

Colin: You let me know the time, and I will not only be at your service, I will service you until you can't think straight and you risk turning into the most orgasmic woman in the history of the universe. Just wanted to give you fair warning.

Elle: Consider me warned.

CHAPTER SIX

The band sang of eyes of the bluest skies, jarring her
awake.

Her ring tone. Guns N' Roses.

Bleary-eyed and still groggy, she fumbled for her phone
on the nightstand.

Squinting, she spied the edge of the red number on her
clock radio—eight-thirty in the morning.

On a Sunday.

Crap.

It was too early for anyone to be calling with good news.

An all too-familiar burst of panic blasted through her
when she saw "unknown number" on the screen. When
Sam had called from his many stints in rehab, the number
had always shown up as unknown. Likewise, the times he'd
rung her up while out partying, plastered and begging her
to take him back, he would block his number.

Logically, Elle knew that Sam wasn't calling her from
the grave. But a rabid fear pulsed through her nonetheless.
She swiped her finger across the screen, sitting up in bed
and doing her best to clear the sound of sleep from her

voice in case it was a client or one of the kids she counseled at the center. They all had her number. It was on the website for the center, along with her bio about how much she enjoyed being involved in helping the kids in the community.

"Hello?"

"Hey. It's Marcus."

"Hey there. What's going on?" Marcus was one of the boys who played hoops at the center from time to time. "Are you trying to get into the center on a Sunday? We don't open until ten. One of the volunteers should be there then."

"No, actually. I'm not," he said, speaking tentatively, the vocal equivalent of shuffling his feet. "I'm sorry to bug you so early. I've been thinking about what we've been talking about, and I'm finally ready to do something."

"Okay. Tell me more." She knew a little bit of his story. He hadn't told her many specifics but he had started coming around the center a few months ago, when he'd graduated from high school and moved out of his family's house. Lately he'd been opening up to her. He'd been raised by his father and a stepmother; his biological mother was out of the picture. She didn't know much more than that, but his biological mother had other children, older siblings he wanted to connect with.

He cleared his throat and seemed to be drawing up his courage. "I just feel like I spent my whole life not knowing anything about my family and where I came from, and now I do. And my dad didn't want me to find them, but they're here in Vegas, and I'm not living at home anymore. So this is my choice. I need to do this."

She tossed back the covers and headed to her closet as she chatted with him. "Then you should do it. Something is compelling you to connect with them, and you need to listen. Family is a powerful pull and a potent bond, and you've never had a chance to get to know them," she said as she pulled on jeans, crooking her head against the phone as she zipped them up.

"But what if they don't want to meet me?" he asked in a flurry, as if he had to spill out all the words in order to say them. She heard the tumultuousness in his voice. One moment he was courageous, the next he was hampered by fear. She wished she could cheer him on in person on this mission.

"Look, Marcus. I'm not going to sugarcoat this for you. They might have zero interest in getting to know you. They might not care. They might be so busy with their lives that they could give a rat's butt. But this is in you," she said, feeling a bit like a football coach giving a half-time speech. "You are trying to take a big step, wanting to connect with siblings you've never known, and that is bold."

There was something quite soap opera-esque about his quest. The long-lost half brother...appearing out of nowhere...showing up on the doorstep of older brothers. But as soapy as it seemed on the surface, Elle had seen enough of the drama and danger in the world to know these scenarios were far more frequent than anyone would think.

"My dad once mentioned that one of them was closest to my mom, so I think I'll start with him. Plus, he has a dog, so he's out and about a lot in his neighborhood."

Her antenna went up. "How do you know that?"

"Um."

"Marcus, have you been following them around?" she asked sternly.

"Maybe," he muttered.

"That's not a good idea. It can freak people out. You need to be direct. If you want to meet them you need to man up and go over there. Don't follow people. It's creepy. Makes them think you're dangerous. You're not, are you?" she said, like a teacher doling out tough love. Some days she had to play that role with the boys and girls at the center. But hell, that was why she went into counseling and social work—for the chance to make a difference with young people who needed it most. Some of the kids who hung out at her center had been teetering on the edge: living in poverty, raised by drug-addicted parents, born to fathers or mothers in jail, or plain damn neglectful ones.

And gangs. Lord knew some of these kids had been tempted. Street gangs, like the Royal Sinners, preyed upon the young and the vulnerable, promising them riches through crime. She hated that gang; hated the way they tempted the kids; hated the way they ruined lives.

"I'm not dangerous. I swear. I'm just..." He stopped speaking, letting his voice trail off.

"You're scared," she supplied, speaking softly.

"Yes," he said in the barest voice.

"Remember what we talked about?"

"*Rise above*," he said, echoing Elle's mantra, which she tried to instill in the kids.

"Yes. Rise above. You can be so much. If your goal is to meet the family you've never known, I'm behind you. But you have to stop stalking them. Do not let fear guide you. Rise above it."

"Okay. I'm going to do it. I'm going to head over to this guy's home," he said, his voice stronger and more confident now.

She beamed as she wandered to the kitchen and grabbed a carton of eggs from the fridge. "Let me know how it goes. I want a full report," she said, then ended the call and began cracking eggs and cooking breakfast for her son, who padded out from his bedroom a few minutes later.

"Hi, Mom."

Her heart went warm all over. Her brain was flooded with pure happiness.

Hi, Mom.

The simplest thing in the world but it was music to her ears.

* * *

Colin scratched his head as he surveyed the six-packs in the beer section at the local Safeway near his brother Ryan's home. He hadn't touched a drop of alcohol in eight years, and he honestly wasn't sure what anybody drank when it came to beer in the first place. But Shannon had told him to grab some brew for their brother Ryan, since he was in some kind of a bad funk, and Ryan was a beer man. If Shannon had asked him to grab tequila, Colin would have been in and out of the liquor store in ten seconds with a beautiful bottle of Patrón—that was like liquid diamonds. Colin could have written a dissertation on the stuff. For many years, tequila was his best friend, his most reliable companion, his steady mate.

Hell, he and tequila had been deeply in love. You never forget your first love, even if you sample others along the way. Colin had started hitting the liquor bottle right after his father was killed when he was thirteen. He'd only flirted with it then—he had friends with older brothers, absent parents, and keys to the liquor cabinet. That was what being buddies with the Royal Sinners did for you. Gave you access to all sorts of shit. Better stuff than alcohol, too. His best friend at the time was Paul Nelson, and Paul's older brother T.J. introduced the both of them to magic pills, because liquor was too risky for a teenager to pull off—the smell on your breath, the bottles in the trash...

But painkillers? They were the golden path to gliding through high school without your brothers, sister, or grandma knowing what you were up to. Colin had needed to numb the pain of missing his dad, hating his mom, and wishing his life hadn't taken that turn into pure hell. Oxy was far easier to hide than booze. Stash it in a sock. Stuff it into the bottom of your gym bag. Hide some in a Ziploc in the toe of your shoe. Nobody looked there. No one suspected. Pop a few of those bad boys in the morning and cruise through trigonometry, European history, English lit.

Getting straight As did wonders to hide the problem and kept his family from discovering all the help he got from his little friends.

College was a dream—he didn't have to worry anymore about his family finding out, so he could party all night, mix pills with tequila, and slam some Adderall the next day to speed up his brain in class. Worked like a charm. He grand-slammed his way through college, acing all his economics and business management classes while high, buzzed, or on speed.

Nothing could stop him.

Nothing except collapsing during the triathlon he'd competed in at twenty-three, dehydrated from spending too much time with Señor Patrón the night before. He'd trained hard for it, too. The Badass Triathlon was not just the standard swim, bike, and run—it also included a rock climb. After you scaled the rock wall, you turned around and did the first three legs in reverse.

It had been hard as fuck. Exhausting as hell. Only for the hardcore athletes, and Colin, a cocky bastard then, was sure he could finish well even hung over.

Nope.

He'd fallen as he climbed, and had he not partied too hard the night before, he'd have fallen correctly, sustaining only a few lacerations.

Instead he landed all wrong, injured his tibia, and passed out in Red Rock Canyon.

Emergency room.

Grandmother called in.

Brothers and sister told.

Job nearly lost.

Rock bottom.

There had been moments in those early days when he'd have given his left arm for another glass and his right for a handful of pills. Now, with eight years clean—no slips, no relapses, no *just one drinks*—he felt steady and calm. He'd made it through the hell of withdrawal, he'd had the support of friends and family in getting sober, and he relied on a solid network of like-minded men in his recovery support group. Every day, he aimed to live according to a new way of thinking—a sober way—and he honestly wasn't tempted anymore when he walked past tequila on the shelf, or saw a glass being served at a bar.

But beer? That shit was nasty. He didn't have a clue what anyone liked, so he grabbed some Corona and headed to the self-checkout. As he slipped his debit card through the register, a flurry of nerves skated up his spine. What if his sponsor Kevin saw him? Sure, he had an iron-clad reason to be buying, but shit, he would sound like such a liar.

"Oh, it's for my brother."

That was the kind of stuff addicts said when they were falling off the wagon. Nobody lied better than an alcoholic ready to sidle up to the bottle again. Colin took solace in the truth, though. He wasn't going to touch this stuff. That was why Shannon had asked him to stop by the store. She knew he could handle it. Hell, he was damn proud of himself for proving to his family that every day he was recovering.

And to himself, too. He intended to do that by competing in this year's Badass Triathlon at the end of the summer. He hadn't attempted it since his epic fail. But it was his personal quest to finish it this time. Whether he came in first or last didn't matter. Finishing sober was all he wanted.

Colin paid for the beer and headed out of the store, ready to see Ryan. His brother had had a hell of a day. He'd spent it at Hawthorne, visiting their murderess mother in prison. Apparently she'd finally confessed to him that she'd had their father killed. Colin had never doubted she was guilty, but Ryan had held out hope she'd been framed, and that with the case reopened someone else would be nabbed. True, the detectives were still looking for the gunman's potential accomplices, but for once and for all, Ryan was as sure of their mother's guilt as the rest of them were. Now it was Colin's job, along with Shannon and Michael, to lend some support to their brother.

As he got behind the wheel of his Audi, something nagged at him. Something he'd meant to do last night after he said good-bye to Elle. He snapped his fingers.

"The picture," he said. The hot sex must have fried his brain. He'd forgotten to text her the image of the kid in the Buick who'd been stalking Shannon—Colin was sure he'd seen the guy around the community center playing basketball. He hunted for it now. But as he scrolled through his photo gallery to fire the picture off to Elle, all his recent images were gone. Right, he'd reset everything on his phone the other day after testing a new fitness app that downloaded a virus. Needless to say, his venture firm wasn't going to fund that app.

He'd simply get the image from Brent another time. Now, he needed to be with his family.

And later this week, he had a date with Elle.

Well, it was hardly a date.

More like a plan to fuck.

But that was okay. He loved fucking her, and if fucking her was the way to win the heart that he wanted badly, he'd be up to the challenge.

* * *

"No one was there." Marcus blew out a long stream of air.

"So you try again another time," Elle said, trying to cheer him up as she untied her roller skates while chatting with Marcus on the phone.

"I guess so," he said, his voice trailing off.

"Look, just because he wasn't there this morning doesn't mean he won't be the next time. Besides, who's at their house anymore these days?" she said with a laugh. She'd just finished her workout at the rink, and over at the arcade, Alex hammered the joystick in what looked like a furious game of *Frogger*. "It'll probably take a few tries before you find them."

"Yeah, you're right," he answered, sounding a touch more hopeful.

She smiled as she tugged off her skates, glad that her words were giving Marcus some kind of courage. "So just go again until you do it. Life is all about risks, right?"

"Risks," he said, as if he were letting the word marinate. "Right. Risks."

As she finished the call, she dropped her skates into her bag then joined her son for a round of *Frogger*, soundly schooling him in the arcade game she'd aced at this very rink back in high school. "It is so much easier to crush you in games at the roller rink than on the Xbox," Elle said, pumping a fist in victory when her frog successfully evaded more cars, trucks, and traffic than her son's.

"As if your retro games even count," he said with a smirk.

"Hey! I didn't see you complaining about my retro games during practice. You were glued to the screen."

He shrugged. "I pretended to like it."

She answered him with a noogie. "What do you say to you, me, fries, and a shake?"

"Mix in a burger and you're on, T," he said, calling her by her roller derby name. Only the "T" stood for more than just her alias – it was her word to live by.

"It's a deal."

CHAPTER SEVEN

The basketball arced through the air, swirling once, then twice, around the rim and dropping with a whoosh into the basket.

"No fucking way!"

Rex stared at the ball in amazement as it bounced on the concrete of the court.

Colin held his arms out wide as he stood on the free-throw line. *I told you so.* "Angle. It's all angle."

"You have got to be kidding me!" the boy said, his big eyes rounder than ever. He'd been doubting Colin, all right. Rex was one of the teens who played in the rec center basketball league. He grabbed the ball and held it as if he were weighing it, then he narrowed his eyes at Colin. "Is this like Playoff Gate all over again?"

Colin laughed and wiped the beads of sweat from his brow. "I assure you, I did not deflate the basketball. But if I did, I would tell you that no matter what the PSI, I'd still have a greater chance at landing a free throw if I had my arms at this angle," he said, demonstrating a wider placement of his arms, "than at this angle." He returned to a tighter alignment. "And I can tell you, too, that if you're behind the free throw line, you need a smaller angle to make the shot, and if you're dribbling…" He began moving down the court, while Rex picked up his pace to stay with him. "And you pass the ball to get away from a defender, passing it at a nice straight angle gives you better odds of keeping the ball on your team. Like this." Colin tossed it neatly to Rex, who snatched the ball and lifted it above his head.

"Smaller angle," Colin said, correcting him, and Rex made a quick adjustment then watched the ball sail into the net.

"Holy shit," the teen said as the ball bounced on the court. Rex's younger brother, Tyler, had joined them, watching from the sidelines, and looked less impressed.

Rex marched over to Colin and slapped his palm. "I still don't believe you, but a deal is a deal is a deal. You get to tutor me now in business math."

Colin beamed. For the last year he'd been coaching the rec league and tutoring the teens at the center in business math as part of his personal decision to devote more time to service. He'd lost out on a big deal a year ago, and had felt the first inklings of the familiar urge to bury his frustrations in liquor. Rather than give in, he'd refocused his energies, pouring his time into others. That had helped him fight the good fight and stay on the straight and narrow path.

"It's all math, man. Everything is math," he said, grabbing the ball from the ground and dribbling it in place. "You will use math in every fucking area of your life. Chance of hitting a free throw from one-third of the way up the court? Math. Chance of landing a slam-dunk?

Math. How much money do I need to pay my bills? Math. Is it worth missing class to sleep in? Comes down to math."

"What he's saying is—math is everything," Tyler said.

"What? You're on his team now?" Rex said jokingly to his brother.

"Listen to Tyler. He knows what he's talking about," Colin said. A few years younger, Rex's brother dabbled in basketball, but his asthma slowed him down.

"And this is the shit you do for a living?"

Colin took aim at the net and watched the ball soar. "See, I'm not some natural basketball player. I only learned how to hold my own on the court by applying math to the way I play. And yes—this is the shit I do for a living. Every day. Evaluate risk. Study balance sheets. Look at profit and loss statements. And take a gamble as to whether some new technology for phones, or TVs, or gaming, or whatever, is going to change the world." The ball slinked neatly through the basket. He tossed it to Rex, who took his shot.

"How much green did you bring home last year?" Rex asked.

Colin laughed, shaking his head, as the younger man landed a shot.

"You're not going to tell me?"

"No. I'm not going to tell you. But I will say this: my portfolio of companies had a twenty-four percent return, and that's well ahead of the stock market, and it's also ahead of the twenty percent benchmark for a venture capital firm, so there you go. Plus, one of the early seed startups I invested in five years ago went public, and my firm netted a beautiful profit from that sale. A thirty times return."

Rex's eyes practically turned into dollar signs, and Colin chuckled. "Don't get ahead of yourself. That money goes back into the portfolio. So we can invest in more companies," he explained, dribbling the ball. Rex was eighteen and headed to community college. He didn't know what he wanted to major in, and Colin was hoping he'd lean toward business. He had some innate interest in it. He just needed a push to see the value in the long term.

"But that's your goal, right?" he asked.

"You got it. Find the diamond in the rough. Bet big on it before anyone else does. Grow it and watch it turn into a money tree."

Rex waved his arms enthusiastically. "Oh man, I want a money tree. I want a big, fat money tree that grows greenbacks all year round. Ty, let's go grow us a money tree."

"Yeah, right, in the concrete pit at our crappy apartment complex," Tyler said with a snort from his spot on the sidelines.

"Hey! Watch it. We'll move up someday." Rex turned back at Colin and pointed his thumb at Tyler. "I gotta look out for him. Mom's working too many jobs. She's never around."

"That's why she makes sure you're here instead of wandering the streets," Colin said, passing the ball to Rex. "And if you study business, you'll have a hell of a better shot at growing a money tree than you would by chasing after some get-rich-quick scheme. Invest, nurture, grow, make more. That's what I do. That's my job. That's my passion." He held out his arm, showing the tattoo there. *Nothing ventured. Nothing gained.*

Rex tucked the ball beneath his elbow and walked closer to see.

"Hey, Rex. I'm hungry," Tyler interjected.

"Give me a second, Ty. I'll make you mac and cheese when we get home. My man Colin is training me to be a venture capitalist. Get over here and join us." Rex turned his attention back to Colin's ink. "So that's your mission at work or something? Nothing ventured, nothing gained?"

"Yeah, but in life, too. Means more to me than just work."

"Like what?" Rex asked.

"It means take big chances. It means stay away from drugs," Colin said, talking bluntly to the boys as he always did.

Rex sneered. "What do you know about that, Mr. Richie Rich? You probably bathe in Cristal."

Colin rolled his eyes. "Dude. You think I was born rich? You think I was rolling in cash as a kid? Wrong," he said, as if he'd just slammed a buzzer on a game show. "My family was fucked up, and I was the most messed up of them all. Painkillers, tequila, and speed in college. I was a mess. All this," he said, gesturing to his arms, covered in ink, "they're my reminders. Eight years clean." He pointed to the art on his body, naming each one. "Lotus, new beginning. Sunburst, truth and bravery. This Chinese character—it's for strength."

Rex raised his chin and peered at an infinity symbol with four interlocking circles on Colin's wrist. "What's that one?"

"Me and my brothers and sister. The four of us. Our unbreakable bond, no matter what."

"That's like us," Rex said, patting his arm where the sleeve of his T-shirt hit.

"What do you mean?"

Rex pointed to his little brother. "Him. I always look out for Tyler. That's why I have this." He pulled up his sleeve to his shoulder. At first Colin saw only a few letters of the word *protect*. His hackles rose, remembering what Ryan had told him a week ago. The guy who'd been following Shannon around had some ink on his arm that said *Protect Our Own*—the tattoo of the Royal Sinners.

Colin spoke sharply. "Do not even. That better not be what I think it is."

Rex furrowed his brow. "Way to freak out, dude. What the fuck do you think it says?"

"That better not be *Protect Our Own*."

Rex laughed deeply, clutching his belly, letting the sound resonate through him. "No. No. No," he said, catching his breath. "No way. No how. Our ink says *Protector. We got ours together." Rex stepped closer to Colin and showed him the full wrap of the word around his bicep. Tyler yanked up his shirtsleeve, displaying matching ink.

"I would whip him good if he messed around with that gang." Rex draped an arm around his little brother.

"Whew," Colin said, wiping his hand across his brow in exaggerated relief.

"I saw some of them a few blocks away the other day."

"Here?" Colin asked, pointing to the basketball court.

Rex nodded. "Nearby. We made sure they didn't come any closer."

Colin didn't like the sound of gang members hovering so close to the community center. He was well aware that it was a risk—this center was located in a section of town that had been a hot bed of crime years ago, but the surrounding neighborhood was improving now. Still, he wanted the center, the kids, and Elle as safe as could be.

"Who's we? What is *Protector*?" he asked, returning to the ink.

"A group of us who are trying to look out for others," Tyler said, chiming in proudly. He seemed to idolize his older brother.

Colin arched an eyebrow. "Like the Guardian Angels?"

Rex nodded. "We model ourselves after them. We're all volunteers. We do safety patrols. Walk the streets. Keep an eye out. Elle inspired me to do it. Rise above, as she would say."

"Did someone say my name?"

Colin turned in the direction of the sultry, sexy voice. She wore tight jeans and a little white summery blouse. The outfit did wondrous things to her fantastic tits and her fabulous ass. Her long, dark hair spilled down her spine, and she gathered it up, creating a makeshift ponytail, then fanned her face with her free hand. A small part of him wished the woman wasn't so damn hot. As Rex and Tyler snapped their gazes to Elle, he could see it in their eyes— she'd featured in their whack-off fantasies. A primal, territorial instinct licked through his veins, and he wanted to pounce on Elle, wrap his arms around her, and claim her.

"Mine," he'd say with a snarl, toss her over his shoulder and cart her off to the woods to take her, mark her, and leave his imprint on her.

Of course, the rational, adult portion of his brain knew that was ludicrous. She was hardly his, and even with what they had, he needn't be jealous of teenage boys. They were boys, and while they might lust after her, they also admired her.

"We're quoting you, Elle. *Rise above,*" Tyler said, raising his fist in the air. Yup, it was a mix of feelings they possessed for the hot-as-sin and caring-as-hell director of the center where they spent many days and evenings.

She held up a hand to high-five Tyler then slapped the older brother's hand, too. "Excellent. You boys do me proud. Are you staying to get a bite to eat? I hear there are turkey sandwiches on the menu tonight."

"I love turkey!"

"More than my mac and cheese?" Rex asked his brother.

Tyler nodded. "But I still love your mac and cheese."

"Fine, we'll stay. We need to work on our angles later." Rex draped an arm around his brother. "Hey, Elle, did you hear? Colin is trying to turn me into the next venture capitalist."

"That sounds like an excellent pursuit," she said.

"I'm gonna earn twenty-five percent and beat his ass."

"After I tutor you in math, you just might," Colin said.

The teen turned to Elle. "He twisted my arm. He's gonna make me learn my two plus twos for community college."

"That's not a bad thing, Rex. And I suspect you'll learn a whole lot more than two plus two."

"Anyway, it's too hot out here. We're going inside. Catch you later, Mr. Cristal," Rex said with a wink at Colin.

As he walked away, Elle raised an eyebrow. "Mr. Cristal?"

"Long story. But it has a good ending."

"Maybe tell me tonight?" She tucked her thumbs into the pockets of her jeans. "Turns out I have more time than I thought. Alex is at a friend's house for dinner, then they're going to see the new dinosaur movie or whatever that thing is that all the boys are watching on the big screen."

"Are you asking me out, Elle?"

"I was just thinking it would be fun to hang out with you. As friends," she added, a reminder of how she saw him. Her voice went a touch softer, "As well as...*you know.*"

Hang out. Friends. Not exactly the words he wanted to hear from her. But he could work with it. "I can do a lot with more time."

"I had a feeling you might be able to," she said, tapping her watch. "Give me an hour to finish up?"

"Perfect. I need to stop at my house anyway. I'm taking care of Ryan's dog since he's followed Sophie to Germany."

"He followed her to Germany?" she asked, bouncing on her toes.

"He did indeed. He's madly in love with her. So I've got Johnny Cash for the week, and I need to go take him for a walk."

"That is so sweet."

"Me taking care of his dog, or him following her to Germany?"

Elle flashed him the sweetest smile. "Both actually. I'm so happy for her," she said, practically glowing as she spoke about the two of them. "He looked so in love with her when I saw them at the Venetian event together. And it's incredibly cool of you to look after his dog." She gestured in Rex's direction. "And to help Rex to focus more on his studies. I've been trying to get him to work on math for the longest time, and I've never seen him connect with anyone else here like he does with you." She reached out to wrap her hand around his arm. "He's such a good kid at heart, taking care of his little brother and everything. But he needs to channel all his money-making energy so he's not taken in by the wrong thing."

"I hear you loud and clear," Colin said, enjoying all the things Elle had just told him, but especially her reaction to Ryan's romance movie-esque pursuit of Sophie. Sure, she was talking about another couple, but something seemed to spark in her at the mention, as if it stirred up a long-dormant longing.

Cool your jets, Colin.

He might be reading too much into it. But Elle had focused so long on other people—on her son, on her ex. She didn't let romance into her life, and now she was only permitting fun in the bedroom. Perhaps, though, he needed to do more tonight than just send her soaring between the sheets. This thing between them might only be about the physical right now, but he had a chance tonight to show her how good he could be for her. Maybe friendship was the key to unlocking the heart that she kept so protected.

"Meet me on Fremont Street and North Las Vegas Boulevard at six p.m."

Her eyes widened and her shoulders tensed. A flicker of fear crossed her eyes. "Are you going to make me do the zip line?"

He scoffed. "Make you? Never. Encourage you? Absolutely."

"Why do you want me to do it?"

"Because it's fun. Because it's a natural high. Because it feels good."

"Lots of things feel good but that doesn't mean I want to do them."

"So let me get this straight. You do roller derby, racing around a rink like a speed demon on skates, and you won't do a zip line?" he asked, challenging her.

She narrowed her eyes, parking her hands on her hips. "Not the same. Roller derby is flat. Besides, I've done it for years, I play defense, and it's *indoors*."

"C'mon, Titanium," he urged, goading her with her roller derby name.

She pursed her lips. "No fair."

"All's fair," he began, but cut himself off before finishing with *in love and war*. He didn't want to hint at love, or romance, or anything close to it. Those were red flags for her, even if he hoped something in the back of her mind or heart might yearn for them. "In any case, it's your choice, Titanium."

"I will consider it as I lock up my office," she said, and those words—*lock up*—flipped the switch on an idea.

He jumped to a new topic. "Hey, would it be okay if I increased my firm's donation to the center?"

She shook her head playfully. "No. God no. Anything but that," she said, waving it off. She rolled her eyes. "Obviously. But why, may I ask?"

"Thought it would be smart to get some additional security while the revitalization is going on," he said, gesturing to the court and main building. "Lots of people coming and going. Construction crews. My donation already went to some of that already. Just a little more for some extra manpower."

"Anything I should worry about?" she asked, arching an eyebrow. "Well, more than usual. I know this isn't the best section of town, but it's getting better."

"It is absolutely getting better. Let's keep it that way. I happen to know some guys in security," he said, since Ryan and Michael ran a security firm.

"Let's do it."

"Three of my favorite words from you," he said, as they walked off the court. He pointed to his car parked down the block. "I'm going to go shower and walk the dog. I'll see you at six."

She fanned herself. "Now I have a nice image of you naked and wet in the shower."

"And that's my cue to go."

He brushed his lips against hers, leaving her a quick, hot kiss to think about.

CHAPTER EIGHT

Elle stared at the crowds along the Fremont Street Canopy seventy-seven feet below her.

Deep breath.

She wasn't afraid of heights, but she was afraid of, well, of *dying*. Or, more precisely, dying stupidly. Like jumping into a lake and cutting her head on a rock. Like parachuting. Like crashing from a zip line. That kind of death.

Logically, she knew a zip line wasn't a dangerous activity in the spectrum of dangerous things. But her rapidly beating heart, which seemed to be fighting its way out of her chest, begged to disagree. Her skin prickled with nerves—the kind she hadn't felt since she was younger and danced with danger. Now, as an adult, she tried to keep her risks manageable.

You can do this, she told the portion of her brain that had zero interest in skydiving and bungee jumping. *Just a zip line. It's exceedingly safe, and ridiculously fun.*

Plus, Colin waited patiently on the other side, hovering in his seat. The parallel zip lines ran down the length of the covered Fremont Street that was the epicenter of downtown Las Vegas—old Vegas, with the Golden Nugget, and slots that still relied on coins rather than tickets. It was Vegas before mega resorts broke ground on the Strip.

Everyone rode the line here on Fremont Street. It was part of the experience. Besides, cruising along a zip line was a perfectly manageable risk. Man-made, controllable. The kind she could handle.

"I'm ready," she said to the attendant. In a rush, so she wouldn't back down, she let go and stepped off the platform, zipping off in her seat harness. She unleashed a rollercoaster shout of excitement. Adrenaline surged through her veins as she soared above the specks of miniature people, and a sense of wild glee engulfed her as she sped, faster and faster. She glanced briefly to the left, where Colin sailed above the crowds on his downhill flight along the canopy.

Screw fear. This was a pure rush, as the summer breeze whooshed past her, reminding her of the thrill she felt when roller-skating, the high-speed chase around the rink. The charge that raced through her overpowered her primal worries. She rode several blocks in the sky.

She flew the final feet to the end of the line. The guy on the platform helped unhook her. "How was it?" he asked.

She gave him a thumbs up, her heart still pumping wildly.

Minutes later, she climbed down from the platform and met Colin on the street. He wrapped his arms around her. "Admit it. You loved it," he said with a gleam in his eyes.

"Loved it," she said breathlessly, her pulse pounding in her veins. "Absolutely loved it."

"Excellent. Tomorrow morning you'll join me for kayaking at the crack of dawn at Black Canyon," he said.

She shuddered. "Kayaking? Like in a lake?"

"That's generally where one kayaks."

"That comes with a chance of flipping over and cracking your head on a rock. Pretty sure this zip line is all you're getting out of me when it comes to crazy sports."

"Kayaking in flat water? Chance of flipping over is slim to nil. So low risk it's beyond low risk."

She patted his chest. "In that case, I have somewhere to be at the crack of dawn tomorrow. Hmm. Where could it be? Oh right," she said, snapping her fingers. "Sound asleep in my bed."

"Mmm. Bed. Another potential extreme sport."

"Now that I might be up for," she said, then lingered in his embrace, inhaling his freshly showered scent—clean, and sexy. She didn't hold back. She pressed her lips to his neck and kissed him, letting herself savor this part, this permission she'd given herself to enjoy the sexy times with Colin.

He drew a sharp inhalation, and asked, "Payback for the other night?"

She nodded and roped her arms tightly around his waist, playfully gripping him, keeping the focus squarely on what they were—friends with benefits. Nothing more. "And now I shall take you to a secret location and smother your neck in kisses that make you turn to putty in my hands. See if it works as well on you as it does on me."

He leaned his head back and laughed deeply. "That's a viable option for tonight. Or I could take you to the Mob Museum and we can find a dark corner there."

"The Mob Museum?"

"Ever been?"

She shook her head. "No, but I've been wanting to go ever since it opened a few years ago. I keep meaning to go, especially considering how much I love gangster movies."

He nudged her with his elbow. "Let's go."

She nudged him in return. "You're holding out on me tonight. The zip line, the Mob Museum. Everything's above the belt," she said, and though those all distinctly felt like the elements of a date, they were also things you'd do with a friend. She wasn't crossing lines. She wasn't breaking promises. This was good, old-fashioned hanging out with someone whose company she enjoyed.

Plain and simple.

* * *

The answer was yes.

He was absolutely holding out on her. He wanted her, but he wanted her to see that they could have amazing sex and an amazing time. They wandered through the crowds, soaking in the neon and lights, the exuberance of the summertime atmosphere, and not once did he feel a lick of envy for the twenty-somethings bobbing around with long, tall plastic glasses full of liquor in their hands. Nope, he was a happy son-of-a-bitch as they walked through old-time Vegas, then up the steps of the museum that documented the history of the mob.

"We're closing in thirty minutes," the ticket taker said in a monotone at the entrance.

"We'll be speedy," Colin said, and they walked inside the stone building, and strolled first through exhibits on famous "made men," both in the mob and popular culture, perusing photos of some of the most notorious Mafiosi over the last one hundred years, like John Gotti. Next, they checked out an installation of movie posters.

"Is there anything better than a mob movie?" he asked, and Elle nodded in perfect agreement.

"Love them. *Casino.* Epic. *The Departed.* Fantastic. *Road to Perdition.* Chilling."

"*Eight Men Out.* Proof that the mob had its hands in everything. Even fixing the World Series."

"Everything," she said, enunciating each syllable as she echoed his sentiment. They stopped at a huge framed poster of Ray Liotta, Robert DeNiro, and Joe Pesci. She pointed. "*Goodfellas.* Best mob movie ever."

"Best closing lines ever, too," he added, and they turned to each other, speaking in unison. "*I'm an average nobody. I get to live the rest of my life like a schnook.*"

He raised his hand and they knocked fists.

"Isn't it amazing," she began, "how being a regular Joe was Ray Liotta's worst nightmare? He dreaded not being a gangster, and somehow you felt for him when it happened. You sympathized with his plight as a regular schnook," she said, her voice rising in excitement.

He gestured to the poster for *The Godfather.* "I don't even know what it is about the mob. They do horrible things and live a life of crime, and yet sometimes we root for them in movies. It makes no logical sense."

"Look!"

She grabbed his arm and tugged him to a series of sepia-tinted photographs from Vegas through the years, highlighting famous moments in the city's history and the role of the mob in each milestone.

"It's just crazy to think how much of this town was built on crime," she said in awe, as they stared at a photo of the

Flamingo Hotel when it opened in 1946. "'Operated by noted mobster Bugsey Siegel,'" she said, reading the plaque.

He tapped the wall next to an image of The Sands Casino in the 60s, a home base for Frank Sinatra and his Rat Pack that was owned by a New York mob man. "And it spread far and wide. Some of the biggest hotels in the city were owned and operated by this wild combination of Mormon businessmen and the mob, so they could have a legitimate appearance on the outside, and money laundering and street muscle on the inside."

"The whole notion that there is the underbelly of crime everywhere, all around us, blows my mind," she said, pressing her fingertips to her forehead and miming an explosion.

Colin nodded in agreement. "Handouts, corrupt cops, men on the take, informants, and the guys in suits circulating around town every day, weaving in and out of casinos. Looking like me, or like one of my brothers, or just anybody."

She arched an eyebrow. "Is this your way of telling me you're in the mob?"

He affected a wise guy smirk. "Doll face, it's time you knew the truth. You're sleeping with a made man. You want to know who I really am? I'll tell you, sweet cheeks." He pointed to an interactive screen on the far wall that read "Mob Nickname Generator."

"Oooh, I'm finally gonna learn my honey baby's real name." She rubbed her palms together as they reached the screen.

He tapped it, and they chuckled at the rubric the screen asked them to fill in: name your racket, with options like money laundering, casino skimming, and blackmail; what's your role, such as capo, soldier, business associate, corrupt judge; and what is your mob era, with choices like prohibition, the swinging 60s, and the modern era.

Elle went first, entering her picks, then reading her status report. "Ooh, I'm a mob girlfriend. Men buy me things and who am I to turn them down? They parade me around town and take me to dinner, and my name is 'Elle 'Moneybags' Mariano.'" She snorted. "Ha. I wish."

"My turn," Colin said, and together they decided he'd be a corrupt politician, and he read the result aloud. "I just take what's offered to me, okay? Nothin' wrong with that. The mob slips me a few things now and then—some cash, a free meal, a bottle of my favorite bootlegged whiskey. What's the big deal? I'm Colin 'Scotty' Sloan."

She dragged her nails through his hair. "Colin Scotty Sloan, you are one handsome fella," she said, in an over-the-top floozy accent. It was jokey, but it still turned him on. Or maybe it was just that her proximity was making an instant impression on certain parts of his anatomy. Because that part was standing at attention now, announcing its intention to have her, and to have her soon.

"I'm gonna take you out for that fancy meal you deserve, sweet thing," he said, snaking his hand down her back and squeezing her ass. "Show you off as mine."

"Oh, I like that, Scotty Sloan. I like it very much." She slid her body close to his, rubbing her sexy frame against him, making contact with his erection. She arched an eyebrow and gazed south. "Seems you like the idea, too, don't you?" She lowered her voice to a sexy purr, dropping the mob girlfriend accent and returning to pure, dirty Elle.

"You think so? What makes you say that?" he asked, egging her on.

She pressed harder against his dick and started circling her hips. No one was in this exhibit room but them, with the eyes of generations of made men watching. "This," she said in his ear, then dropped her hand to his jeans, grabbing him through the denim as she palmed the outline of his cock. He groaned from her touch. "This fantastic hardon makes me say you like the idea of parading me around town."

He jerked her even closer. "No, this hard-on says I like doing much more than parading you around, Elle Moneybags Mariano." He grabbed her hand, walked her to the exit sign, pressed hard on the heavy door below it, and entered a stairwell.

Ah, stairwells. The perfect locations for a little something.

Her eyes blazed with mischief as he spun her around and backed her against the wall. "Like I said, I'll do more than parade you around. Since that's what you want," he said, cupping her face with his hands and gazing at her. He drank in her absolute fucking beauty with his eyes, savoring the way she looked. The lusty expression, the parted lips, the racing breath.

She was so sexual, so raw in her needs, and he loved it. Loved it so damn much. He lifted his thumb to her mouth, brushing it against her lips. "Do you realize I've never gone down on you?" he asked. "What the fuck is up with that?"

"I know," she said, breathily. "I want it so badly."

"Why has this not happened yet?" he asked as he stroked her bottom lip softly with the pad of his thumb.

She shook her head. "Because we're always screwing? Because we go straight to the main attraction?"

"Maybe."

"Or because we've never been someplace private enough?"

"Maybe that's it. Because when I go down on you, I want you without a stitch of clothes on. I want to spread you out, worship your sexy body, and take my time licking and kissing and sucking you all over. I want to taste every inch of your skin before I bury my face between your legs," he said, dropping his hand to her jeans and cupping her. She moaned as he felt how hot she was through her clothes.

"Are you going to do it here?" she asked, and she sounded so damn desperate and hungry and horny that he was dying to strip her jeans to her ankles, kneel before her, and taste her heat. But no. He had patience. He was going to have her when he had time to feast.

"No," he whispered. "But when I do, it'll be like this." He angled her head slightly, then flicked his tongue gently over her parted lips. She gasped, shuddering as he lightly brushed his lips over hers. He ran the tip of his tongue over the seam of her mouth, as if he were tasting her sweetness. The possibility of lapping up her sweet pussy electrified him, sending heat roaring through his blood as he licked her as if he was going down on her. She trembled in his arms as he showed her precisely how he intended to lavish attention on her, how he'd kiss and suck and then devour her. God, he wanted her. He wanted her so badly. On his mouth, flooding his tongue, all over his lips, drenching his chin. He kissed her like that. Like a man consumed. Like a man who had to have her, taste her, touch her. His hands clutched her cheeks, his lips fused to hers, and his mind raced with images, sensations, and fantasies about how she'd taste with her legs wrapped around his neck, writhing and bucking as she grabbed his hair and came hard on his tongue.

Fuck.

He couldn't take it anymore. In a mad fury, he unzipped her jeans, and dipped his hand inside her panties. Oh hell. This was wetness. This was lush, delicious heat. He stroked her and in seconds his fingers were coated.

"Look at you," he said, breaking the kiss. "Look at how fucking wet you are." He pulled his hand out of her panties and brought his fingers to his mouth. His eyes rolled shut as he tasted her—like sex. She tasted like sex and lust. He opened his eyes to find her staring at him hungrily, jaw agape.

"Don't tease me," she said, gripping his shoulders.

"I'm not going to tease you. I just needed a taste," he said, then returned his hand to her panties, sliding his fingers in the delicious crease between her legs. The stairwell was dark and echo-y and every sound, every moan bounced on the heavy walls as he stroked her.

"I want you to taste me soon. I want you to eat me. I fantasize about it all the time," she said on a sexy groan as he rubbed her clit, a hard little diamond—swollen, wet and begging for his touch. He slipped a finger inside her heat, thrilling at the instant reaction it elicited from her. She clasped a hand over her mouth, capturing her own moan. Her knees buckled, and he used his free hand to steady her. Gripping her hip, he moved his mouth to her ear. "Fuck my hand," he told her.

She rolled her hips, riding his fingers as he thrust inside her tight channel. "You fantasize about me a lot? About me eating you?"

"Yes," she moaned as she rode his fingers. "God yes. Every night."

"You think about me fucking you?"

"Fucking your hand. Fucking your face. Fucking your dick. I picture it all," she said, her voice broken and breathy as she rocked into his touch.

"God, I love how much you want to fuck me," he said, in a ragged voice. His dick was so hard it was practically staging a mutiny in his jeans. It was ready to bust out and take over. To sink in and spend the whole night inside her.

But he wanted her pleasure more. Her release. Her bliss. And he knew how to find it. He knew the way around her body because he'd never wanted anyone with this kind of raging intensity. He crooked his finger, hitting that magic spot that sent her flying. She curled her fingernails into his shoulders, digging in, holding on, as her mouth formed a perfect *O*. He sealed his lips to hers, swallowing her cries of pleasure as she came hard on his fingers in the stairwell.

"The Mob Museum is closing in ten minutes. Attention, museum-goers. The Mob Museum is closing in ten minutes. If you don't wish to spend the evening with the ghost of Bugsey Siegel, we strongly suggest you wrap up your visit. Don't say we didn't warn you," the voice on the loudspeaker said in a Jersey accent.

Elle's shoulders shook, whether from laughter or the aftershocks of her orgasm or both—it was hard to tell. But deciphering the finer meanings of her reaction took on less importance than his need to be inside her.

Now.

CHAPTER NINE

"Come with me," he said, quickly zipping her jeans, straightening her top, and guiding her in her woozy, buzzy state back into the exhibit hall, where a security guard dressed in black barked, "Closing time in ten minutes."

Colin saluted him. "Yes, sir."

Elle kept her head down, her hair forming a curtain around her face as he led her through the made men room, down a hall, and to the bathroom. He pulled the door open, locked it behind them, and grabbed her waist.

"Put your hands on the sink now."

Obeying, she slammed her palms against the marble counter.

"Look at me in the mirror," he said, and she met his gaze in the reflection as he yanked her jeans down her legs. "These jeans are so fucking tight," he muttered as he kneeled, tugging them to her knees, then just below. He stood back up, and tapped her ankle with his foot. "Spread wider."

She obliged as he unzipped his own jeans and rolled on a condom.

She bent her back and lifted her ass, and he smacked it once with his palm. "Can't resist," he said playfully. "Too tempting."

"Don't resist."

"Never," he said, and slid the head of his dick against her heat. "So wet. Did I do all this to you?" he asked, as if he didn't know the answer.

"I'm pretty sure this is the eighty-seventh pair of panties you've melted right off me," she said with a sexy glint as he rubbed himself against her. His dick was pointing its way home, begging to be deep in her, but oh, did he love just savoring the slickness before he sank inside. He fucking loved coating his dick in her slippery heat before he felt her clench around him.

"Eighty-seventh? That's it? I need to work harder."

"Speaking of hard—"

Her words were silenced as he buried himself in her. "Oh fuck, Elle," he said on a groan, as he savored that intense moment when he was first inside the woman he craved. He picked up the pace, meeting her eyes in the mirror. Her amber eyes were glossy and full of lust, and her cheeks were rosy from the glow of her first orgasm. "I love looking at you as I make you come. I want to watch you fall apart again as I fuck you," he said, low and husky in her ear.

"I want that too. So badly."

Setting a fevered rhythm, the second hand ticking in their ears, he stroked into her. She moaned on each thrust, panting as he filled her. "You tasted so damn good on my fingers," he said huskily. "I can't wait to have you. When I do, I'm going to show you exactly why you came so many times alone at night thinking of me."

"I did, Colin. I did," she said, swiveling her hips as he pumped into her. "I thought about fucking your face all the time."

Oh hell. Those words were like a straight shot of lust through his bloodstream. They set him on fire. They flipped switches all over. He groaned deeply. "I bet you were saying all sorts of filthy things to me in your head. I bet as you fucked yourself alone in bed you were saying *Oh Colin, fuck me with your tongue. I want to ride your face.* Did you say that?"

Her body answered with an epic shudder, a wild tightening against his dick, which was so damn hard inside her. Her slick walls gripped him as he slammed in and out of her, pulling back so only the tip was in her. He paused momentarily, then whispered in a low, dirty growl in her ear, "*Colin, I'm going to come all over your face. I'm going to come so fucking hard on your face,*" he said to her, and her eyes glazed over, and her body trembled, and everything, everything, everything in her reaction told him he was not only right, but she was there, finding her way to a second coming. He let go of her hip, and glided his finger across her clit. "Say it," he commanded, as he fucked her deep and rubbed her clit.

"I'm going to come so fucking hard," she said, her voice falling to pieces as she came on him. She started to cry out in ecstasy, but he clamped his palm over her mouth. He fucked her furiously, holding in all her screams, keeping her quiet as his balls tightened and his own orgasm tore through his body, consuming him like a torrential storm ripping across the coastline.

He cursed as he came hard.

He wanted to collapse onto her, to wrap his arms around her and just exist in this sated, blissful state. He looped his hands around her sexy waist, holding her close. He brushed his lips against her collarbone, and she shivered then flashed him a small smile.

"Attention, the doors are closing in two minutes. Thank you for visiting the mob museum. Bugsey is not alone tonight. We have just received word that Al Capone is haunting the premises."

"Al Capone!" Elle said in a stage whisper. "Oh no!"

Quickly, Colin pulled out and disposed of the condom. They straightened up, and a minute later, walked to the exit, thanking the ticket taker and the security guard who locked the door behind them.

On the front steps of the museum, Elle grabbed his hand. "Let's play some poker, Colin Scotty Sloan."

He wished he didn't like it so much when she kept her fingers locked through his as they spent the next hour wandering through Fremont Street, playing slots, then a round at the five dollar tables.

When it was time for her to go, he walked her to her car. "I had a really great time," she said, but before he could say "me, too," she brushed her hands together, as if she were wiping the evening away. The night was over. It had a before and an after. "That's that. Now I'm off to be a mom."

Her voice changed. Her tone shifted. Her whole demeanor transformed. She was moving from Elle the sexy, wanton woman who was dirty and bold and who liked to fuck hard, to the other Elle.

The one who had no room in her life for him. The one who erected walls and ramparts to keep him out. His heart sagged, knowing he might never be able to knock those down. They might simply be unscalable because of how he'd lived and who he'd been before her.

Choices had consequences. Every single one. He'd made some terrible choices when he was younger, and even though those days were far in the rearview mirror, he was feeling the repercussions as he walked her to her car and said good night before she drove off to her real life.

* * *

Fun.

That was good, plain fun.

That was basically the best night she'd had in ages.

She shook her head in amazement as she slowed her car at a red light on her way to pick up Alex.

"*Fun,*" she said out loud, as if the word was a new concept.

In many ways, it was to her. Elle hadn't had that sort of evening in…well…in many years. Sure, she always had a blast doing roller derby, but that was more of a necessary outlet, her own therapy to handle living with an addict, since she'd started on the team when she was with Sam then continued when she kicked him out. And, yes, she and her son had gobs of fun playing zombie games, going bowling, and challenging each other in Pac-Man at the roller rink after her matches.

But adult fun? Date fun? Fun as a woman?

That had been eons ago. Like, maybe the Paleolithic period. Getting knocked up as a teenager didn't give you many opportunities for fun.

Tonight though, from the zip line to the museum visit to hand holding along Fremont Street…every single second was lovely, and a small part of her heart already longed for another night like it.

She never thought she'd have a bad time with Colin, but she hadn't imagined they'd have such a good one. It made perfect sense that they'd gel, she reasoned, as the light changed and she hit the gas. The two of them had clicked from day one. They'd chatted easily when they first met, sharing a similar view on the value of community service, the importance of being role models for youth, and the benefit of giving kids a chance to have fun, too. But tonight she learned they had even more in common, little things, like their shared affection for mob movies and their fondness for the stories of Vegas.

Then there was the sex. Oh, the toe-curling, sheet-grabbing, mind-blowing sex. As she turned onto the street where Alex's friend lived, her chest tingled with the memories of how he'd taken her against the sink after sending her over the edge in the stairwell. He was direct and dirty, and he seemed to embrace that she was, too. He was also commanding and intense, and relished telling her exactly what he wanted from her.

She wanted all the same things.

And admittedly, a quiet part of her wanted more of him. A part she rarely acknowledged. Try as she might to keep him in the friend zone, being friends with him only made him more appealing. But she had to stay strong. Had to maintain the boundaries. That was the only way to protect her son, and to keep her promises to herself. Colin was a great friend and an amazing lover, and surely she could have him as both for some time. No need for complications.

She pulled into the driveway, cut the engine, and walked to the door. Her girlfriend Janine answered, greeting her with "You all set for the match next week? Friday evening."

Janine was the jammer on the Fishnet Brigade, their roller derby team.

"Absolutely. Gotta block for my Cool Hand Bette," Elle said, using Janine's skate name.

"Excellent. I'll pick you up and drive?"

"It's a plan."

Minutes later, she was driving Alex home.

"How was the movie?"

"Awesome," he said, then proceeded to tell her about how intensely realistic the velociraptor attack had seemed. Elle smiled and laughed, all the while thinking she could so do this.

Nothing was going to stop Elle "Moneybags" Mariano from having her cake and eating it too.

Not a damn thing.

Not even the crack of dawn.

Because that piece of her that had longed for more woke her up early the next day. It tugged at some untended spot within her, like a small child grabbing her mother's shirt, asking for another cookie. She didn't entirely know what her heart wanted. She wasn't even in tune with the language it was speaking. But *something* compelled her to go.

As she peeked out the window, the sky turned the shade of dark blue that comes before the sun rises.

She pulled on shorts, a tank top, and a pair of her white roller skating socks with the row of red skulls around the knee, left a message for her snoozing son, and took off to surprise Colin.

CHAPTER TEN

This was a perfect dawn. Calm, quiet, and beautiful.

The craggy canyon rocks loomed larger as he drew closer to the lakeshore. The cool waters were still and serene, reflecting the soft rays of the rising sun that peeked over the horizon. Colin only had an hour free before he was due at the office, but he'd seized it. Times like these were precious.

The near-silence surrounding him was like a natural tranquilizer. Only the splash of the paddle with each stroke broke the quiet. He'd already gone for a swim, and tomorrow he'd tackle a morning climb as part of his training regimen for the triathlon. The event was less than a month away, and he was nearly ready. Way more prepped than he'd been last summer. He'd planned to try the triathlon again a year ago. But his last girlfriend, Kayla, hadn't understood his drive to redo the race, and she'd needled him again and again to stop spending so much time working out. Rather than rock the boat with Kayla, he'd abandoned his quest to compete. The relationship fizzled out a few months later when he realized the obvious—he and Kayla weren't right for each other, and he didn't want to be with someone who didn't understand what mattered to him. When he broke up with her, she'd left him a slew of angry messages—the kind that made him wish text messaging had never been invented.

At least Elle understood why he wanted to do this race. She got it. She got him. She understood that these moments before the day turned hectic and wild had become essential to his wellbeing, and to his recovery. At first he thought he could run faster, bike harder, or kayak longer to prove that he'd left addiction in the dust. Then he began to accept that recovery wasn't something you could muscle through to a finish line.

It was a daily practice.

He practiced it with intense outdoor exercise that burned in his muscles and made his heart pound. He'd always been active, but getting the bad shit out of his system had given him the chance to become an athlete in a new way. The rigor of his workout was part of how he gave back—to *himself*. After years of pouring crap into his body, he now chose to do the opposite. To treat his body like a temple.

Of course, there were other ways he enjoyed being good to the body, and last night was a prime example. He replayed the stairwell, the sink, the sexy sounds she made, and the sounds he didn't let her make.

Splash.

He nearly missed a paddle stroke, and he laughed quietly. Picturing Elle's hot body, and remembering her ravenous appetite, was not conducive to focused morning exercise. He repositioned the paddle and continued rowing closer to shore.

No time to linger on the woman while in the water. *Just concentrate on finishing the workout.*

He raised his eyes to the edge of the lake and blinked. What the hell?

A woman with long, wavy brown hair, and a badass skater girl outfit waved to him—big, broad, wildly happy waves. She cupped her hands around her mouth. "What do you think? Can I wear this kayaking?"

Striking a playful pose, she gestured to her outfit. She was a sight all right, in her tattered jean shorts and wife-beater tee, displaying the ink on her arms and wearing those crazy socks. She didn't look outdoorsy at all, but who fucking cared? He cracked up as a surge of happiness bounded through him. The last thing in the world he'd expected to see this morning was Elle. But the furious beating in his heart as he dragged the kayak ashore had little to do with the exertion and more to do with the utter delight of his unexpected morning visitor.

He tapped the side of the fiberglass hull. "So you decided to take me up on my offer to hit the lake?"

"Not entirely," she said, with a coquettish little grin and sway of the hips. "I don't think I have the right gear. But I thought I could take you out for a quick breakfast to say thanks for getting me out of the house last night. I had fun. I did some Yelp research and there's an organic cafe that serves steel-cut oats and handpicked blueberries on the way back to town. I'm guessing that's the only thing you put in your body in the morning?"

He fought back a grin. She knew him too well.

"Don't know where you got the idea that I was some kind of health nut," he said, with a "who me" to his tone.

"It's a mystery to me, too."

The real mystery though was why she was here. This wasn't like her. Not the Elle who had defined lines, rules, and boxes for him. On the one hand, maybe this was another acceptable sliver of time. But on the other, maybe she was here because he'd changed his approach and shown her a fun date last night. He hoped it was the latter, but whatever the reason, he'd gladly take it, and not just because those sexy socks made him think how insanely hot she'd look if they were the only thing she wore.

But because she was here.

* * *

"Where's Alex?" Colin asked after they ordered at the Ampersand & Pie, an off-the-beaten-path cafe with chalkboard menus and wooden chairs painted sky blue. They'd opted for a table on the outdoor patio.

"Not sure if you know this about teenage boys, but they have a thing for sleeping in," she said, tapping her watch. "It's seven a.m., and he'll be sound asleep 'til at least nine."

He gestured for her to come closer then dropped his voice to a whisper. "I do know that about teenage boys having once, you know, been one," he said, and she laughed. He reached for his coffee. "It was quite a surprise to see you at the shore."

"Not a bad one, I hope?"

"Never a bad one. But tell me. Why didn't you want to go kayaking? I would have gone back out on the water with you."

She shrugged and reached for a napkin on the table. "I figured there wasn't really time."

He arched an eyebrow, clearly not believing her. She folded and unfolded the napkin but didn't say any more.

He dropped a hand onto hers. "Okay, obviously, it's not about whether you had enough time to kayak. You're nervous, like you were with the zip line."

She squeezed her eyes shut momentarily. This felt less like fun and more like talking. But, something inside her *wanted* the talking. Not just about movies and the mob, but other things—the things that had brought them together in the first place. Talking about life. Was this why she'd felt the urge to find him this morning?

She worried away at her lip then sighed as she answered. "It's not that I'm afraid of kayaking. I just don't like activities that have a high possibility of death. Car racing, bungee jumping, kayaking..." She added, pointedly, "Or rock climbing."

He laughed. "You can't keep me away from that sport. And fine, the first two, sure. They can be dangerous—"

"So can rock climbing. You broke your tibia doing it."

"And lived to tell the tale. In fact," he said, tapping his calf, "everything works just fine in both legs. But let's get back to kayaking. You can swim, right? Wait. Don't tell me. Elle Mariano can't swim and my next project is to teach her how to dog paddle?"

She tossed the napkin at him, pinging his shoulder with it. "I can totally swim!"

She just didn't like to anymore.

"So what is it?" he asked, tilting his head, waiting. Simply waiting. Giving her time to answer, as well as time to study his handsome face. Dark scruff lined his jaw—that sexy, all-over stubble that she loved to feel against her. His brown eyes were the shade of espresso, and focused intently on her. She'd made a career out of listening to others, but she suspected she could learn from him, because this man made her feel as if he was hearing every single word.

She half wished there was some deep, dark reason for her mini phobias. Okay, not really. But it would be easier than the truth, which was that it hadn't taken much for her to become a fraidycat when it came to certain activities. "It's not as if there's some terrible traumatic story from my childhood, like I was caught in a current, or was attacked by a jellyfish, or that I nearly drowned. But when I was younger, a bunch of us used to go swimming at a lake, and jump off this rock ledge into it. One time when I did, I cut my head on a rock."

He winced. "Ouch. Were you okay?"

She nodded quickly. "Yes. I mean, there was a lot of blood, and my mother did her best impression of a calm nurse as her daughter's head bled and she took me to the ER. I got a few stitches right under my hairline, and everything was fine," she said, pushing her hair away from her ear to show him that she had no scar, no marks. "But still. It freaked me out. And I just realized that I didn't want to take chances like that again. That I could be safer if I *didn't* do stuff like that."

"But you do roller derby," he said in a gentle voice.

"Ah," she said, holding up her index finger to make her point. "The seeming contradiction. But see, I've always skated, and it's indoors, and there are no rocks, or dangerous currents, or cliffs to fall off of. And I like to be active, so skating seems the more reasonable risk. But that's also why I'm a blocker, not a jammer."

He raised an eyebrow in a question.

"Blocker is defense. Not as many injuries. It's the safer position."

"I see." He nodded slowly. "So you avoid things like zip lines and lakes and cliffs to stay safe?"

She parted her lips to speak but stopped to gaze at the wood of the overhang, and truly considered her answer. "I suppose so. I like life. I like living. I want to keep it that way. Seems I have the greatest chance if I can minimize risk by not, say, parachuting or rock climbing or anything else that might shorten my life."

"It might. It also might expand it," he suggested.

A tiny bead of defensiveness zipped across her. "Are you saying I don't have an expansive life?"

He shook his head. "No. Hell no. I just think there are reasonable risks and unreasonable ones, and you have to know which ones can enrich you."

"It's easy for you to say. Your whole job is about risks."

He wiggled his eyebrows. "I know. And I fucking love it."

"And I love helping kids at risk avoid more dangers in life," she said, matter-of-factly. She turned philosophical. "Funny, how both our jobs are about risk. But in very different ways."

He held his arms out wide, tapping an imaginary point with each hand. "That's true. It's like we're triangulating a problem. Approaching it from different sides."

Something about his analogy was so very Colin, and it amused her. "You really can see everything through the veil of math, can't you?"

He laughed deeply, flashing a big smile as he did. "Guilty as charged." He leaned forward. "So why did you come this morning, since you clearly had no intention of kayaking?"

That was the question, wasn't it? Last night as she'd returned home, she'd held tight to the notion of embracing the fun parts of their arrangement. She'd believed she was seizing the day and biting off a whole, yummy corner of a delicious chocolate cake. But the morning had rolled around, and she'd wanted something else.

Something she couldn't even name.

"I don't know," she said softly, holding out her empty hands. "I think I just wanted to surprise you, even though I don't want to go kayaking, Colin."

He reached for her hand, threaded his fingers through hers, and squeezed lightly. His touch was like turning on a light switch in a basement. It flickered briefly then started to light up the dark. Her heart fluttered for a moment, then settled into a peaceful rhythm. "Maybe some days you'll want to kayak and some days you won't, and whatever you want is fine by me," he said. It sounded like a metaphor, and somehow it left her a little sad, a little wistful.

The waitress arrived and set down their food. He dug in. "This is some fucking badass steel-cut oatmeal right here," he said, and she laughed as she bit into her toast.

When they were done, he took her to her car and kissed her good-bye, a fierce, hot kiss that felt different from the night before. Perhaps because it ended at that—just a kiss.

Maybe that was the answer to why she'd been compelled to get out of bed and drive to Black Canyon at dawn. This trip had never been about kayaking. Perhaps she'd come to see if they could have this kind of moment—without contact, without lust, without ripping off clothes.

She wasn't sure why she'd needed to know this. She was

well aware that this brief affair with Colin existed solely in the bedroom. But still, some part of her had been curious, and she'd needed to scratch that itch.

She'd scratched it, right?

CHAPTER ELEVEN

Colin: That thing you want me to do to you…

Elle: I'm all ears.

Colin: Come over tonight.

Colin: I mean, when can you come over? (See my attempt to be all polite rather than just demand your body, even though you want me to just demand your body)

Colin: Let me rephrase. When can you come over so I can make you come countless times on my face?

Elle: I'm sorry, what did you say? I was suffering from an intense bout of text message–induced lust.

Colin: I have just the cure for that.

Elle: You are the cure for all my lust.

Colin: Excellent. Let's keep it that way. So…tonight?

Elle: I want to, but can't. Busy with the boy. But my mom offered her services tomorrow night, so let me get back to you on a time. Actually, she offered her services anytime I want to get serviced by you!

Colin: You better not get serviced by anyone but me.

Elle: As if I need anyone else's services.

Colin: Also, that is an awesome offer. You should take her up on it.

Elle: I know. I'm lucky that she wants me to have a booty call. Though, I don't want you to think I'm only into your body. You have a nice brain, too. And you're fun. :)

Colin: Why thank you. I'm honored you've noticed more than my cock. So does that mean you'll grace me with your presence for, say, Thai food after said booty call? You know, since that's fun. :)

Elle: As long as I can order the super-spicy, burn-your-tongue-off pad Thai.

Colin: Like I'd order anything else.

Elle: I can't wait…for pad Thai and that thing I want.

Colin: Hmm…Can't remember now…what is that thing you want?

Elle: What you said to me in the stairwell.

Colin: I think I remember. You wanted a back rub, right?

Elle: Yes. Absolutely.

Colin: Or was it a foot massage?

Elle: Please. I can't wait for you to touch my toes.

Colin: Or maybe, it was something else? Refresh my memory, please.

Elle: Braid my hair. I want you to braid my hair.

Colin: Ah, yes. I am going to braid it so good you sing my name to the heavens.

Elle: You're on.

* * *

The face was eerily familiar.

Colin nearly stopped in his tracks as he rounded the corner on his way to the game room at the center. *That guy.* Walking toward him. Colin had noticed him shooting hoops a few times. He'd seen him in a math tutorial a couple of months ago.

But he'd also seen him in a photo on Brent's phone.

His eyes widened as he studied the guy heading in his direction. That was the dude who'd been stalking his twin sister. Brent had taken a picture of him outside Shannon's home one afternoon more than a month ago.

What the hell?

The hair on his neck stood on end. A primal instinct to protect his flesh and blood kicked in. He wanted answers. Wanted to know why the fuck a teen at the community center had been parked outside Shan's house...more than once. The guy had dark eyes, dark hair, and ink covering his right arm. He wore jeans. His boots clunked on the linoleum floor.

Colin hadn't yet gotten Brent to resend the image so he could forward it to Elle. Now the guy was here, and Colin was going to cut out the middleman.

"Hey," he said to get his attention.

The guy stopped short and peered around, like he was making sure who Colin was talking to. He pointed at himself and mouthed *me?*

"Yeah. You," Colin said, tilting his head. One part of him wanted to demand an answer. But the other part, the rational, logical, adult portion, told him not to jump to conclusions.

Give him the benefit of the doubt.

"What's your name?"

"Marcus," the guy answered, shifting on the balls of his feet.

Colin motioned him to the side of the hallway, next to the bulletin board layered with announcements for center activities. A poetry class. The free lunch schedule. Basketball leagues.

Marcus joined him. Colin scrubbed a hand across his chin, then dived into business, meeting him square in the eyes. "This might sound weird. But I'm pretty sure you were hanging around outside my sister's house a few times. Shannon Sloan. What's up with that?"

He answered immediately. "It's not weird." Marcus pulled up his right shirtsleeve. Colin flinched, but quickly relaxed when he saw the ink. It matched Rex's arm. *Protector.* "I do safety patrols with the Protectors," Marcus added.

"If you saw me somewhere, that was probably why. We go to a lot of neighborhoods."

He blinked. "Really?"

Marcus nodded. "Yup. We do. And I do."

A smile broke out across Colin's face. Color him impressed. "Rex was telling me about the Protectors. Like the Guardian Angels."

"That's where we got our inspiration from. Rex and I do patrols together sometimes. By the way, it's nice to meet you officially." He extended a hand. Something that looked like happiness flashed in Marcus's eyes as they shook. Colin wasn't sure what to make of it.

"Sorry, I should have given you my name. Colin Sloan. I volunteer here. Good to meet you, too. Truth be told, I was worried you were part of the Royal Sinners. We thought you might be when I saw you outside Shan's house. That you were targeting my sister for something."

Marcus held up both his hands, a sign he had nothing to hide. "No. God no. I want nothing to do with them. I was just checking things out. We've been scoping out a bunch of neighborhoods, even nicer ones. Just to make sure."

"Make sure of what?"

"That the streets are safe. No matter what." Marcus tapped his arm. "Always."

"That's awesome. Keep it up, man," he said. He couldn't wait to tell Shannon and Brent that there was nothing to fear, and that this kid was doing a good thing for the community. Colin knocked fists with the young man. He started to walk down the hall, when Marcus called out to him.

"Hey."

Colin turned around. Marcus swallowed then cleared his throat, as if he was about to say something difficult. "I sat in on one of your math sessions a few months ago. When I first checked out the center."

"You did?"

Marcus nodded several times and ran a hand over his chin, a gesture that Colin often did. Well, it wasn't unique to him. Lots of people did that. Still, he felt as if he was looking in a mirror for a second, seeing a young man trying to do good. "Yeah. Learned some stuff about P and L statements. I'm going to college in the fall."

"Good. I'm glad. Let me know if you need any more help. Math is kind of my forte. I'd be happy to work with you if you need anything."

Marcus smiled briefly. "I will. Thanks. That means a lot to me," he said, and his voice sounded like the very definition of the word hopeful. Odd, considering they were talking about math. For a moment, Marcus seemed as if he was about to say something more but he cut himself off. "I gotta run."

"Take it easy," Colin said and turned the other way.

He had an appointment with Rex to work on advanced algebra, thanks to the bet he'd won on the court the other day. As he headed to the homework room, his phone buzzed in his back pocket. His heart beat faster with the hope that it would be Elle, confirming a time for tomorrow evening. Then he nearly smacked himself for being so damn eager to see her.

Take it easy. Play it cool.

But hey, what man wouldn't want to see the woman who willingly and beautifully embraced the kind of pleasure he and Elle shared? Memories of her flashed before him, but his hopes were dashed when his brother Michael's name appeared on the screen with a text message.

M: Detective wants to meet again tonight re: some new info. Ryan has some details. He's going to call you a little later when he's in a better cell zone. I'm going with you to see the detective.

Colin heaved a sigh.

It didn't matter to Michael that the detective liked to meet with them alone to discuss the reopened investigation into their father's murder eighteen years ago and his search for the suspected accomplices. Determined as ever, Michael would have his way. Colin suspected this was Michael's means of making up for something that had never been his fault. After Colin's drinking and pill problem came to light, Michael had blamed himself for the trouble that his brother had gotten into in high school, especially because of the company Colin had kept as a young teen.

"You're crazy. Those are my mistakes, and I'm taking responsibility for them," Colin had said to him one night a few years ago, when his older brother told him how shitty he felt for not having known about his addictions. "I've accepted and moved beyond the fact that I made some bad choices and picked the wrong friends. Let's just learn from the past and let it go," he'd said, relying on the advice he'd leaned on in his recovery group.

"Fine, but I'm here for you now. Anything and everything," Michael had answered, like it was a new blood oath they were taking.

Anything and everything apparently included meeting with the detective to discuss new wrinkles regarding drugs and murder. Michael was probably coming along as some sort of buffer between the past and the present, as if he could shield Colin somehow. Colin didn't need that protection any longer, even when talking to the detective about the friends he'd had when younger. But Michael needed to be present more than Colin needed him, so he let his big brother be the big brother. That was part of Colin's own letting go—accepting that the people he loved wanted to give of themselves in the ways that they could.

He fired off a return text.

C: Working with the kids now. Should be done in an hour or so and hope to catch Ryan then. Did he give you the details?

As Colin walked into the game room, a reply arrived.

M: The call kept breaking up. Something about that pattern. Sounds like it's a hell of a lot more than a few names and addresses.

The pattern again. That damn pattern Ryan had told him about. When he'd first learned whose names were in it, he couldn't believe that he'd known both men many years ago. Now they somehow held clues to his father's murder.

CHAPTER TWELVE

A construction crew jackhammered outside her closed window, smashing the broken sections of the basketball court in preparation for smoothing them over with a fresh concrete surface. A pair of new security guards patrolled the block, courtesy of Colin. The sight of them brought a smile to her face—the man had moved quickly to make sure the center was safe during a time of transition.

As Elle surveyed the signs of change, she chatted on the phone with some of the center's biggest donors, making her round of calls to thank them for their contributions.

She'd started sending letters and flowers earlier in the week, and was following up today with personal calls. She dialed another number and spoke briefly with a benefactor in San Francisco named Charlie, who'd attended the Beethoven event. "We couldn't have done it without you. We're already starting the work, and I'm thrilled to say it's going well so far," Elle said as she gazed out the window. "I'm watching them rebuilding the basketball court right now. And the boys spend a lot of time there, so your contribution is being put to good use immediately."

"It is a pleasure and an honor to help such a worthy cause."

"If you're in Vegas again, I do hope you'll stop by the center to see our work."

"I come to Vegas often. Once a week now, it seems, and I will take you up on it. And please, you can count on me to be a regular contributor. The center is a worthy cause, and it also allows me to right some wrongs from my past."

"It does?" she asked, curious as to what he meant.

He sighed with a note of regret, but his voice seemed hopeful too as he answered her. "I made some mistakes when I was younger. I held onto a debt longer than I should have. This is my amends."

"I'm a big fan of making changes," she said, smiling as they talked about redemption and all its possibilities. So refreshing to hear him speak openly about amends. Sam had never truly embraced that concept, though she'd desperately wished he had. Even during his rehab stints, he'd never tried to apologize for his past sins and omissions. His behavior sober was remarkably similar to his behavior when he'd been high—yet another reason why she'd never trusted his recovery. It had never stuck, and he never truly changed.

Clearly.

He'd died in her arms smashed on cocaine.

Colin, on the other hand, seemed to live a recovering life. He gave of his time. He opened his heart. He'd learned from the past. The man she knew now was exactly the kind of man she could see herself falling for. Colin cared about kids, and he was kind, smart, passionate, and sexy as hell. For a brief moment, she imagined their relationship with no rules, no boundaries, no lines, and she could see Colin fitting seamlessly into her life.

As more than her friend.

She wondered, though, what he'd been like when he was addicted, and if she would even have recognized him. Not physically, but emotionally—was he the same guy she knew now? Or was he more like Sam? Or even Charlie, who also seemed determined to live a changed sort of life.

After the call ended, someone rapped on her door, so she swept aside her musings about Colin and making amends. She rose and opened it, delighted to see Marcus on the other side. But her smile fell quickly—his face was white as snow.

"I need to talk to you. Badly." His voice shook.

Worry coursed through her, a prickly flurry of nerves as she shut the door. "Of course, come in. What's going on?"

He sank onto her couch and dropped his head in his hand, running his fingers roughly through his hair. Her heart lurched toward him.

"I need to talk. About some heavy shit. And you can't tell anyone," he said, raising his face.

"Are you going to tell me something I'd *need* to tell someone else?" She looked him in the eye, making it clear that she'd keep his confidences if they didn't cross certain lines. "Because if you tell me you're going to hurt yourself or someone else, there's no confidentiality."

"No. God, no," he said with a brief laugh, but it was a joyless sound. "I just need this to be between us."

While she wasn't technically Marcus's social worker, she'd been trained as one. And as the center director, she strove to abide by proper guidelines. That meant she'd keep whatever they discussed between the two of them.

"My family, who I've been trying to meet? My brothers? My sister?" he said, as if he needed to prompt her.

"Yes."

He sighed deeply. "You know one of them."

She cocked her head, trying to figure out who on earth it could be. "I do?"

He nodded and gulped. "You do. He's a volunteer here, and I knew that when I first came to play hoops. He's the reason I started coming around the center. To see what my family was like. To get a sense before I met them."

The world froze. Everything and everyone became a statue as she swayed, absorbing his news.

"Colin Sloan is one of my brothers."

She clasped a hand to her mouth. Then it was her turn to sink down, as she fell into her chair and tried to rearrange her shock so she could lend her support.

"My dad never wanted me to meet them," Marcus said. "He always told me I was safer staying away from them. So I respected his wishes while I lived under his roof. I worry he's going to be pissed when he finds out, but I don't care. I have to do this. I need to go back and try again. Especially since I just talked to Colin in the hall."

"Does he know?" she asked, her voice papery.

Marcus shook his head. "No. Not yet. But he seems like a good guy, and I want to do this right." He talked more about his parents and the twisted tale of how his dad met his mom, and how his dad felt about her. When he was done, he took the biggest inhalation in the world, it seemed, and relaxed into the couch, spreading his arms across the back of it. "You're the only person I've told about this. God, it feels good to finally say their names. To finally be able to talk to someone and share all the details."

He was unburdened, buoyed with relief. Meanwhile, she'd taken on the weight of one of the biggest secrets she could ever imagine keeping from someone she cared for.

Cared for.

Holy shit. The realization crash-landed in her that Colin wasn't just the man she was sleeping with. He was more to her. Even if she couldn't have it, she realized she wanted more than friendship with him. More than just these sexy nights.

This wasn't the plan. This wasn't supposed to happen. He was supposed to be her no-strings lover.

Which made this new situation that much harder. Because she'd just spent the last hour in a strange state of suspended animation as she counseled a boy on how to reconnect with the family of the man she was involved with.

Never in her life had she wanted to clone herself like she did now. Never had she so badly needed to be two Elles at once.

* * *

Colin closed the math apps on his laptop, pleased with the progress that Rex had made. After winning the basketball court bet, Colin had expected some resistance from Rex, but the teen had taken quickly to the business math they worked on and had decided to sign up for a math placement test at community college in just a few days. Their tutoring had become a crash course, and Rex had been excelling.

As a reward, Rex attacked a fleet of zombies as he played video games with his brother Tyler and Elle's son Alex.

Colin glanced over at the boys, firing away at the living dead on the TV.

Alex pointed, practically stabbing the screen. "Get that one. Do it now!" he shouted to Rex.

Sometimes, it was odd to be in the same room with Alex. Not because Colin knew what the kid's mom looked like naked and falling apart in his arms. And not because there was any weirdness with Alex—there wasn't.

The issue lay with Colin. He was keenly aware that Elle had drawn a line in the sand regarding who she let into her son's life. Given what happened to Alex's dad, he understood her need to protect him.

"Rex, look out! There's another one. You have to book it to the safe house!" The warning came from Rex's little brother. Rex narrowed his eyes in fierce concentration, jamming his thumb hard on the controller, firing away at a zombie and blasting him to smithereens.

"Oh yeah! You did it. Man. You don't suck as much as I thought," Alex said to Rex, then punched him on the shoulder.

"I don't suck at all. I rock hard. And I will school you soon enough," Rex said as he raised his arms in triumph.

"You wish," Alex said, picking up his controller to get ready for his turn. "I am the master."

Rex craned his neck to catch Colin's attention. "Hey, man! Got any tips for us on angles and shit?"

"You know anything about video games?" Alex asked as Colin stuffed his laptop into a messenger bag.

"I know a bit."

"Give me a tip," Alex said. "I need to up my game."

Do something cool for Elle's kid? This was a no-brainer —he liked working with the boys, and he liked that he could be a positive influence rather than a bad one. That had to count for something. Plus, Alex was a good kid. "Here's your tip. It's all strategy. You just devise a strategy and follow it. But don't be afraid to pivot if things change, and then to pivot again," he said, then let his own advice register. Because, as he noodled on the words, he realized they might apply to his approach with Elle.

His strategy had been to focus on the physical, then on the fun and friendship, despite her big reservations. The approach had worked, to a point. Each encounter they'd had was hotter than the last, and each moment together seemed to show how good a time they could have. The question was, when would all the fun and games tip over into something more? Something deeper. He'd sensed an inkling of emotion from her at the Mob Museum, and even more the other morning at the cafe by the canyon. Was it time to pivot once again?

"Strategy," Alex repeated, then tapped his temple as he played. "I'm working on my strategy as we speak. Thanks, man."

Alex held out his free hand for a low high-five, and Colin obliged.

As the boys returned to the game, Colin tapped the back of the couch and told them he'd see them later in the week. On the way out, he walked past the vending machine. The Diet Cherry Coke had been restocked. A rarity. He plugged some quarters in and snagged a cold one, then stopped at Elle's office to say a quick good-bye.

A chaste good-bye. A friendly good-bye. To show her he could care for her not only in bed, but also during the regular rhythm of her day. She loved Diet Cherry Coke in the afternoon. A pick-me-up. Yes, it was a small thing. But wasn't it the little gestures in life that often mattered the most?

The door was shut. He knocked and heard some rustling and the squeak of a chair. There was no answer. He waited ten seconds before he knocked once more.

"I'm busy now." Her voice was tinny from behind the walls.

He set the can on the floor and left, sending her a text that the soda was from him.

A few minutes later, as he drove home, his phone rang with a call from an international number. He swiped over the screen immediately, eager for the details from Ryan.

"How's Johnny Cash?"

Colin laughed deeply. Only his dog-loving brother would focus on the four-legged beast first. "I'm on my way home to take care of him now. He is a prince among canines. I took him to the dog park the other night and all the lady dogs ran up to him," Colin said into the speakerphone as he slowed at a red light.

"They can't help themselves around him. You can use him as a wingman if you think he can help you land a woman. Wait. What's the latest with the woman from the benefit?"

Colin tapped the steering wheel and blew out a long stream of air. "Like I said before you left, it's complicated. Speaking of complicated, you know that kid who was following Shan? I've got great news for you." He told his brother what he'd learned an hour ago about the Protectors. "So it's all good. We don't need to worry about him," he said, pressing the gas as the light changed. "Now, why don't you tell me why the hell you're calling from Germany at midnight your time when you should be focusing on your woman?"

"Don't you worry. I'm still focusing on her, but you will not fucking believe what she found out the other night."

"Lay it on me."

"Sophie was jet-lagged and couldn't sleep. So she was working on deciphering the rest of the pattern that I told you about." Ryan was talking about the sewing pattern that their mom had passed onto him before she went to prison. She'd asked Ryan, then just a fourteen-year-old, to hold on to it for her, telling him that it was a prized pattern for a dog jacket that she wanted to make when she was freed. He'd held onto the hope that she might be innocent, and so he'd saved the pattern for her, only to discover a week ago, when Sophie tried to make the jacket, that it was a code of sorts. The first row contained addresses that corresponded to the homes of the shooter, and of the two alleged accomplices in their father's murder. Sophie had said there was more to the pattern, and she'd need extra time with it.

"What did she find out? What were the rest of the lines?" Colin asked.

"It's a list of more addresses. They had missing numbers and symbols, but she worked on it and she figured out all of them. She gave it to John, and when he put it together with the leads he's been looking into, he believes the pattern is a hell of a lot more than just those two guys. You better be sitting down," Ryan said, his voice heavy and intense.

Colin slowed the car, pulled over, and cut the engine. "Talk to me. What is it?"

Ryan heaved a sigh then told him the newest wrinkle.

Colin was damn glad he'd pulled over. His head fell back against the headrest, the shock of Ryan's new revelation echoing in his bones.

When he reached his home and leashed up his brother's dog, his phone buzzed once more. Elle had messaged him. At last. But when he read the note, frustration seared him to a crisp.

Elle: I'm so sorry. I have to cancel tomorrow. Something came up.

CHAPTER THIRTEEN

Johnny Cash trotted perfectly by Colin's side as Michael pulled up in his black BMW, a mountain bike on the roof. Colin slowed his pace and met Michael as he stepped out of his car. His brother must have come straight from the office. He wore his usual striped button-down, tie, and dark pants. When he reached Colin, he whipped off his sunglasses, his cool blue gaze sharp as ever. "Did you talk to Ryan? You ready for the detective?"

Colin pushed his palm down as if to say *let's take it easy.* "It's just a talk. I've got nothing to hide."

Michael clapped him on the back. "I know that, man. That's not my point. I was just asking. Just making sure."

Colin brushed off Michael's hand. "I get it. But the point is I'm neither worried, nor surprised about anything related to our mother," he said, though that wasn't entirely true. He'd been shocked by the news Ryan had shared about her, but only for the first few minutes. At this point Colin was accustomed to hearing that she was a less than stellar citizen.

What had him so prickly was Elle's cancellation of their plans tomorrow with zero explanation. Nothing. Not a word. That confused the hell out of him, especially because he had no right to ask her what was up. She'd been direct from day one about what she could give and what she couldn't. They were friends-plus-more, and that was that. She'd made no promises, and he had no reason to feel slighted.

Except…she'd been giving off some serious *I want more* vibes at the café the other morning. He'd been damn sure they were crossing into the unchartered territory of *more*— exactly where he wanted to be with her.

But, hell, maybe that had been wishful thinking on his part. Maybe he'd been reading too much into one small, sweet little moment. Because this Elle—the hot and cold one—was the one he'd been used to. Push, pull. Move forward, retreat. Fuck, freak out.

Time to wise up and accept what she would give, instead of angling for something he'd never have. Elle was the summit he'd never reach, thanks to his past.

Right now, Colin's present involved a detective, who parked his Nissan Leaf at the curb in front of his house. Colin nudged Michael and dropped his voice. "I never, never, never would have pegged the detective as the owner of an electric car."

Michael laughed. "Doesn't he know he's required to drive a sedan? Four doors, dark blue, unmarked. Just like the movies."

John walked over to the two of them, took off his shades, and said hello. Johnny Cash barked at the man. Colin tugged on the dog's leash, giving him a quick correction. "It's okay, Johnny Cash. If you're nice to him, the detective won't throw us in the pokey," Colin said.

John rubbed the dog's head. "Nice first name for a dog. And I don't have any plans to throw you in the pokey." He paused, then added, "At least, not today." John shifted his gaze to Michael. "Good to see you again, too, Mr. Sloan."

Michael nodded. "I know you were planning on talking to Colin, but I see no reason why I can't be here."

John nodded and shot him a closed-mouth smile. "Not a problem. Happy to chat with both of you about the latest. Do you want to talk inside? Or chat on the porch?"

Colin's street was quiet now, so he opted for the porch.

John dived right into the heart of his visit. "Here's the deal." He took a piece of paper from his pocket then spread open a copy of the sewing pattern on his lap. Johnny Cash lifted his snout to sniff it. "We knew from Sophie's first attempts that this pattern contained more than just a few names. Now that she's figured out all the addresses in it, we were able to track them to who lived in those houses at the time of the murder. We believe that this was a drug dealing route," the detective said, sharing what Ryan had told Colin on the phone.

There it was. The official mention of how unbelievably fucked up their mother was. What gnawed at Colin the most wasn't that he shared genes with her, but that he shared *choices*. The choice to use—coke for her, pills and liquor for him. The one solace he found was that even before he'd stopped, he'd stopped at using. He'd never moved into the selling, as she evidently had.

"Surprise," Michael said with disdain. "Inmate 347-921 was a drug dealer, in addition to being a murderer. What next? She ran a child pornography ring? Oh wait. She probably operates an underground sex slave business from prison." Michael shoved a hand into his dark hair. "Every fucking time it's something else with her."

"Sorry to be the bearer of this news." John's voice was steady, a stark contrast to Michael's. "We believe these men were at the top of the pattern not only because of their potential involvement in the murder, but because of their role in the drug ring, and we think below them is the list of people Dora was selling to regularly. Presumably she hid her route in the pattern so no one in her family would know what she was doing. We'd previously thought Stefano was her dealer, but it seems he was a step up. He was her supplier and provided the drugs she sold. That's why she owed him money—for the drugs she procured from him." John turned to Colin. "But we don't believe Stefano was the one who recruited her for it. Do you know anything about how she got involved? Can you remember anything?"

Michael raised a hand and cut in before Colin could say a word. "Why are you asking him?"

"Because of the friends he had when he was younger," John said to Michael in a cool, even tone. "That's why I'm here talking to him."

"I'll answer it," Colin said firmly, taking the reins. He loved his big brother, adored him to the ends of the Earth, but Colin wasn't a kid anymore. "The answer is no. I have no clue how she got involved in dealing drugs. I had no idea she was selling, but it doesn't surprise me because she was a fucked up, desperate woman. But if you're asking for details about the drug business the Royal Sinners were in, I'll tell you anything I know. I've been upfront with you from day one, Detective. When I was thirteen, I hung with the wrong crowd. I was friends with the wrong people, and yes, I was friends with the brother of one of the men whose address was in the pattern. T.J. Nelson's brother Paul. He was fifteen and I was thirteen, and when Ryan told me T.J's name was in that pattern, I was shocked—and frankly embarrassed that I was ever friends with his brother. We did stupid shit. Egged houses, TP'd them. That was as far as we went. But we knew what the older guys were doing because we heard them talk."

"What did you hear?"

"They were always talking about territory. They claimed 'hoods' for fencing their stolen goods, and when they moved deeper into drugs, they claimed sections of neighborhoods for selling those, too. They marked everything that was theirs with gang logos, insignia, personal graffiti. They'd have a field day on Facebook today with the way they tagged stuff."

John nodded. "The gang culture, oddly enough, loves social media. They post pictures of themselves online, on Instagram and Facebook, holding wads of bills from their drugs, or showing off phones they stole."

"That's what it was all about then, too, in an old school way."

"What do you know about T.J. Nelson?" John asked.

"He's the guy you think brokered Stefano's hits, right?" Michael chimed in. After Sophie uncovered the code in the pattern, and Ryan delivered some fresh details on potential names, the detective had enough info to pinpoint the suspected accomplices. A pair of cousins, T.J. and Kenny Nelson, were believed to have helped Jerry Stefano pull off the murder. When Stefano wound up going to prison for the crime, he never gave up their names. But the detective had new evidence pointing to their roles—T.J. as the broker and Kenny as the getaway driver.

John nodded. "We think that's a strong possibility. We want to know more about him, and how big his role was."

"Big? Like he was a mastermind of the whole thing?" Colin asked, trying to get to the heart of what the detective needed to know.

But John kept certain details close to the vest. "There are a number of possibilities we're looking into. Tell me what you know of him."

Colin sighed deeply, rewinding to his days as a thirteen-year-old, picturing T.J. Nelson, the towering older brother with the short mohawk, gold earring, and menacing smile. His arms were made of steel, and he had a head for strategy. He was always plotting. "What I remember overhearing was T.J. talking about who was handling what in the Royal Sinners. He was very focused on which guys were responsible for which areas. The territories, they called them," Colin said. "And they also talked about the protection of them."

"Of the territories?" John asked, his voice tight and clipped, a shift from his previous tone, as if he were holding something in.

Colin nodded. "Yes. I didn't have any of the details, but that's some of what I overheard when he was around. Who handled the fences. Who picked up the drugs. That sort of thing." Colin held up his hands like an innocent man, telling the whole truth. "I had no clue my mom was selling, dealing, or using. But given what you figured out with that pattern, maybe that's what she was doing talking to them. Maybe she was picking her territory for selling."

"Seems she got a prime one," John said. "Any idea why she would?"

"She probably blew somebody," Michael said with a sneer.

Colin leaned forward, speaking in a stage whisper. "John, I wanted to let you in on a little secret. You might not have picked up on this, but Michael's not a fan of our mom."

John laughed lightly; the momentary tension had vacated. "That's coming through loud and clear."

"To answer your question, I have no idea why she would get a prime route, as you say. Except that she was desperate, and maybe she had some strings to pull, because she was willing to do whatever she had to do to get what she wanted. That's what I know to be true about her. Maybe she and Stefano were working together," Colin said, because that seemed plausible to him.

Michael cleared his throat. "What's going on with the Royal Sinners these days, Detective? I follow the news; I've been reading up on them, seeing more and more stories about them rising in power. More crimes, more problems, more trouble. More organized, too, than their rival gangs. I keep hearing 'Don't mess with the Sinners.'"

"Yeah, we've upped the security at the center during the repairs just to make sure the kids are safe," Colin added.

A somber look flitted into the detective's eyes. "You hear right. They're a top priority for Metro, and my men are working hard on gang enforcement and prevention. We've got an anonymous tip line for concerned citizens to report suspected gang activity, an anti-gang initiative, and public education is going strong. We're doing everything we can on the enforcement front. Last week, we had a few more arrests of Royal Sinners members for grand theft auto, and some from rival gangs for burglary."

"Glad to hear it's being taken seriously. Some of my other clients have also been asking about it and increasing their security services based on what they've been reading in the news," Michael said. "They want to protect themselves, and to know the authorities are working hard on it, too."

"I assure you, we are. And you can let your clients know that you've talked to Metro and that we're committed to this," he added. "We're doing everything we can to dismantle the gangs, member by member."

That last word latched onto Colin's brain, making him wonder if his old friend Paul had gone down the path of his brother into the Sinners.

"Hey, what happened to Paul? We didn't stay friends."

"Paul Nelson is dead," John said, matter-of-factly, and Colin's blood froze. "Shot three times in a drive-by shooting a few years ago. Retaliation from another gang over a murder. One we think T.J. was involved in. Both T.J. Nelson and Kenny Nelson are on the run now. They're wanted for other crimes over the years."

His whole body turned to ice. "Wow," Colin said heavily, grappling with the shocking news. "Paul died before he was thirty."

"Gangs are a young man's business," John said. "You don't find many old men in street gangs. The young men usually die or wind up in prison by the time they hit thirty. Like Stefano. Like Paul."

"What about T.J. and Kenny Nelson? They must be in their forties. What's their secret to a long life as a gang man?"

"I'd like to know. Because they're the exception to the rule," John said, then thanked them for their time and walked away.

* * *

The bell above the door jingled. Marcus looked up from his math book as a guy in jeans and a black T-shirt entered the convenience store where he worked.

Marcus nodded a hello then returned to the page in front of him, as his mind replayed the day. Talking to Elle had unburdened him, and he was more fired up than ever about his plans. College, living on his own, getting to know his unknown family—he'd wanted all of that for so long, and he was close to having it. Living with his dad had been stifling for so many reasons. Sometimes he missed seeing his stepmom and his little sisters now that he was no longer at home with them, but Marcus was glad to live with his friends. He was on a path to becoming an assistant manager here at the store, and that was helping him make ends meet, along with his savings from little jobs over the years.

As he worked through some equations, the guy grabbed a bag of chips and sauntered over to the counter. He was about Marcus's age, maybe a year older. He had a goatee, light eyes, and a black and blue fingernail on his right hand, as if he'd slammed it in a car door.

The guy tossed the bag on the counter, as if it were a prize he'd won at a fair. "I'll take this tasty bag of barbecue chips, *please*," he said, stretching out the last word.

"Sure," Marcus said, scanning the bag. "That'll be a dollar and two cents."

The guy jammed his hands into his pockets, riffling around. He pulled out a flip phone and set it on the counter, eyeing it dismissively. "Someday I'll get an iPhone." Stuffing his hand into his pocket again, he produced a wadded-up bill, then spread it open. "Shit. I only have a one."

"That's cool. I got it," Marcus said, reaching into the change tin to grab two pennies.

"You are the man," the guy said with a too-wide grin as he pointed his index fingers at Marcus like guns.

"No problem."

The guy glanced at the textbook and stabbed his finger against it. "You learning algebra or something like that?"

Marcus nodded, not bothering to explain that he was well beyond ninth grade math at this point. "Studying for school."

"College?" the guy asked, as if he'd never heard of it before.

"That's the goal."

"Man, that shit looks hard. I can't even imagine."

Marcus smiled faintly. He wasn't worried. He wanted the challenge. Wanted to meet it and exceed it.

The guy ripped open the bag with a loud pop and stuffed a chip in his mouth, crunching loudly, like he was showing off how well his teeth worked. "My goal is to never need college," he said, then cocked his head like he was studying him. "See you later," he finally said, then walked to the door and stopped to add, "*Marcus*."

A chill swept through him as the bell jingled and the guy left.

How the hell did he know his name?

He glanced down at his work shirt and laughed at himself. His nametag was on. "Duh," he said, and he returned to his textbook.

* * *

Colin's bike pounded against the bumpy trail, vibrations thrumming in his bones. He leaned into the curve, relentlessly focusing on the single track beneath the wheel and the 180-degree turn ahead of him on the descent.

Whipping past the switchback, he stomped the pedals, chasing speed, chasing adrenaline, and finding it on the hills of Red Rock Canyon with his mountain bike. Dirt churned up beneath him as he attacked the toughest trail, leaving the latest twists and turns in the never-ending saga of their mother in a swirl of dust.

When he reached the bottom, his heart hammered mercilessly, but he'd beaten his brother.

Michael had determination on his side, but Colin possessed that too, along with a more potent dose of fearlessness. Sometimes fearless meant you were faster on a downhill. Tonight, with the sun sinking low on the horizon, the time on the bike was therapy—it was necessary to shed the frustrations he felt over Elle, but also the guilt he still harbored over his mistakes as a kid. Riding a rocky downhill required extreme concentration, and the rattle and hum of the wheels on the ground had forced everything else from his brain, narrowing his focus to only the bike and the trail, and besting his brother.

Michael rolled up next to him, stopping his bike.

"Streak's still intact," Colin said, his breath coming fast as he wheeled to the water fountain at the base of the hill. "I continue to reign supreme on two wheels."

"Watch it. You're lucky I still ride with you," Michael teased, as he unsnapped his helmet.

After a drink of water, Colin let the therapy continue, this time with words. Because he wasn't done. The silt on the riverbed of the past had been well and truly stirred up tonight. "Michael," he said, stripping away the macho bravado. "I still feel like shit for being friends with those guys."

His brother got off his bike, resting his palm on the seat. "You're not responsible. Your friendship played no role in the murder."

"But what if I hadn't been friends with Paul? What if I'd never known them? Would things be different?" he asked, letting the question hang in the air.

Michael dropped a hand to Colin's shoulder. "Forget the 'what if.' Focus on the real. And that's this: she didn't find Stefano through you," he said, his voice firm and clear. "She found Stefano on her own. She found those others on her own. Hell, for all we know she might have found them through her lover. The one thing I know for certain is she didn't find them through you being buddies with T.J's little bro when you were twelve and thirteen. That is not how it happened. But even if it had, for the sake of argument, let me ask you this. Who arranged for the murder?"

"She did," he said softly.

"Who hired Stefano?"

"She did." His voice picked up volume.

"Who planned a murder?"

"She did." His tone was strong and certain now.

"Exactly," Michael said, bending to the water fountain and gulping up a stream. As he rose, he wiped the back of his hand across his mouth.

"But I've made the same mistakes she made," Colin said quietly, guilt stitched into his voice, into his goddamn heart and soul. Most days, he didn't beat himself up. But some days, he did. Some days he was consumed with the emotion.

Michael raised a finger and pointed it at Colin. "You didn't do what she did. You made mistakes that are fucking forgivable. You made mistakes that hurt yourself. You made mistakes that a human being makes. You did not kill a man. You are not like her."

Colin pressed his thumb and forefinger against the bridge of his nose and exhaled, visualizing letting go of all this guilt.

Soon, soon, he had to say good-bye to it.

"Speaking of what ifs, have you ever heard from your 'what if' girl?" Colin asked as they loaded their bikes on the roof rack a few minutes later.

Michael shook his head. "Not lately. That's why she's a 'what if' girl."

As they left, Colin asked himself if he'd be happy letting Elle become a 'what if' girl.

CHAPTER FOURTEEN

Big dots of primary-colored light swirled in a speed race across the slick hardwood floors, as the music of the B-52s pulsed throughout the rink.

"All right, my crazy skaters, I want to see how excited you get when you go to the looooooooove shack." The directive came from Elle's sister Camille. Mic at her mouth, she worked up the crowds at the Skyway Roller Rink, where she was the manager.

A flurry of teens, sprinkled with a few moms and the regular crew of older skaters who still rocked out on the quads nearly every night, motored around the oval, picking up the pace to the popular skating tune. The song was an appropriate number for the conversation Elle needed to have with her little sister, considering Elle and Colin were having a "Love Shack" kind of relationship.

The getaway kind. The sneak-off-and-get together kind.

Or was it more accurate to say they'd *had* that kind?

That was why she was here: to figure out if she needed to cut things off with him. But she flinched from the mere

thought of ending the sweetest thing she'd had in ages—
their secret, sexy, wonderful affair.

"That's right!" Camille shouted. "Skate like there's glit-
ter on the highway!"

Camille held up a finger and mouthed *one more minute*.
As Elle waited for the upbeat song to end, she dropped her
head to her hand, Marcus's confession echoing in her
mind. There was no way she could tell Colin about his
brother. That would be wrong. It wasn't her place. But she
felt awful knowing this news was barreling toward him and
that any day he'd learn he had a long-lost brother.

There was something so very soapy about it, as if she
could be reading the crib notes to a storyline on *As the
World Turns*.

*The character of the mother becomes pregnant before the
murder of her husband. The mother hides her pregnancy during what turns out to be a speedy trial. She goes to jail six
months pregnant. No one in her family knows about the baby
in her belly. The only one the wiser—besides the medical staff
at the correctional facility—is her lover on the outside. The
lover whose hands were clean of the crime.*

Elle shuddered as her sister encouraged the crowd to
"bang, bang, bang on the door."

*Then the half-brother is born in prison and handed over to
his father, who moves far, far away from Vegas with his baby
son. He's not required to tell a soul. There are no prison rules,
nor federal ones, requiring a parent to disclose to half-siblings
that they have a new little brother.*

*The father meets a new woman in San Diego, falls in love
with her, fathers more children, and returns to Vegas a few
years ago with his oddly blended family.*

Elle had started to replay the rest of the story when the
song ended and Camille introduced an MC Hammer tune

then set down her mic. She nodded to the little gate at the edge of her DJ booth. Elle rose and followed Camille to the skate racks as she began straightening pairs of rental skates. Elle joined in, knowing the routine well from having helped out here before.

"So what's the story? Time to spill," Camille said in her no-nonsense tone as she tucked some laces into a pair of skates.

"The problem is, I can't even tell you what the problem is," Elle said, frustration thick in her voice as she adjusted the wheels on another pair.

Camille arched an eyebrow and stared at Elle with her deep brown eyes. "What's that supposed to mean?"

"Just what I said. I'm sworn to secrecy."

"Well, unswear yourself, girl, so I can help out," Camille said, nudging Elle with an elbow. "Or do I need to tickle it out of you, like when we were kids?"

Elle stepped away and held up her hands in surrender. "Not the tickle! Anything but the tickle."

"Fine. I won't torture you like that. But tell me what's on your mind. I have ten minutes of MC Hammer and Vanilla Ice queued up before I need to get back there, and I want to help you," she said as she worked her way down a row. Camille's dark hair was twisted into a looped-over ponytail, and she wore jeans and a T-shirt. She'd been managing this rink since after college. Both sisters had been avid skaters growing up, and Camille loved music and happy places, as she liked to say, so the job fit her perfectly. She'd been the one to encourage Elle to try out for the Fishnet Brigade a few years ago. *Perfect therapy to deal with your crazy-ass baby daddy,* she'd said. Camille had never been fond of Sam, and with good reason.

Elle sighed and tried to figure out how to begin to ask for the advice she couldn't even truly ask for. "So there's this guy…"

"Ah, the plot thickens."

"And I like him."

"Oooh. It's even thicker."

"But it's not serious."

"Because of you or him?"

Elle stopped unknotting a gnarled lace to consider the question. Did Colin want to be serious with her? From time to time, he'd seemed to. But he never pushed her. He understood her boundaries. "Both of us are fine with the way it is," she answered before she had time to delve any deeper into why she'd been experiencing more moments when she wanted to shed the boundaries and erase the lines between them. To dive in full speed ahead, damn the consequences. "But the thing is, I learned something about him and his family that he doesn't know."

"Oh, now the plot is molasses thick," Camille said, her eyes glittery with excitement from the prospect of a juicy tale.

"And I can't divulge what I know because of confidentiality guidelines as a social worker, and it's kind of a big thing, so I just have to wait and see if this other person will divulge it to him. And ugh, Camille, I just feel like a mess in here," she said, grabbing her belly. "I'm all twisted and turned, and I feel like I'm lying to him, but I'm not. I just can't tell him. It's not my secret to tell."

Camille's expression turned serious and she stepped away from the row of skates. She parked her hands on Elle's shoulders. "You can't solve every problem. If this is something you can't do anything about, you need to try not to let it eat away at you. You worry too much, and you take on the weight of everything. And I get it. You've had some tough shit to deal with yourself."

"But do I keep seeing him while knowing this secret and not being able to say it?"

"Do you want to see him?"

Elle nodded. Easiest question of the night.

"If your hands are tied, your hands are tied. You can't untie them, just like you couldn't make Sam a better dad," she said, reminding Elle of how hard she'd tried to fix the things beyond fixing. "Lord knows, if you're having a nice time with this new guy, you deserve it. Let go of the things you can't control." Camille snapped her fingers. "That reminds me of a song. Lace up!"

Elle grabbed a pair of skates, tied them quickly, and rolled over to the rink, eagerly anticipating her sister's musical choice for her life.

Camille returned to her perch at the mic. "Boys and girls, men and women of all ages. I need to take a break from Vanilla Ice because every now and then we must heed the advice of the one and only Ice Queen, Elsa."

Elle cracked up over her sister's choice. Only Camille could find inspiration in the insanely popular Disney song that blared through the rink. Maybe the verses of "Let It Go" weren't entirely on point where Elle's problem was concerned, but the chorus and the final few lines gave her something else she needed.

A reminder that this battle wasn't hers to pick and choose. It wasn't hers to fight or not fight. All she could do was stand on the sidelines.

Let the storm rage on.

Whatever was brewing in Colin's life wasn't Elle's storm. It would rage on of its own power, whether or not she saw the man again.

* * *

Later that night, Alex grabbed an extra composition notebook from the school supplies aisle at Target and showed it to Elle. "For planning."

"Always good to plan for school."

He shook his head. "Nope. This one is for *State of Decay*. I came up with a new strategy today, and I want to write it down and test it out, step by step."

She shook her head, bemused. "Look, sweetie. I'm glad you like the game, but your freshman year of high school starts in about a week, and you do need to start focusing on schoolwork. Maybe we should get you a history review book, and you can work on how World War I began instead of your zombie attack plan."

"Don't worry. It was the assassination of Archduke Franz Ferdinand, and I'll still bring home straight As," he said, flashing her a toothy smile. He wasn't exactly a straight-A student, but he earned enough of them that she didn't stress much about his grades.

She snagged the notebook from him and dangled it like an offering. "Tell you what, mister. I won't worry about your strategy plans, if you agree to review history facts like that one every day for the next week—*before* you spend any time on your new project."

He held out his hand to shake. "Deal."

She dropped the notebook into the cart. "And now, we are off to find a history review book."

He shot her a look like she was crazy.

"What? You just said you'd study up on history facts?"

"I will. But seriously, Mom. A book? Maybe an app with history quizzes or something instead?"

She held up a hand, but gave in. "Fine. But track it down by tomorrow, and show it to me."

He pumped a fist in victory. "Awesome. And listen, I came up with a whole new approach to *State of Decay*," he said, his voice rising in excitement as she rolled the cart to the highlighters. "That guy at the center, Colin, told me to."

She stopped immediately and tilted her head. "He did?" she asked, unsure what to make of Colin's chat with her son. True, the two had talked before. But still, she was damn curious what they had chatted about.

"He said you just devise a strategy and follow it," he said, sweeping one hand across the other and pointing forward, like a general launching into battle. "But don't be afraid to change if it's not working."

As he dropped a yellow highlighter onto their pile of supplies, she had her answer. Funny that it came from Colin through her son.

Time for her to change her approach.

CHAPTER FIFTEEN

From the twenty-ninth floor of his office building, the icons of the Strip looked like Monopoly hotels. Up here, they became little Lego structures with playful shapes and Lilliputian charm—the pyramid of the Luxor, the miniature Eiffel Tower, the rollercoaster that wrapped around the New York-New York hotel...

The view from miles away was akin to how an idea took shape for Colin. It started small, but as he zoomed in closer it had the potential to become a glittering star on the skyline. That was what he was looking for today from his team of venture capitalists as they presented the startups they were considering funding.

When Larsen, one of the youngest and brightest staffers at Redwood Mountain Ventures, finished his presentation, Colin leaned forward in his chair, ready with questions.

"What is your risk analysis? Is it worth it?" Colin asked, wishing he could apply a simple mathematical formula to understanding Elle and her radio silence like he did with scrappy little startups. But as Larsen shared both the potential of the advertising tech firm under consideration as well as the risk, Colin was reminded once again that even black-and-white business decisions weren't rubber stamped through mathematical equations. There was no formula to tell if a company was the next PayPal, Google, or Uber.

It was math plus intuition. It was analysis plus gut. In business, Colin had always relied on razor-sharp instincts. He'd leaned on them, too, with Elle. But all of a sudden, they'd stopped working. She'd stopped writing, stopped talking to him, stopped engaging. And he had no clue what to do next.

"I'm not convinced consumers want this technology yet," he said to Larsen, and the sentiment was eerily similar to how he imagined Elle felt about him.

When the meeting ended and the other team members left, Colin pulled Larsen aside. "Thank you for all your hard work. As always, your presentations are top-notch. I want you to find the next game changer. You're close. Keep searching."

"Thank you, Mr. Sloan," the young man said before he scurried out.

"It's Colin," he shouted in a light-hearted voice. "How many times do I have to tell you it's just Colin?"

"Probably a lot. Thank you, Colin," Larsen said from down the hall.

As he headed to his office to dive into work, his assistant rang. "There's someone here to see you. She has a delivery of flowers."

* * *

The big bouquet of orange lilies and purple asters hid her face. Clutching the blue glass vase tightly, Elle walked into Colin's office, nerves bouncing across her skin.

She had no clue if he was pissed at her.

She had no clue if he even wanted an in-person delivery.

But this was the least she could do.

She'd never been to his office before, and from her spot behind the vase, the first thing she noticed was the burgundy carpet, then a soft beige couch and a shiny oak coffee table arranged in front of his desk. Slowly, like in a game of peekaboo, she moved the vase and revealed her face.

Holy shit.

She nearly dropped the flowers.

The view from the window was stunning, but it had nothing on Colin.

He stood, resting casually against the edge of his desk, wearing the hottest two pieces of a three-piece suit. He didn't have a jacket on; he wore tailored pants, a white shirt, and a vest, and she had to force her lips together so she wouldn't start panting, drooling, or just gaping at him. The sleeves of his shirt were rolled up twice, revealing a hint of the infinity symbol on his forearm.

She wanted to lick it. She wanted to lick him. If ever there were a more perfect image for edgy businessmen than this one—Colin, with his dark eyes, sexy scruff, rolled-up sleeves, and that vest, that fucking vest that was killing her with hotness—she wouldn't believe it. Nope. The evidence was in front of her, and she had to have him. She had to somehow cordon off the secrets she couldn't reveal from the man she couldn't resist.

Two Elles. Plain and simple. Here and now, she declared herself cloned.

She cast her gaze to the bouquet. "They call it a carnival of color," she said, her voice dry.

He didn't move an inch. His arms were crossed. "It is colorful. What do *you* call it?"

She stepped closer. "A thank you. An in-person thank-you for your firm's amazing generosity in supporting the community center."

He walked to her, took the flowers, and set them on the coffee table. "You're welcome," he said as he sat on his couch.

Her chest tightened with nerves. "It's also an apology."

He cocked his head. "For what?"

"For canceling."

"You don't have to apologize for that."

"I do, though," she insisted. "Because I didn't want to cancel."

"Elle, you don't have to say you're sorry. I don't expect an apology. I don't expect anything."

Maybe he didn't. Maybe she'd trained him to expect nothing from her because she felt like she had nothing to give.

And while she couldn't give him the full truth, she could offer him *her* truth. So she marched to the door and shut it, giving them complete privacy, and returned to him, sitting on the edge of the coffee table.

"I know you don't expect anything, but I just left you hanging, and that's not fair, no matter what this is," she said, gesturing from him to her. "I just had a lot of stuff on my mind, and I kind of freaked out, and that's why I was out of touch." He parted his lips to say something, and she kept going in a rush. "But right now, I only have one thing on my mind."

He raised an eyebrow, this time inviting her to say more.

She reached for his right wrist, tracing the infinity symbol, forcing away the thoughts that threatened to touch down in her head—he'd gotten this ink to symbolize the connection between him and his siblings. The four of them. But there were more. Except *this* Elle didn't know that. This Elle was the one having the affair with Colin Sloan.

She stroked the lines on his wrist. He hissed in a breath as she made contact with his skin. She raised her chin and met his eyes. "You look so fucking hot," she said in a whisper.

"So do you," he said, his eyes blazing.

She glanced at her attire—a summery skirt and a sleeveless top. Hardly her hottest outfit. She let go of his wrist and leaned closer to him, dropping her hands to his thighs, so strong and firm under her touch.

"I bet I'll look hotter when I do this," she said and palmed him through his pants. A burst of sparks ignited in her belly as she stroked his erection, loving that he was already rock hard, that all it took was this momentary closeness, the heat of suggestion, and a few words to ratchet him up. But then, maybe he was just like her. Maybe he'd wanted her from the second he'd laid eyes on her today, too.

In a flash, she unzipped his pants, pushing them open so she could see his newest ink. Her breath caught as she gazed at the Phoenix tattoo on his hip. She ran her thumb over it then lowered her lips to flick her tongue across it. She raised her face. "Does your door lock automatically?"

He shook his head. "But they know not to come in if it's shut."

She arched an eyebrow, her unsaid question clear. *Have you done this before?*

He shook his head. "No. They know because I like to be able to focus at times. And when I need to focus—ah, fuck. Could you just lock it so we can get to the good part?"

She laughed and practically vaulted over the chair and table to flip the latch on the door. When she turned around, he'd pushed his pants to his knees and was stroking himself. Her mouth watered as he worked his fist slowly up and down the length of his gorgeous shaft.

"Don't do that," she said as she stared at him, so turned on by the sight of the man's hand wrapped around his hard-on. "I want it all. I want all of you in my mouth. All to myself."

"You can have all of my dick anytime you want," he said, and in seconds she was on her knees, licking the head. They groaned at the same time, their sounds making it clear how much they both wanted this. She glanced up at him as he watched her draw his cock into her mouth.

"I definitely accept your apology now," he said with a light laugh then threaded his fingers into her hair, pushing it all over to one side so he had a perfect view of her face.

She flicked her tongue along the hard length of him as she sucked.

"You can cancel on me anytime," he said.

She grinned even with her mouth full, then her smile vanished as he groaned louder and gripped her hair with both hands. There was no time for smiling or laughing with his cock all the way in her mouth. All she cared about was making him feel good, because he'd only ever made her feel amazing. Beautiful. Craved.

She wanted him to feel the same. She drew him in deep, opening her mouth wide but sucking hard, the way he liked. Friction, lots of friction, and speed. She'd only done this to him once before, in a bathroom at a Japanese restaurant off the Strip one night after they'd finished an appetizer of edamame and were waiting for their sushi. He'd come hard and fast, and she'd loved it. But not as much as she loved it now—on her knees, in his office, with the stunning view of Las Vegas splashed behind them.

"Suck me harder," he urged in a heated whisper, and she couldn't resist. She loved that he was vocal and direct. That he told her exactly what he liked. She moved faster, cupping his balls in one hand, playing with them as she licked, sucked, and aimed to steal every last breath from his lungs with a blow job that would blow his mind.

"Ah," he said on a moan. "Like that. Just like that. I fucking love it when you do that."

She knew what he meant, so she moved her hands faster across his balls, gently tugging as she showed him how incredibly much she loved his cock. Heat blasted through her like a rocket. She was so goddamn turned on from blowing him. Another pair of panties melted—wetness pooled between her legs, and she ached. Her sex pulsed with need. She could practically come like this. She rocked her pelvis as he fucked her mouth. Her hips moved back and forth because she wanted to be riding him so badly. But she wanted this more—all of him between her lips.

"Yeah, that's perfect. So fucking deep," he said as his fingers gripped her skull, and he kept her head firmly in place.

Faster and harder, more frenzied than ever, she sucked his cock, imagining him as king of this town, presiding over partnerships, striking deals and making decisions, but here, for these few moments in his office, she controlled all of this man's pleasure. With her mouth. With her tongue. With her lips.

With her ravenous appetite for him. With her bottomless desire to touch him, to taste him, to feel him.

He groaned louder, and rocked up into her mouth. A quick, hard thrust. Then another. He was starting to lose control, fucking her mouth harder than he ever had before. She nearly gagged.

But she didn't, because she needed his pleasure desperately. Had to give it to him. Had to take him deep.

He shuddered, grasped her head as if holding on for life, and grunted. There were no words left to say. Only feelings. Only pleasure. Only release. She swallowed every last drop of him then licked his cock up and down before letting go and meeting his eyes.

"Can I come over tonight?"

* * *

There was only one answer.

Still, he wanted to know something. Pulling her up on his lap, he adjusted her skirt so she straddled him. "You said you kind of freaked out. Why did you freak out?"

She gulped. Pushed her hair—slightly messy from his hands—away from her cheek. She looked him in the eyes. "Because I like you."

Oh hell. There it was. His heart hitched a ride on a hot-air balloon, sailing away to the sky. He was hopeless with her. "I like you, too," he said, looping his arms around her and planting a quick kiss on those wickedly talented lips. "Does that scare you?"

"To like you? Or that you like me, too?" she asked.

He smiled. "Both."

She nodded. "Both scare me."

"Just be honest with me. That's all we have, Elle," he said, cupping her cheek, keeping her gaze on him. "That's all I ask of you. I respect your boundaries and your wishes. All I want is your truth."

She closed her eyes. Her face looked pained and she sighed, but when she opened her eyes, she nodded.

"So listen—no strings, no promises, nothing more. But if you cancel, don't say something came up. Say I have to see my sister, or I'm too tired, or I need to work late, or I don't want to see you again. Or I met a guy with a bigger cock, and—"

She grabbed his hand and squeezed. "Just go ahead and strike that excuse. Because you know that will never happen."

He wiggled his eyebrows. "Good. It's my secret weapon."

"You can use that weapon against me anytime."

He gave a quick thrust up, showing he was always armed around her. "Another option would be: I'm going to surprise you at your office tomorrow with flowers and the blow job of a lifetime."

A grin spread across her face. "Was it the blow job of a lifetime?" Her voice was so damn sweet as she asked.

"Fuck yeah. It was so good I might even add some new ink that says 'I am a lucky son-of-a-bitch. I've had the best blow job ever.'" She cracked up, then her laughter was cut short when her phone buzzed.

"That's probably my son texting me again."

"Everything okay?"

"Yes. But apparently it's *impossible* to find a decent history quiz app in the entire app store," she said drily as she stretched back to her purse, grabbed her phone, and slid open a text. "Yup. That's him. He claims he still can't find one."

"He really tells you that?"

She rolled her hazel eyes, and grasped his shirt, tugging for emphasis. "I made him a deal—if he studies history before school starts, I'll let him try his new strategy for *State of Decay.* By the way, thank you for sharing that little tip with him. Very analytical," she said, and he nodded a *you're welcome.* "But he claims he can't find a decent app at all. That a good history app doesn't exist."

The corner of his lips quirked up. This was too easy for him. This was a piece of cake. "I know a few. We were pitched on an e-learning company a few weeks ago. We didn't invest because there's no huge market upside, but I was pretty damn impressed with the ease of use, and the focus on actual facts rather than earning points in gameplay or something."

Her eyes widened, and she gripped his shirt even harder. "Are you serious?"

"Totally serious. Let me go back through my notes and send it to you later."

"You can send it to him directly, if you don't mind. I'll text you his number. But copy me, so I know he got it."

He grinned. Progress. This was a big step forward. "Absolutely."

She leaned forward and dropped a kiss on his nose. "Thank you," she said softly. Then once more, in an even quieter voice, "You are my hero."

That's all I want to be.

But aloud he said, "I'm glad I can help you."

"Isn't there anything I can do for you? Help you find the next Snapchat to fund?" she asked, teasing.

"I'm always on the hunt for the next thing."

"Or should I just get to work on topping the blow job of a lifetime?" She winked. "Now that you've set the bar so high for me."

"Yes. That. Do that. And you set the bar yourself with this fantastic mouth," he said, running his fingertip across her lips. "But you know what I also want?" He dipped a hand under her skirt and stroked her damp panties. Ah, nothing he loved more than the evidence of her desire.

She moved gently against his hand. "What do you want?"

"God, I want to fuck you right now," he growled as he slid a finger inside her underwear, feeling her slick flesh.

She gasped. "Do it."

He shook his head.

"Why not?"

"Because I want you to want it."

"You think I don't?" she asked, as she rocked into his fingers gliding across her.

"I want you to want it so much it drives you crazy."

"I'm pretty much insane right now," she said, her breath coming faster.

It was his cue to slow down. "I know. But I want you to come over tonight already hot and wet. I want you to spend the day thinking about me, and what I'm going to do to you, so when you show up you'll be a live wire, and I can fucking devour all your sweetness."

"Oh God," she said, shuddering as she moved faster into his fingers.

He had to exercise phenomenal control. He could have her coming all over his hand in less than a minute, but that would ruin tonight.

He bent his head to her ear, and whispered, "I want to taste you coming. I want to fuck you so hard. I want to feel you beneath me as you writhe and moan and scream. And I want that in exactly nine hours. See you at seven."

He smacked her rear, giving her a sharp crack to remember him by all day. He zipped himself up, kissed her goodbye, and showed her the door.

He wasn't imagining it when she shook her ass at him in a sexy "see you later" as she walked away.

CHAPTER SIXTEEN

Soon. Please let it happen soon. Let this day end any second. She stared at the clock on her wall, willing it to tick faster.

But the tortoise speed of the second hand was either a cruel joke or a reminder that Colin was right. He was all she thought about as she finished up some paperwork about the status of the center's programs.

And since he was all she thought about, she was hot, she was bothered, and she was horny.

Great. Just fucking great to be parked at her desk, filling in information about the poetry nights and the hot meal plan, when her skin was sizzling from that morning encounter at his office.

She pushed back from her desk, walked to the ladies' room, and splashed cold water on her face, then dried it with a scratchy paper towel. Ugh. The damn towel was rough. She made a mental note to look into new paper towel vendors, and as she left the restroom she gave herself a virtual pat on the back for having successfully turned off the latest bout of lust.

Good thing because when she returned to her office, Marcus was rapping on her door.

Tension crashed into her, but she reminded herself of her new approach. *Be two people.* With Marcus, she was only Center Director Elle. The other side of her ceased to exist.

"Hey there," she said.

"Do you have a second?"

"I do." She guided him into her office and shut the door. "Is this about..." she asked, letting her voice trail off in question.

"Yeah. You didn't tell him, did you?" Marcus asked, terror in his brown eyes. For a brief moment before she answered, she studied his eyes. They were dark brown, like Colin's. Another secret she had to bear—a small one that was folded into the big one. But still, she now knew they shared a family resemblance. That gnawing in her chest resurfaced, and she tried valiantly to swat it away. She clenched her fists and refocused away from Marcus's eyes and back to his question.

"Of course I didn't say anything. I told you I wouldn't, and I meant it. Now, tell me what I can do for you?"

"Sorry. I didn't mean anything by it. I know you wouldn't tell him. I'm just..."

"You're nervous," she supplied, as she placed a hand on his shoulder. He was shaking. "Hey, it's going to be okay. Talk to me."

"What if they don't believe me?" he blurted out. "I'll just be showing up out of the blue and saying 'Hey, I'm your little brother. I was born in the pokey. We don't even have the same dad, but isn't it cool?'" He swung his elbows back and forth in mockery of a too-happy person. "I mean, my mom never told them. My dad never did. I don't think they have a clue."

"Show them your birth certificate. You have one, right?"

He nodded. "Yeah, I have a copy of it," he said, his gaze drifting to his feet. "Says right there in black and white how I was born behind bars."

"There's no shame in where you came from. We all came from different places. My son came from an eighteen-year-old high school graduate and his father is dead from an overdose. I do not let him feel shame about any of that," she said firmly. Marcus raised his face again. "So don't let a few words on your birth certificate affect how you see yourself."

"I just feel like I'm trying to hit them up with proof," he muttered.

"But you are, and there's nothing wrong with that. You need to be smart about this and be prepared, because it is hard. Maybe that's why no one was home the other time you went there. Maybe the universe knew you needed to have all the evidence before you went."

"I need to do it soon. The detective called about the reopened investigation. He wants to talk to me. I don't want to talk to him, though."

She held up both hands and backed away. "You shouldn't tell me more on that. I can talk to you about the family stuff, but anything involving the case, I need to stay out of."

He flashed a small smile. "I won't. But thanks again. I think I'm going to rip off the Band-Aid. Do it next week."

Next week. Each piece of information was another cut to the flesh.

When he left, she glanced at the clock. The good news was their discussion passed some time.

The bad news was she was going to need to go home and take a cold shower to wash off this new download of intel she wished she didn't have to store in her head and her heart.

Both ached terribly.

* * *

A female Elvis impersonator with drooping breasts dangling out of her jumpsuit mugged for the camera on the street below. She draped her arms around two guys with sunburns and foot-long plastic drink glasses. With their free hands, both men mimed grabbing a breast. The Elvis outfit was made *modest* by pasties on her nipples.

The woman laughed, and so did the guys. Until one stopped laughing, started hacking, and promptly heaved into the nearby garbage can.

"And that's all, folks, in today's five p.m. Parade of What We Might Have Been," said Kevin, Colin's friend and mentor from his recovery group. The two of them stood on the elevated walkway at the corner of Bally's, surveying the madness and mayhem of happy hour on the Strip. This was one of the many faces of Vegas—the city embodied glitz and glamour in its classy hotels, sex and sin in its nightclubs, beauty and class in the fountains of the Bellagio, but also the seedy in the late afternoon crowds weaving up and down the sidewalks, drunk as skunks.

Colin held up his iced coffee and toasted. "Here's to my best friend. Coffee," he said, since caffeine was the one "vice" he allowed himself to have.

"Hear, hear. May it never ever be banned," Kevin said, swallowing the last of his drink then returning to the conversation they'd started before She-Elvis had arrived on the scene. "So, the meeting with the detective and talking about the past, did that stir anything up?"

"Not really," Colin said quickly, glancing at his watch, calculating how much time until he saw Elle.

Kevin shot him a steely stare. "Really?"

Busted.

Colin forced his mind away from the anticipation of tonight, and back in time to his conversation with Michael at the base of the mountain after they'd met with John. He sighed, dragged his free hand through his hair, and shrugged. "Guilt. It brought back a lot of guilt."

The other man nodded sagely. "That makes sense. But you need to keep working on letting go of that. Guilt—and I mean the misplaced kind—can eat you up. When you start to feel that way, the things that we think will take the pain away seem a helluva lot more appealing. Tequila looks a lot prettier the worse you feel."

"Yeah. That's true," Colin admitted. The moments he'd been most tempted to crack open a bottle were when he felt the shittiest about himself.

"Just be aware that revisiting the past can mess with your head. So keep doing the things that make you feel centered. Your exercise. Your work. Your meetings. All of it. Okay, man?"

Colin's gaze drifted to his arms, to the inked reminders of the man he wanted to be. The strong one, the kind one. The man who didn't live a wrecked kind of life. Strength, love, passion, family, truth. They were his touchstones, his hallmarks, and his guides. "I will."

"Because something this big could knock you off your game. Falling in love. Breaking up. Losing a shit-ton of money. Even good things, like landing a new deal. Hell, just learning something out of the blue. *Anything can be a trigger.* That almost happened to me a few years ago when I fell in love with my wife. You'd think falling in love would be this wonderful thing to keep me straight. But I very nearly popped the pills again because I didn't know if she was feeling the same thing, and I felt so out of control."

Kevin's admission knocked the air out of Colin's lungs. He'd never imagined falling for someone could have those kinds of consequences. "Seriously?"

Kevin nodded. "Love nearly kicked the shit out of me."

"How did you deal?"

"I told her how I felt. I was honest with her. I spoke the truth, and she loved that I was open, and the rest is history."

The words struck a chord. He'd delivered worlds of pleasure to Elle between the sheets, he'd proven he could show her one hell of a good time out of bed, and now there was one last thing to do.

Open his heart.

CHAPTER SEVENTEEN

At last.

She blasted the AC in her car and cranked up the music, rocking out to an upbeat Katy Perry song as she drove to Colin's home. Her mom had picked up Alex already, and the two of them had planned a festive night of bowling, arcade games, and the Chinese buffet. He'd also reviewed his history facts for a full thirty minutes, thanks to the app that Colin had found and sent to the two of them. The best part? Alex said the app was fun. From a fourteen-year-old boy, that one-word description was the best she could hope for.

As for Elle, she sighed happily as she imagined the night ahead of her now that she was on her way.

She shivered as the images flashed before her. This was a sex date all right, but it was also more, given the words they'd both said that morning at his office.

I like you.

They were three simple words, said in many ways every day. They were young words, breathed by middle-schoolers and teenagers, and yet they felt adult, too. They were an acknowledgment of caring, a way of stating that what was between them was more than sex, but not quite hurtling toward that scarier four-letter word.

There was no way they were going in that direction. No way at all. Not even possible. She wouldn't let *that* happen.

As the song segued into the chorus, she sang along, letting the music keep her mind on the moment and far away from the afternoon. Just as she blocked on the roller rink for the jammers, she was blocking out the sides of her that had not been invited to play tonight.

Her outfit too was pure After Hours Elle. No steady, reliable flats and jeans-wearing Elle here. She'd decked herself out in her sexiest high-heeled shoes, a short black skirt that hugged her hips, and a clingy tank top. She was strong and toned from exercise, and she knew Colin liked to see as much of her skin as possible, so she'd picked this outfit for him.

As she turned off the highway, she dialed his number to see if he wanted her to call in the Thai order they'd talked about. It went straight to voicemail.

She went ahead and ordered anyway. Dinner would be her treat.

* * *

After the meeting with Kevin, he'd managed to carve out forty-five minutes pre-date for a trail run. He'd pushed himself extra hard with a punishing uphill route in the early evening heat. But he'd needed it, because Kevin was right. The challenging workout had helped settle his mind and heart, dislodging some of yesterday's latent guilt and also strengthening his resolve to share his feelings with Elle.

Now, he stood under hot jets of water, rinsing away the remnants of the sweaty workout. He shut the shower, dried off, and wrapped a towel around his waist so he could get ready for his date—*in his house*. The best kind of date. As he finished brushing his teeth, his phone rang, so he tossed the toothbrush on the edge of the sink and grabbed the phone from his bed in case it was Elle.

It wasn't.

Rex was calling.

"Hey, man, what's up?"

"Okay, here's the deal. I am *almost* ready," Rex said, stretching out the word. "I'm like ninety percent ready. And I want to just kill it on this test. But there's one problem that's making me absolutely bat-shit crazy."

"Lay it on me," Colin said, as he opened a drawer to grab a pair of boxers.

Rex rattled off the details, and Colin walked him through the steps to solving the equation as he pulled on black briefs and hung up his towel. The other line rang as he reviewed how to crosscheck the work, but he didn't look to see who was calling since he was mid-explanation.

"Awesome," Rex said, relief and exuberance in his voice. "You are clutch, man. You are so clutch."

Colin smiled at the compliment. "Need anything else?"

Rex cleared his throat, then said, "*Um.*"

Uh-oh. Rex never hemmed and hawed. The guy was the king of boldness.

"What is it? Just tell me."

Rex sighed. "Shit, I hate to ask. But I need a ride tomorrow to the test. My mom is taking the car for a job interview, and Marcus's ride is in the shop—his tires are being rotated. So he can't drive us."

"Us?" Colin asked, curiously. "He's taking the math placement test, too?"

"Yeah. He heard I was taking it, so he signed up as well. He's a fucking math whiz though, just like you. He's done all the studying on his own, and he's trying to place into calculus or some shit like that. He's trying to find a ride, but I just figured I'd take the initiative and ask you. I guess I could take Uber though."

"No, you won't take Uber," Colin said with a wide grin. He was so damn grateful to be hearing this—that both boys were eager and ready to learn. "Tell me where to pick you up and I will gladly be your driver."

Driver.

That word clanged loudly in his brain. His dad had been a limo driver and would have been proud of him— not for driving per se, but for helping the kids who needed it, especially when it came to math. His father had never gone to college, but he'd tried to work on his own number skills during the last year of his life, taking accounting classes at night school. Maybe Colin had picked up where his father had left off, carrying on his memory as the numbers guy of the crew.

Rex gave him the address, and Colin wrote it down. "Got it."

His bell rang, sending Johnny Cash straight out of an evening snooze and into a brief bark-fest at the door. He headed to the entryway and peered in the peephole.

Even through the tiny window, Elle looked edible.

He glanced down, realizing he'd only managed to put on boxers.

So be it.

He opened the door as he finished his call with Rex. "I'll be there at eight a.m. That work for you?"

"Absolutely. You're the best," Rex was saying as Elle stepped inside Colin's home and mouthed "wow" as she raked her eyes over his hardly-dressed body.

"See you then." He hung up, tossed his phone on the entryway table, and kissed her.

A soft kiss for a mere few seconds.

Then a hard and furious one that had hands wrapped around bodies and fingers diving into hair and breath coming fast from both of them. They were a collision of lust and heat. They clawed at each other, grasping, grabbing, needing contact. Fierce and fevered contact.

She giggled, breaking the kiss.

He shot her a curious look, and she pointed downward. Johnny Cash was licking her calf.

"I think he likes my lotion."

"Is it eau de filet mignon?"

"No. It's Body Shop. Satsuma oranges. All their stuff is made with no animal testing, so maybe that's why he likes it."

"Either that or he has scurvy." He pointed to the living room. "Go lie down, Johnny Cash."

The dog obeyed, trotting to the rug in front of the gray couch.

She gestured to his briefs. "Nice boxers," she said, and he followed her gaze. She was staring at his erection, a full tent against the cotton fabric.

He gestured to her. All of her. "Nice everything."

"Who are you meeting at eight a.m.?" she asked, as he reached for her hand and led her into his home.

"Rex. He needs a ride to take his math placement test tomorrow."

She beamed. Absolutely fucking beamed. Her whole expression lit up with the biggest smile he'd seen in ages. "That is so cool of you to do that. I'm so thrilled," she said as she reached for his arm, running her fingers along his skin. "I love it when you help them. It kind of turns me on."

"I'm taking Marcus, too. Does it turn you on twice as much that I'm driving two of them?"

She blinked. Once, twice, three times. Her face seemed to freeze, and her smile turned into a deletion.

He frowned, confused at the shift. "Are you okay?" She closed her eyes for a second, squeezed them hard, then pressed her fingers to her temple. "Elle. What's going on?" he asked nervously.

She opened her eyes. "Sorry. Sometimes I get these headaches. It's nothing." She waved her hand as if to dismiss it. She reached for his shoulders, grasped them, and walked backward to his couch. "You know what really turns me on?"

"Tell me."

"Thinking about you all day. Like you wanted me to," she said as she reached the couch. "I've been hot and bothered since I left you."

She sank down on the couch and he followed her there, kneeling over her as she lay down.

"Did you count down the hours?" he asked as he ran a hand up her bare leg.

She nodded as she settled into a pillow at the end of the couch, her chestnut hair spilling across it. "It was pure torture."

"Were you wet just thinking of me?"

"Yes. Just like now. I was turned on constantly. I ached for you," she said, as he glided his finger across the damp panel of her panties. His cock twitched against his boxers as he touched her. His delicious, wet, horny Elle. God, he loved how much she wanted it. He loved turning her on. He loved touching her. Pushing her tight little skirt up to her waist, he groaned as he saw her panties—black lace with a tiny bow at the center.

"You need to be naked, right now. Completely naked," he said, tugging off the panties and removing her heels, too. The shoes were sexy as fuck, but a plan was a plan was a plan. He needed her in her birthday suit for the first time. "Nothing on. Nothing but you, naked from head to toe, as I bury my face in this sweetness." He slid a finger through her slick heat as she arched into him, wriggling out of her top at the same time.

She moved to her bra next, freeing her tits. His breath hitched. There she was, down to nothing but her beautiful bare self and the shimmer of desire evident in the flush on her skin. Her eyes, so dark and hungry, told him that she had indeed been one tortured woman all day long.

"I almost feel bad for making you think about me for nine hours straight," he growled, as he pressed his hands on the insides of her thighs.

Her legs parted, and he groaned as he drank in the sight of her wet pussy. She was so fucking sexy, and so damn turned on, and he wanted her more than he'd ever wanted a woman in his life. "But I can't find it in me to feel bad when you're this worked up already."

She ran a hand through her hair and panted. "I am. Oh God, I am. You're the only thing I could think about. I've been so turned on since I saw you this morning, and I'm dying for you."

Her words stoked the raging fire in him. It crackled and burned with rampant desire as he opened her legs further, savoring the utterly intoxicating view of this beautiful woman arching her hips toward his mouth.

His dick ached. His erection throbbed against his boxer shorts. His mouth watered as he settled between her legs, hooked them on his shoulders, and at last, at long fucking last, he kissed her sweet honey center.

* * *

Oh God.

Oh dear fucking God in heaven.

She rocked into him the very second he touched her sex. It was like a match on tinder, igniting her instantly. She groaned, she moaned, and she cried out his name. She was a live wire, exposed, ready, and waiting. She'd wanted this for so long, had pictured it often, and had fantasized about it so many times.

Sure, they'd had sex on a handful of occasions, and she'd taken him deep in her mouth twice, but this was virgin territory.

It was a first for them, and if it happened right, it would be a first for her.

She'd never come like this. Sam hadn't been into it, and she hadn't been with many others. This was her ultimate fantasy. The one she devoured in her erotica. The one she dreamed of, rode her fingers to, and fucked herself with toys to images of.

As he swept his tongue across her pussy, she bowed her back, so ready to sing, to shout, and to scream. He was a fucking dream. His lips were soft, and his stubble was rough, and his tongue was insistent as he flicked it up and down along her swollen, aching clit. She grabbed his hair as if her hands were a steel grip and she couldn't let go. She wouldn't let go. She rocked into his face. Electricity crackled through her, lighting up all her nerves, sizzling her skin.

She cried out his name, and for a second he broke contact to look at her—his eyes were heated, full of the same wild longing. That moment was like a thread between them, a tight, neat line that tethered her to him. To share in this lust for another person was the greatest high, the sweetest intoxication, and, hell, did they have it. She wanted his mouth as much as he wanted to consume her.

"Tell me what you say when you fuck yourself," he said in a dirty growl. "Talk to me like you did all the times I devoured you in your fantasies."

Another wave of desire crashed through her, and she dug her nails into his scalp. Gladly. She'd gladly tell him. She'd used him so many times; she'd gotten off to him countless nights; she'd come to his image over and over.

"Fuck me with your tongue," she said, panting as she thrust into him.

He moaned as he licked her, cupping her ass and pulling her closer. His tongue explored her. His sinfully delicious lips devoured her, and she'd never felt so lavished, so cherished, or so utterly craved. His hot kisses turned her into a wet, writhing collection of sparking nerve endings and rushing blood cells.

She closed her eyes, sharing with him all the dirty things she'd said in her head as she'd masturbated to him. All the filthy words she imagined she'd say when she finally felt him do this. "I want to ride your face. I want to fuck your face so hard," she said, in broken gasps. His tongue kicked into some kind of overdrive, flicking her wildly. He let go of his grip on her ass and grabbed her hands, clasping them tight, clutching them as he feasted on her. Hands in hands, this act became all the more intense.

Closer. She felt closer to him than she ever had before as he held her tight, their fingers laced together, while he drank her in. Her muscles tightened. The first wave of pleasure crashed over her, and it was happening.

"I want to come all over you, Colin," she said, as the sensations rolled through her, overwhelming her, flooding her brain with nothing but beautiful bliss.

"Oh God," she cried out, losing control, letting go, and giving in to everything she felt with him. "I'm going to come on your face. Just like you want." He gripped her hands so damn tight as he ravaged her. "Just like I've pictured. Oh fuck. Oh God. It's so fucking good."

Then she screamed, and nothing else existed in the whole damn world but this perfect moment of pleasure, this unparalleled ecstasy with this man who was so unbelievably good to her in every way.

CHAPTER EIGHTEEN

Rock. Hard.

His dick was steel. His stubble was coated in her gorgeous, glorious, delicious wetness. He could still taste her on his tongue. Like sin and honey. Like longing and lust. Like the woman he had to have completely.

She sighed happily as her eyes fluttered open, so dreamy and sexy.

"Hi," she whispered as he rose up. "That was…"

"You are…"

Neither one of them could seem to finish their sentences. She scooted back into the pillows then lifted her hand, tracking the lotus design on his chest. She traveled lower, over his abs to his waist. She pushed down his briefs. He was sitting on his knees, still between her legs. No better place to be.

She ran her tongue across her lips as she freed his cock, then took it in her hand and stroked him. Shuddering, he felt a bolt of desire tear through him as she rubbed her hand slowly up and down his dick. He loved how she touched him. Absolutely fucking loved everything about it, from the way she ran her fingers over him to how her breath came fast and heavy as she gripped him.

Mostly though, it was her eyes. It was the way she gazed at him. She looked at him with so much want, so much desire, and so much more. Like she wanted him in all the same ways he wanted her.

His breathing turned erratic the more she touched him, the more she rubbed her hands all over him. The craving inside him multiplied; it rose exponentially as she stopped at the head of his dick, spreading a bead of liquid over him. He groaned.

She whispered his name.

"Yes?" he answered, as he pushed off his briefs. His voice was soft, but it echoed, the only sound in his quiet home. It vaguely occurred to him that he hadn't stopped to turn on music or anything. He hadn't needed it though. The noises she made were all he wanted in his ears.

"I want to know how it feels without any barriers," she said, wrapping both hands around him now, leading him closer to the promised land.

The prospect of flesh against flesh, skin on skin, electrified him. But a kernel of worry set up camp, too, and he remained stock still as he asked, "Are you sure? I mean, should we?"

"I'm on the pill."

"But…"

"I wasn't when I was younger. The condom broke. The pill has been fantastic. But we don't have to if you're not comfortable."

"No, I want to. I just want to make sure it makes sense."

She nodded. "It does. It works."

He positioned his cock between her legs and rubbed the head against her wetness. Roping her arms around his neck, she drew him closer. She spread her legs, wrapping them around his hips as he sank into her. He trembled from the absolutely exquisite feel of her hot pussy gripping his dick. "You're so fucking wet," he said as he hitched her leg up higher, giving himself a better angle.

"I always am with you," she said, then raised her face to his and claimed his lips. She kissed him, and he fucked her, and soon that was all he knew. The deep and primal drive to fill her. The heat flooding his body. Her fingernails running the length of his spine. And her mouth, her decadent, sinful lips fused to his, kissing him greedily as he took her.

Hard.

Deep.

Rough.

She let go of his mouth and yanked him closer, kissing his neck, his face, moving her lips to his ear. "I love the way you fuck me," she whispered, her voice fevered.

So fiery. She was so damn fiery and passionate. It drove him wild. "Fucking you is amazing. Do you have any idea why it's so good?" he said in a heated voice as he stroked.

"Tell me."

"Because it's more than fucking." The words tumbled from his lips. He hadn't planned to tell her now, but he couldn't hold back. He couldn't pretend. She was more than this. She was so much more than the physical. He pulled back to look at her. Maybe he'd scared her. Maybe she'd freeze up again. But her lips were parted, her eyes were wide open, and she gazed back at him, not letting go.

"I know it is," she whispered, the words like poetry to his ears. Sweet, gorgeous music.

"It's more than what it used to be."

"So much more," she murmured as she moved with him. They were finishing each other's sentences, filling in what the other was saying. They both felt it. There was no other way.

Their bodies coiled together. She was slick and hot, and so was he, and he couldn't get close enough, couldn't have enough of her, couldn't imagine this stopping at just sex. No, this was way more than fucking. It was fucking and falling at the same damn time, and nothing—no drug, no drink, no high-flying parachute dive—had ever felt as good as coming together with the woman he desired madly.

Coming together...and falling apart.

* * *

She shivered as he ran his fingertips over her sparrows. "These are my favorite," he said, kissing them.

She trembled in his arms, her back to him as he held her. She barely felt like herself. She was some other version of Elle Mariano in these stolen moments with Colin. And she loved this version. She savored being this woman. Not a mom. Not a social worker. Not a woman with secrets that couldn't be shared. She wore only her bra and panties, and he was clad in his briefs. They'd eaten Thai while watching the final ten minutes of *Goodfellas*, reciting the closing lines together. Then they'd managed one more quick round, and now the clock was racing closer to the end of the night. She had to leave in thirty minutes.

"Why do you like them?"

"Because I love your neck, and these birds are like a homing beacon to me."

"That's why I got them."

"To draw me to your neck?"

She laughed and shook her head. "No. Because in olden days, sailors would follow birds to land. That's how they knew when they were coming close to shore. There's a legend about a sailor who found his way home by spotting sparrows. I just love the idea of finding your way home."

"When did you get this one?"

"Five years ago. Things were really rough with Sam then. It was his third or fourth rehab stint. I lost count. But I needed the reminder that I could find my own way home," she said, glad it was a topic she could freely discuss. Though they'd talked about their ink before, they'd never delved into it in great detail.

"I like that idea. I believe that's true. You can find your way home," he said softly, and she craned her neck to look at him. The sun had dropped below the horizon, and night had fallen. Dark shadows lined his face from the waning light in the windows; he'd only turned on one lamp.

"I believe it, too. And sometimes you have to rely on something outside of yourself to do that."

"Who or what did you rely on?"

"My mom, my sister, my son. Basically, my family," she said.

"I love that you're so close to them. It's the same with my brothers and sister," he said, and she tensed momentarily, wondering what would happen to that tight-knit foursome when they learned they were five.

His hand dropped to her hip, traveling across the cherry blossom tree that decorated her side up to her rib cage. That had hurt like hell, given the location, but she loved the intricate design and symbolism of it. "Wait. I was wrong. This one is my favorite," he whispered, dusting a kiss across the blossoms. "It's beautiful and sexy, like you."

"I had this one done in San Diego when I took Alex there a few years ago. The tattoo artist who did this gave me a similar design to the one he made for his wife. It's on her neck, and it's gorgeous. He said in Japan it's a symbol for the preciousness of life. With tattoos, it represents femininity and beauty."

"Both are perfect."

He traveled across her body, landing on the script-y *T* on her wrist. "But this one truly is my favorite. Titanium. You told me you got this after Sam died."

She nodded and swallowed. Her throat hitched with the memory. "Yes. My reminder to stay strong. *Obviously*, since that's what titanium is." She inched around, facing him, meeting his eyes. There were other truths she'd been sworn to protect, but her life, her past, and her pain were hers alone to share. She'd never told him all the details. And now, as they came closer together, the time seemed right. "He died in my arms."

His jaw dropped. "Shit, Elle. I'm so sorry. I knew he OD'd but didn't know the details."

"We weren't together. We hadn't been for a long time. But he showed up at my house, smashed, sick as a dog, white as a sheet. He stumbled inside, and I started to call my mom, since she's a nurse. But then he just started convulsing." The cruel memory flickered in her mind—Sam's eyes bugging out, his breath coming in spurts, his chest seizing up. She'd called 911 immediately then crouched on the floor, holding him, desperately waiting for the ambulance to show up. It was too late. The medics pronounced him dead on the scene. "Alex saw the whole thing."

Pain sliced through her, and she winced from the memories.

Colin wrapped his arms around her. "That's such a terrible thing for him to see. I didn't watch my dad die, but I saw his body a few hours later, when my mom found him. I'll never forget the image. It must be so hard for Alex."

"It was," she said. Her voice broke and a tear slipped down her cheek.

He kissed it away.

"Colin," she said, her voice thin as air. "That's why I'm scared."

"I know. But that's not me. I won't be like that."

She nodded, though she was certain they both knew no one could make that guarantee. But it wasn't fair of her to ask either, especially since he'd already proven that he could rise above. He was the best man she knew. The kindest, smartest, most thoughtful gentleman she'd ever met. The guy who helped the boys at the center. Who drove them to tests. Who helped them study. Who inspired them in gaming strategy and tracked down history apps. He was the man who treated her like a queen.

She placed her finger on his lips. "You can't make that promise. And I can't ask you to. But..."

"But?"

The fear escalated, whipping through her. She hadn't come here tonight expecting to want so much more from him, but she couldn't walk out that door the way she came in. Every second she spent with him, naked or clothed, she became more connected, more linked to this man. This was no longer about sex. It was about *why* the sex between them was so spectacular. Because of how they felt.

She looped her hands in his hair and tried to push past that fear. "You make me feel things I've never felt."

"It's the same for me. I've never felt anything like this," he said, and the look in his eyes was one of pure joy. She wanted to remember it always. She clutched that emotion tighter now, because it was giving her the strength to say the next thing—to tell him she was ready to try.

She'd just parted her lips to speak when her phone buzzed.

Fuck a duck.

"That might be Alex," she said, sitting up and reaching for her purse. "As you learned earlier, he texts a lot. Which is good. I want him to. But—"

She stopped speaking when she saw her mom was calling. Her mom never called when she was with Alex. Worry flooded her and she answered instantly. "Hey, Mom. Is everything okay?"

"Everything is fine. I just dropped Alex off at home though, because the hospital called. They're short-staffed tonight, and I need to get to work an hour early to fill in. But he's totally fine by himself. He's not even playing video games. He's practicing his history facts. I think he wants you to quiz him tomorrow," her mom said.

Elle breathed easier, but still stood up and started hunting for her clothes. "Did you have a good time?"

"The best. We always have the best time. I beat him at bowling, but he beat me at some crazy motorcycle game. Anyway, I just wanted you to know that I won't be there when you get home, but you still are under orders to have a good time."

Elle found her skirt and pulled it on. "I had an amazing time," she said, locking eyes with Colin, who'd tracked down a pair of gym shorts. He smiled at her as she slid into her shoes.

"Then you need to do it again."

"I do need to do it again," she said, wiggling her eyebrows at him. "I love you, Mom. I'll see you soon. Are you coming to my match on Friday night?"

"As soon as my shift ends I'm there."

She said good-bye and turned to Colin. "I need to go. I know he's old enough to be home alone, but I don't feel right being here and doing what we've been doing and just leaving him on his own. You know?"

He nodded. "I get it."

She pulled on her tank top, wishing she could have finished what she'd started to say. But maybe this was the universe's way of slowing her down. Elle had been prone to rash decisions before. Perhaps, she needed to meditate more thoughtfully on what to say. Or maybe what she really needed to do was talk to her son. She'd been protecting him, keeping him safe from the kind of hell he'd witnessed with his father. Rather than tell Colin she wanted to try with him, she should tell her son what Colin meant to her.

Then perhaps the three of them could hang out after the match.

"Hey," she said softly. "Would you like to come to the match, too? My mom will be there. Alex usually goes. It would be fun to have you there, too."

"Ryan comes back the night before. So he'll probably swing by and get Johnny Cash, and once he does I can come see you. Are you going to be wearing those super hot socks that go to here?" he asked, tapping her above the knee.

She laughed and nodded. "I will."

He adopted an intensely serious face. "So when I come up and say hi, I need to act like I don't have fantasies of fucking you while you're wearing nothing but those socks?"

A sweet rush of heat spread down her spine. "Yes. Pretend you're not thinking that."

"And that I'm not thinking how you'd look in them with these beautiful legs wrapped around my neck, Skater Girl?"

Oh dear lord. A gentle pulse beat between her legs, as she shouldered her purse. "Yes. That. Pretend you're not thinking that when I see you."

"I'll just pretend I'm one of your loyal volunteers at the center come out to support you."

She leaned in and kissed him. "Pretend for now. Maybe not much longer," she whispered, then turned on her heels to go.

That was all she could manage for the moment. She had so much more to say. She felt so much more in her heart.

* * *

Holy shit. Kevin was right. *Be honest.* He'd told the woman he cared for her, and the result was better than he could have imagined.

Fine, fine. No commitments were made. No promises were exchanged. But they were breaking down walls. As he kissed her good night, he was more determined than ever to be the best man he could be.

For her. For her kid. For himself.

He wouldn't let anything get in the way.

CHAPTER NINETEEN

Her heels clicked on the concrete steps as she walked two flights to her apartment. She slid the key into the latch, but there was no give. The door slipped open.

Alex appeared, a *gotcha* look in his brown eyes. He pointed at her. "'The New Deal was a series of domestic programs started by President Franklin Roosevelt to help the United States recover from the Great Depression. *Boom*," he said, raising his arm in triumph. "Now, where were you tonight?"

Heat spread across her cheeks. She'd only said she was *going out* when she'd left earlier. She hadn't uttered the word *date*, and she certainly hadn't said with who. But her attire said it all.

"Out," she said sheepishly, slipping past him. He shut the door behind her, letting it close with a loud bang.

"*Out.* Is that his name? You were out with *Out*?"

She laughed as she headed to the kitchen and poured herself a glass of water. She took a long gulp then figured now was as good a time as any. Speaking the truth—at least the start of it—to Colin had been such a refreshing change from holding back. Perhaps telling her son would have a similar effect. Besides, it was the right way to handle this blossoming relationship.

She walked around to the stools at the counter and patted one. "Sit."

"Uh-oh," he said as he plopped down. "Am I in trouble?"

"No." She took the other stool and crossed her legs. Nerves beat a path through her chest, but she glanced down at her tattoo. *Be strong.* "Alex, I made a promise when your father died that I would never put us in that situation again."

He furrowed his brow. "What situation?"

"Me being involved with someone who's addicted."

"Is this the part where you tell me you met a hot meth head and you have bags of kitty litter in your car?"

She laughed softly and shook her head. "No. But major points for a good joke. Though you do know there is no such thing as a hot meth head, right?"

"Yeah. I know. Meth heads are nasty."

She crinkled her nose. "So gross," she said, then returned to the topic. "I've been seeing someone—"

"You're dating a junkie?"

"God, no."

"You said 'being involved with someone addicted.'"

She nodded. "Right. I know. Because that's the promise I made to you, and to myself, and to us. Our family. To *not* get involved with an addict. But, I want you to know I've been seeing someone who's a recovering addict."

"Oh," he said, his voice flat. She didn't know if that meant he didn't care or he was disappointed.

"And I think he's a really good guy," she added.

He arched a skeptical eyebrow. "Like my dad was a good guy?"

"No. Good guy like the real deal."

"Okay," he said, his tone light and easy now. "So what's the issue?"

"I want to know how you feel about that. He's been in recovery for eight years. He's a good, solid, strong man who hasn't relapsed."

He shot her a look as if she was nuts. "I don't get it, Mom. What's the problem? He sounds cool."

"He is cool. You know him."

She could see the gears turning in his head. They clicked, and he wagged his finger at her. "No way! You're dating Colin."

She couldn't help but grin. "How did you guess it was him?"

"Duh."

She jutted out her chin. "Duh, what?"

"I can't believe you thought I wouldn't guess him," he said, laughing at her, clutching his belly and guffawing. Her son was actually guffawing.

She straightened her spine. "I'm sorry, but did you have radar installed?"

He stared at the ceiling as if he were deep in thought. "Hmm. Let's see. Could it be the way you flirt with him at the center?"

"I don't flirt with him."

"Could it be the fact that he sent me a history app?"

"Oh, excuse me. Did it say 'I like your mom' on it?"

"No. But get real. What guy does that?" he scoffed.

"A nice guy," she said insistently.

"Exactly. That's my point. He's a good guy. He volunteers. He helps Rex for free. And I've seen the goofy look you get when you're texting."

She was so busted. "Would you prefer that I don't go out with him?" she asked gently, giving him the out that she felt she needed to. Alex was her top priority, and even though she prayed he'd say no, she'd have to honor his wishes if he said yes.

"No," he said with a laugh. "It's fine."

"Do you mind if he comes to the match, and maybe we can all hang out and get a coffee or Coke or something?" she asked, with a cocktail of nerves and hope that she hadn't felt since she herself was a teen asking out a boy. Such a strange feeling, to want her son's approval so badly.

He shrugged happily. "Sure."

"Does it bother you that he's a recovered addict?"

He shook his head. "Mom, he's not a thing like Dad. We're cool." His phone rattled, and he grabbed it. "Oh man, James just got a new cheat code."

That was that. He'd moved on. She'd clung to fears of what their life might be like if she ventured down this path, but Alex was resilient. He'd taken his punches and gotten back up.

She was the one who'd been living in fear. He'd been living his life.

Time for her to do the same.

Fully. In every way. Not only as a mom, but as a woman, too. A woman who was falling hard for a man.

* * *

"I owe you, man. The Cristal's on me," Rex said, offering his hand to shake as Colin pulled up to the building at the community college where Rex and Marcus were slated to take the math test. "Wait. I meant the Shirley Temple's on me."

Colin waved him off. "Get out of here. Happy to do it."

"What are you doing today? You gonna go find the next Google to buy, or go scale the side of a mountain with your Spidey hands?"

"Both," he said. "Work. Some climbing, a run, then a swim."

"You're nuts."

"You should go with me sometime."

"Now you're really crazy," Rex said, laughing with his mouth wide open. "But I will cheer your badass ass on when the day comes."

"Excellent," Colin said, then looked into the backseat as Marcus grabbed his backpack. The kid had been quiet the whole ride. Then again, Rex tended to occupy the majority of the conversational space in any room. "Good luck, Marcus."

"Thanks for the ride. I didn't know 'til Rex told me this morning that you were the one picking us up."

Colin furrowed his brow for a moment, wondering why it mattered that he was the one picking them up. But he figured Marcus had more important matters on his mind. "Happy to help. You guys will do great."

He went to his office, where Larsen greeted him with a coffee and the sheer excitement of having found a kickass startup.

"Talk to me. Tell me why I want in," Colin said as they walked down the hall. By the time the sun dipped low in the sky, he'd worked on a term sheet for the first round of funding, then headed for an evening trail run with Johnny

Cash. The day was made perfect by the photo that landed on his phone that night. An image of Elle's legs from the thighs down in her roller derby socks.

The message said, *See you tomorrow.*

* * *

The whistle blared loudly, and Janine took off around the track, hell-bent on scoring more points. Elle and the other blockers joined in, jostling and jockeying against the Resurrection Girls' efforts to score on the Fishnet Brigade. Elle's quads burned, and her heart beat furiously. Her focus narrowed, as it always did during matches, to her mission —protect the jammer and win the game.

On the next lap, Elle held out a hand for Janine, who gripped it for a few seconds, then let go as Elle sent her shooting faster around the curve. As Janine sped past a Resurrection Girl, an image of Colin popped into Elle's head. She shook it off. She couldn't think about him now. Couldn't think about the fact that he wasn't here. Hadn't shown up. The match would be over in two minutes. Her team was ahead. The point Janine just scored from her assist was more padding on the total.

Maybe by the time they finished he'd be here. He'd show, right? He had to. He'd better fucking show.

A brief burst of frustration powered her around the track, her muscles cursing at her. She didn't want to believe that the man would fail to show up for her and her kid.

The only thing that would hold him back would be—

Her wheels slipped out from under her, and she crashed hard onto the sleek wood.

* * *

As soon as he heard the rumble of Ryan's truck, Johnny Cash whimpered and thumped his tail against Colin's floor. "He's back," Colin said to the dog, who wagged harder. "C'mon, boy. Want to go see Ryan?"

The tail became a propeller, moving so fast it could power a motorboat. Colin opened his front door, and the Border Collie took off like a shot, tearing across the lawn to greet his master. Colin joined the two of them on the sidewalk. "Looks like someone missed you."

Ryan stood up and gave Colin a quick hug. "Thanks for watching him. I appreciate it."

"He's easy. Welcome back. How was it?"

Ryan cocked his head and seemed to consider the question for a few seconds as he pet his dog. "I'm going to ask her to marry me next week."

"Holy shit. Guess you had a great time." He shook his brother's hand in congratulations and proceeded to pepper him with more questions.

Ryan answered them all then capped it off with a simple truth. "Sophie's the best thing that's ever happened to me."

Colin parked a hand on Ryan's shoulder and looked him square in the eyes. "She is. And don't ever forget it."

"I won't," he said, then opened the door of his truck for the dog. An engine rattled down the street, as Colin patted Johnny Cash good-bye.

"He's back," Ryan said in a hiss. "He knows where we all live. Sophie told me he stopped by more than a week ago."

Colin furrowed his brow and was about to ask "who's back" when he heard a familiar-sounding "hey."

"What's the deal?" Ryan said, and Colin nearly stumbled when he turned and saw who his brother was addressing. "My fiancée told me you stopped by my house the other day. Just man up and tell us what you want."

Shit. Colin had told Ryan about Marcus and the Protectors, but he'd had no idea that the kid had stopped by Ryan's house before. What the hell?

"Marcus?" Colin asked, trying to figure out why he was here, and how he knew where he lived. Was he here to share his math results? But then why had he gone to Ryan's house a week ago?

Ryan turned to Colin. "You know him?"

He simply nodded. He tried to form words, but he wasn't even sure what to say. He was used to assessing situations, but this one had him perplexed.

Marcus cut in. "I want to talk to both of you," he said, a touch of nervousness in his voice. "We all have something in common."

"Why are you here?" Ryan demanded of Marcus, then to Colin, he said, "Who is he?"

Colin was about to say what he knew—*I drove him to his math test, he's friends with Rex, Elle knows him, he's a member of the Protectors*—but all those words crumbled to dust when Marcus spoke next.

"My name is Marcus. I was born seventeen years ago at the Stella McLaren Federal Women's Correctional Center. My mother is Dora Prince. I'm your brother."

All the sound in the universe was vacuumed up. His heart stopped, his brain short circuited, and the ground began to sway.

CHAPTER TWENTY

He was frozen, but he wasn't cold. His breath didn't fit in his chest. His skin was two sizes too small.

"Who—" he started, but got stuck on the question. "Who is your father?" Colin managed to say, the words thin and tentative as he tried to make sense of the way north had become south, and down was now up, and who the hell this kid's dad was. Had their mother been knocked up courtesy of Stefano? That thought churned his stomach. Or did they share the same dad? But if Marcus had been born to Thomas Paige, he and his other siblings would surely have known about his existence, because the prison would have turned the baby over to Thomas Paige's parents to raise – Colin's grandparents.

Which meant...

"My father is Luke Carlton," Marcus supplied, and Colin blew out a long stream of air. His mother had not only cheated on his dad, she'd gotten pregnant from the affair. Course, that was the least of her crimes.

"So she was pregnant when she went to prison?" he asked, the words tasting like chalk.

"I guess she had to have been," Marcus said from his post on the sidewalk. The three of them stood in their places like actors on their marks.

"Pregnant? She was fucking pregnant?" he asked again, as if repeating the facts would assemble them into a neat, orderly package.

But before Marcus could respond, Colin turned to his other brother. Ryan's jaw was open. He hadn't moved. He didn't blink. "Can you believe this?" he said to Ryan, holding his hands out wide. He'd barely batted an eye when the detective had told him last week that Dora had been dealing drugs.

But this—this was something else entirely. This was the true bombshell.

He had another brother. One who was fourteen years younger. One he'd never known existed.

This was a meteor crashing into his backyard, slamming a crater in the earth. This was him standing over it, trying to figure out what to do with that gaping maw in the ground.

"No. This is insane, even for her," Ryan said, the look in his eyes mirroring Colin's.

He snapped his gaze back to Marcus, who rubbed a hand over his chin, a gesture that Colin did often, too. He flinched at that one small, shared trait. "I can't believe she was pregnant that whole time, as all the shit went down. And she hid the pregnancy through all of that?"

"My dad told me she didn't want anyone to know. She was scared of it getting out," Marcus said. His early nerves seemed to have evaporated, replaced by something that sounded like relief. He straightened his spine, standing taller. He still wasn't as tall as Colin or Ryan, though. Perhaps, the height genes among the Sloan men had come from their father. Somehow, this small detail mattered to Colin—mattered because he'd loved his dad. Because he missed his dad.

"When did Luke tell you that?" Colin asked, using Marcus's dad's first name.

"When I was older. I think ten or eleven."

"When were you born?"

Marcus gave them his birthday. Three months after their mom went to prison. Which meant she would have been six months pregnant when she was locked up. Colin tried to remember how she'd looked then, during the trial and her arrest. She wore baggy clothes, if his memory served. A seamstress, she'd have known how to make the right outfits to hide a growing belly. The thought of her planning a whole deception hit him like a sledgehammer.

"Holy shit."

There were no other words for this situation. Just none. He backed up, reaching for a railing, a tree, something to hold on to.

Nothing was behind him—only sidewalk, yard, and the utter surprise of the foursome becoming a fivesome. He grabbed Ryan's shoulder, and his older brother steadied him, as the news started to register as real.

His own mother had methodically hid her fifth child, keeping him secret as the tsunami rocked their family.

Five.

He was one of five, not one of four.

And none of them had a clue.

He started traveling back in time, trying to add up the facts and make some sense of this latest machination of their mother's. "So she was pregnant when she was arrested," he said, thinking out loud, taking a minute to process the absolute fucking weirdness of *that* detail. "And she was clearly pregnant when she was sentenced and went to prison." His brain kicked back into gear and started reconnecting the parts to the whole. And as he lined up the pieces, his jaw nearly dropped with one cold, stark realization. He brought his hand to his mouth, started to speak, but his voice was vacant. Then he found words again, managing a bare whisper as he turned to Ryan.

"She was pregnant when Stefano pulled the trigger." And the corollary to that hit him like a harsh smack in the back of the head. *Motivation.* "Was that why she did it? Was that her motive?" He shifted his gaze to Marcus. "Did it have something to do with you?"

Marcus held up both hands as if he were surrendering. "I have no idea. I wasn't even born."

He didn't mean to imply that Marcus was the motivation for the murder, but even so, it had to have played a role in their mother's thinking. She probably wanted the life insurance money so she could run away with her lover and her unborn child.

Colin spun to face Ryan, who looked like a mad man still—like this new wrinkle was rattling him to the core.

"Do you think this had anything to do with it?"

"I think *what the fucking fuck*. That's what I think," Ryan said, clenching and unclenching his fists. "I seriously cannot believe that she hid a pregnancy. But then, this is the woman who buried names of her accomplices, along with a goddamn drug-dealing route, in a dog jacket. That woman could hide anything. She's like a squirrel hiding nuts."

"She must have killed it in hide and seek," Marcus said softly, and a sliver of a smile formed on his lips. Colin glanced at Ryan, their eyes locking, sharing the realization that Marcus had just made a joke about their mother. *Their mother.*

Theirs.

One and the same. The green-eyed, husband murdering, drug dealing, cheater of a woman who had slept with this kid's father while she'd been married to Colin's dad.

Such a twisted, sordid tale. *Dateline* would have a field day with this new development.

There was a rustling sound as Marcus took a sheet of paper from his jeans pocket and unfolded it. "I brought this. I wasn't sure if you guys would believe me. But here it is," he said, then handed over a birth certificate. With steady hands, Colin held the paper and read every detail, Ryan by his side, peering at the document, too. From the state of Nevada. Marcus Carlton's birth certificate. The mother's name was Dora Prince. The father's was Luke Carlton. The date was three months after their mother became inmate #347-921.

In black and fucking white.

"Have you always known?" Colin asked as he handed it back and studied Marcus's face, looking for clues, for the family resemblance. Michael, Ryan, and Colin had plenty of differences, but they all looked like brothers.

Did Marcus fit the mold, he wondered. Marcus had the same eyes as Colin. The same square jawline. Colin saw shades of himself in this boy, and it was odd to be looking at him in this new light.

"Pretty much. Even if my dad and stepmom had wanted to hide it, they wouldn't have had much luck. My stepmom has, um"—Marcus held up his arm—"darker skin than me."

"Ah, got it," Colin said, speeding onto the next questions. There were so many, they were piling up, but he desperately wanted to make sense of this. "So there was no hiding that you weren't her biological kid. And you knew who your biological mom was, but Luke swore you to secrecy when you were younger?"

Marcus nodded. "Exactly. He told me they were threatened. That's why he left Las Vegas in the first place. He said once she went to jail, my mom and dad were threatened that I'd be hurt." He paused, drew a breath. "And I guess you guys, too."

Ryan flinched. "Are you kidding me? He said that? That we would all be hurt?"

Marcus held up his hands. "I don't know every detail. I was really young. All I know is what my dad told me—that it was too dangerous for us to stay in Vegas so he moved to San Diego with me and met my stepmom there."

Ryan dropped a hand on Colin's shoulder and exhaled, hard. His words came out dry and crackly. "You know what she said to me the other week? The last time I was there?"

"When she finally confessed to you?"

Ryan nodded. "She said, '*They told me they'd hurt you all. They told me they'd come after my babies if I said a word.*' I bet it was T.J. and Kenny who said that."

The hair on Colin's arms stood on end as the full meaning registered. "Do you think she meant all of us?" Colin tipped his chin at Marcus.

But Ryan didn't answer. Marcus did. "That's what she's told me, too."

"*She?* You've seen her? You've met her?" Ryan asked then stopped himself, halting the conversation. "I gotta get Johnny Cash out of the car. Let's go inside."

A few minutes later, Colin let his older brother, the dog, and his younger brother into his house.

Younger brother.

The notion still didn't compute. "You go see her?" he asked the boy who had once just been another kid at the center trying to *rise above*. Now he was flesh and blood.

"I have before. A few times. Look, It's not like I have some deep relationship with her," he said, his tone somewhat apologetic. "Obviously she never raised me. I'm closer to my stepmom. But I've visited a few times. My dad took me. He knew it was important for me to go, and I wanted to know who my mother was."

"What was that like? Seeing her?" Colin asked, as he headed to the fridge to grab sodas. It was a natural instinct —invite someone into your house, offer a beverage. Maybe he needed one normal moment in the midst of this madness.

Marcus bit the corner of his lip, then answered. "She's…" He let his voice trail off, searching for words. "She's emotional, and she's not really—"

"She's fucking crazy. You can say it." Ryan heaved a sigh. Colin handed out the sodas then clapped his older brother on the back. Ryan had been hit hardest by their mom's incarceration, since he'd held onto the hope she might be innocent for so much longer than the rest of them had. It was only fitting that he'd be the one to voice the descent Dora had taken behind bars. "She's losing her mind."

Colin snapped his fingers as more puzzle pieces lined up. "Ry, that must be why she spiraled," he said, like he was the detective now, figuring out the clues. "That's why she started going crazy. She killed the father of her children, went to prison with another's man's kid in her, hid that child, and had the baby in prison. No wonder she's gone off the deep end."

"Prison alone would be enough, but add in the other things and she probably never stood a chance at staying sane," Ryan said sadly, cracking open the soda can.

That familiar action jarred Colin—the three of them drinking sodas at his kitchen table. This was the definition of surreal—the trio parked at the same table where he'd eaten his free-range eggs this morning, a slice of avocado on the side. Now, he was chatting with the instant brother who'd fallen from the sky and into his life this afternoon. And yet, he hadn't just appeared out of nowhere. He'd been skirting the perimeter. "Why are you here now, Marcus?" Colin asked. "Why did you want to let us know who you are?"

Marcus gulped. "I wanted to…" He broke off then dropped his head in his hands.

Colin's instinct to help kicked in. "Hey. What is it?" he asked softly.

"I feel so stupid," he mumbled.

"Don't feel that way, just tell me. Tell us."

Marcus raised his face. Glanced away. Swallowed. Looked back at them. "I just feel so disconnected sometimes from my family. I love them, but I feel like I'm not part of them. Like I'm not part of anything." He levelled his gaze with theirs. "My dad and I don't always see eye to eye, and my stepmom tries to include me, but she's busy with my little sisters, and I just felt like I was grafted onto their family. Like they were all just stuck with me. They had no choice but to take me." His voice turned colder, but sadder, too, as he added, "I was nobody's choice."

Colin's heart ached for the kid. His family had been blasted to pieces, but he'd always felt tethered to his siblings and his grandparents. "Is that why you were following us?"

Marcus nodded, a confession in his dark brown eyes. "I wanted to see what you guys were like. That probably sounds stupid, but once I moved out from home this summer, I just couldn't stop thinking about it. I didn't lie to you about why I went to Shannon's. I'm part of the Protectors, and I went to Shannon's street as part of a patrol. But also to keep an eye on her. And since I knew your names, and found out you volunteered at the community center, I started going there to hang out."

Colin's breath caught as he processed this new detail. Marcus *had* been stalking them, but not to cause trouble. Rather to see what the Sloans were like. To gather intel. Colin had no idea if he'd have done anything differently in Marcus's shoes. "You knew who I was when you came to my math tutorial?"

"I did," he said with a nod, and a brief smile formed on Colin's face. He couldn't deny that he admired the hell out of the way Marcus said those two words—*I did*. Because he owned it. He owned his actions. He stood by the fact that he'd been spying on them. "I wanted to know if you all seemed…well, cool."

Colin turned to Ryan, whose expression had softened. The initial shock in his blue eyes had been replaced by something else. Concern, maybe? That was certainly what Colin felt. This kid had been left unanchored in a crazy world, born in the strangest of circumstances, told to keep secrets. All he wanted now was a connection.

"Did we? Seem cool?" Ryan asked, a playful note in his voice for the first time since this conversation had started.

Marcus laughed lightly then gestured to Colin. "Well, you're the only one I talked to. And yeah, I think you're cool," he said. "And I think it's cool that I'm good at math, like you are."

"Me, too," he said with a smile.

"You need to meet Michael and Shan. They're pretty awesome as well," Ryan added.

"I'd like that."

Colin wasn't ready to invite the kid over for Christmas dinner, nor to break out the family photo albums. He wasn't going to take him out for an ice cream and a pizza. But he didn't intend to show him the door either.

He did what he knew was best. Speak the truth.

"Look," Colin said, moving his chair closer to the table. "I don't know what to say. I'm floored. I mean, part of me feels like you were tricking me by talking to me while knowing what you knew." He chose bluntness. His mantra. His mission. No more lies; no more secrets. "But on the other hand, I get it. I probably would have done the same. You had a shitload of stuff to deal with, and now I get why you made that comment in the car yesterday about not knowing it was me who was going to be driving."

"I didn't want you to think I was taking advantage of you. Of the fact that we're…" The careful words came out awkwardly, like he was afraid again to say "brothers."

"That we're…" Colin stuck on the word, too, then pushed past it. "That we're brothers."

That sounded so immensely weird. Even stranger without Michael and Shannon being there. He'd call them in a few minutes and invite them to share this bizarre moment. Then he remembered where he was supposed to be right now. At Elle's match. Looking at the time, he realized it was probably almost over, and a small bout of frustration coursed through him. He'd call her soon, too, and explain why he'd missed the match, and surely she'd understand. There was no doubt in his mind that she'd not only be cool with it, but she'd be keen to hear this news. Probably excited, in a way, that one of the boys she watched out for had done something brave.

Because that was what Marcus's appearance here today was. Yes, it was weird and bizarre and shocking. But at the core, Marcus was downright brave.

"I'm sorry to just spring it on you. There's not really a handbook for introducing yourself as the long lost brother. Or a Hallmark card. I was trying to figure out what to do and say, and then you talked to me in the hall at the center," he said to Colin. "That's when I realized I needed to get my act together and just man up and see you and introduce myself. That's what Elle helped me with."

The house went silent. His ears rang with that name, and a chill ran down his spine. "What did you just say?"

"Elle helped me," Marcus repeated, as if this was no big deal.

When it was a big fucking deal. A huge deal.

"Elle? Elle at the center?" he asked, as if there could possibly be another Elle.

Marcus nodded enthusiastically. "I've been talking to her since the beginning. She's been counseling me. She's kind of amazing."

That definitely described her.

Kind of amazing.

But for the first time ever, other words popped into his head. Words he'd never associated with her before. Words he didn't *want* to associate with her.

If he'd felt the slightest bit tricked before, that was nothing on how he felt now.

Elle Mariano was a liar.

CHAPTER TWENTY-ONE

Her right thumb was trying to secede from her body. It was a lemming, fighting its way off the cliff of her hand.

Because...the pain.

The slicing, searing pain ripped through her hand in a tornado of hurt. She gritted her teeth, not wanting to cry. *Don't let the opposing team see you weak.*

Play had halted. Her teammates skated over where she was curled up in a ball on the rink. Janine wrapped an arm around her waist and helped her up.

"C'mon, girl. Let's get you some ice," she said softly, guiding Elle off the rink.

She whimpered as she skated slowly to the carpeted floor. Camille was there, ready with an ice pack. "Here, let me help you."

With her left hand, Elle waved Janine back to the floor. "Go. Finish. I'm fine," she said with a wince, as another wave of agony crushed the life out of her hand. Her right hip joined in the pity party, too, aching from where she'd smashed onto the hardwood of the rink, her hand and hip taking the brunt of the fall. Carefully, she sat on a bench at one of the tables.

The whistle blasted and her teammates returned to the track, the music blaring again, and the emcee bleating loudly on the overhead PA system. As the game whirled behind her, her sister pressed the ice pack on her traitorous thumb, wrapping it around to the wrist.

Elle flinched from the cold as the biting chill swept over her hand.

"You're going to be fine. I bet that smarts like hell though," Camille said gently.

"Is it broken?" she croaked out.

"In my humble opinion as a self-appointed orthopedic nurse, I'm going to go out on a limb and say nope. But you should get it checked out."

Alex walked over and slid in next to her. "You okay, Mom?"

Elle lifted her face and smiled faintly at her son. He patted her back gently.

"I'm going to be fine."

He raised an eyebrow then peered at her hand. "You should get it checked out. Like Aunt Camille said."

Tough Elle slid back into place, and she shoved off the pain. "I'm okay."

"No. We need to take you in to get it looked at. Make sure it's not anything serious," Alex said, slipping into his role as man of the house. He dipped his hand into the pocket of his cargo shorts. "By the way, your phone went off. I didn't look, but here it is."

He placed it on the table, and the text message icon flashed on the screen.

Several times, indicating several messages. Her stomach plummeted when she saw who they were from.

She hurt a thousand times worse as she gingerly unlocked the phone with her left hand and read each one.

* * *

He pictured raging waters sloshing over the front of the kayak as he paddled through a rough spot. He jammed the paddles harder into the water than he needed to, but the current—the tension on the rowing machine—pushed back. He rowed faster, the equipment at the row club screeching loudly, as if it were about to snap. Part of him didn't care. Part of him cared deeply. Another part of him was pissed, and the only thing that mattered was the battle he was waging with the machine.

And himself.

Maybe he shouldn't have said those things. Maybe he should have been smarter, kinder, softer.

But at the very least he'd been honest.

That had to count for something, didn't it?

The machine had no answers. As it simulated a river, the rowing machine simply jerked and pulled, and he fought back, wishing he were on the water for real, far away from land and able to totally disconnect.

But it was eleven o'clock at night, and this was the only way to fight the demons that whispered temptation in his ear. He was mad, he was frustrated, he was ashamed, and beneath it all, he was strangely happy, too.

For Marcus. For the chance the kid took and the chance Colin had to get to know him in a new way. For Shan and Michael as well. He and Ryan had taken Marcus to meet them, and it had gone well. But dammit. Today should have been something positive and good. Something that could represent a fresh start.

But the day turned sour when he'd overreacted. He'd been a total asshole to Elle. Like Kayla when he broke up with her. He cringed at how shitty he'd felt about himself when he saw her messages, and he hated thinking that Elle might feel that way now.

He wished he could erase those messages. Wished he could do the day over again. Pick up the phone. Call her. Or better yet, just show up at the rink and talk to her. Instead, he'd given her a taste of her own medicine.

But with far too much dosage.

Now, all he wanted was to spend the night with his one-time loves.

Patrón and pills.

Instead, he rowed. He paddled. He gripped. The sound of the gears slammed in his ears over and over. Soon, soon, it would drown out his horrible longing. It had to.

Oh God, please, it has to.

* * *

Her mother dangled the white pill in front of her, waving it back and forth like it was a dinosaur vitamin for a three-year-old. "Just take one."

Elle batted it away.

"It'll taste so good," her mom said, in a singsong voice.

She shook her head. She didn't want to make a bigger deal of her crash. "I don't want it."

Her mom shot her a glare as Elle settled into the couch. "You have a dislocated thumb, and you're in so much pain your sister said you were squealing. Now stop being such a pigheaded lady, miss."

"I was not squealing," Elle insisted. "And please. It's a dislocated thumb. *Thumb*," she said, emphasizing the extreme mildness of her injury. The urgent care doctor had diagnosed her with a simple dislocation. Then he'd clasped Elle's hand in both of his and manipulated the thumb back in place.

Sounded easy. Hurt like a son-of-a-bitch.

Fine. Maybe she *had* squealed then. Possibly she'd shed the tears she hadn't let slide down her cheeks at the rink. Perhaps they'd even served double duty—tears of pain and tears of sadness from Colin's barrage of notes.

She'd deserved them.

Still, they'd hurt.

The doctor had placed a metal splint on her thumb and told her she'd be fine in a day or so. "These type of injuries hurt like the Dickens when they happen and for the next twenty-four hours, but then it's pretty much over and done. But just in case, I want you to have some of these," he'd said as he wrote out a prescription for pain meds.

Camille had filled them at the pharmacy as she took Elle and Alex home, and her mom had arrived as soon as her shift had ended. Now Elle reached for the light blanket on the back of the couch and pulled it over her legs, then shifted to her side and yelped.

"What is it?" her mom asked, her eyes wide, worry written in them.

"My hip. It's not dislocated, though. It just hurts since I landed on it, too." She rubbed the spot where she'd fallen. Using her right hand. Which made her thumb throb. That pain radiated through her hand, up her forearm, and straight to her damn shoulder. She winced. "Guess I shouldn't use this stupid thumb to rub my stupid hip."

"Sweetie, just take one. You'll feel better."

"I don't want to," she said. She needed to stay strong. She couldn't let a *simple dislocation* rattle her.

"Mom." She turned her focus to the hallway door. Alex had popped out of his bedroom. "Take the pill. You'll feel better. You were crying all evening."

"I was not," she said with a huff.

Her mom heaved a sigh then shrugged and addressed her next words to Alex. "Nothing we can do about this stubborn lady."

"People. You act like I fell off a cliff. This is nothing. I'll be back in business tomorrow."

"But you're out of roller derby the rest of the season," Alex said, pointing out those doctor's orders, too. No contact sports for two weeks. Nothing that could lead to re-injury. The season was over in fourteen days.

"Ugh. Thanks for reminding me. Maybe I should take one now. To numb the pain of missing my games," she said, cracking a small smile.

"Now you're talking," her mom said and held out the glass of water.

"But just half of one, please. I don't want to be all dopey."

Her mom nodded and broke the pill in half, dropping one part back in the bottle and handing the remainder to Elle, who swallowed the pill. She only had ten in the prescription, and she'd probably just take this one. She didn't need to spend a sleepless night tossing and turning from the lingering pain.

"Hey. Speaking of missing games, what happened to Colin? I thought he was going to come today, and we were going to hang out," Alex said, as he sat cross-legged on the floor. Her chest tightened, and she met his eyes. This was hardly the letdown of a lifetime, or even a big letdown in the scheme of things.

Still, she hated that Colin had cancelled the first get-to-gether with her son.

"He couldn't make it. Something came up," she said, both lying and telling the truth.

"Well, that sucks," Alex said, annoyance in his voice. "I was kind of looking forward to all of us hanging out."

"I'm sorry."

"It's not your fault, Mom. It's his. If you say you're going to be somewhere, you should show up."

"I know, sweetie. But something came up for him, and he had to deal with it."

Alex scoffed. "If you say so."

Elle had to wonder if she sounded the way she had when she'd defended Sam and his unreliable ways, back in the early days.

"She does say so," Elle's mom chimed in, intervening as she shooed Alex back to his bedroom.

All alone on the couch, Elle reached for her phone, and reread the messages.

Each one made her cringe. Because they were all true.

Colin: I'm so sorry. I have to cancel today. Something came up.

Colin: Wait. That's not what I meant. Let me try again. Because I want to be completely honest, like we discussed.

Colin: Here goes.

Colin: I have to cancel today. Why, you ask? I just met my new brother!

Colin: Crazy, huh? Who would have thought I had another bro?

Colin: Oh, wait. Silly me. YOU would have thought that because you knew.

Colin: I have to cancel today. WTF, Elle?

Colin: I have to cancel today, because you've known for weeks. AND YOU DIDN'T SAY A WORD.

Colin: I have to cancel today because I know I should understand that you had no choice, but I don't know how to do that.

Colin: Mostly, I have to cancel because… I don't know how I feel about any of this.

Colin: Or you.

She took a deep breath, sucking it in, letting her chest rise and fall on that last one. It was a jagged little knife, chopping at pieces of her heart.

Those two lines weren't cruel. They weren't mean. They weren't underhanded digs. That was what made her heart ache even more. He'd spoken the bare truth, and she'd known this could happen—that his feelings for her might alter when he learned she'd kept Marcus's secret.

Still, it hurt so much that this choice meant the end of the sweetest thing she'd had in ages. She'd been falling so hard for him.

Maybe she should take the other half of the pill, to lessen the pain. She reached for the bottle, but it was so far away on the table. She barely had the energy to fumble for it now.

Soon, her eyes started to flutter closed, and the aching in her thumb subsided. The pain padded away, slinking out of the room on quiet cat paws, leaving her with only this whitewashing, this smooth, easy feeling in her body.

But before she slipped into slumber, she tapped out a short response with her left hand.

E: I'm so sorry. There was nothing I could do.

She hit send then decided she wanted to fall asleep on a happier note so she skipped over to the Facebook page for the Fishnet Brigade to see if her roller derby friends had posted any photos from the game. She smiled at an image one of the blockers had shared of the team before the match, then of Elle sending Janine around the curve during the game. She posted a smiley face in the comments then ran her finger over the picture as she yawned, the pills working their magic on her brain as well as her hands.

She clicked back to the page to search for more when a notification appeared. Someone had replied to her comment, but it was from a weird name she didn't recognize, and the words made an eerie warning.

Be careful who you get involved with.

"What?" she mumbled, but she was already floating on a cloud of comfortably numb, and the mystery slipped away with her cares.

CHAPTER TWENTY-TWO

The phone rang, and rang, and rang.

But then, if he were her, he probably wouldn't answer either. Tossing the phone onto the counter, he grabbed his cup of coffee and downed a hearty gulp.

Honestly, he shouldn't even have called her so early. He should let her sleep. She'd probably been up celebrating last night, anyway. He'd looked up the results online and pumped a fist in victory over her team's win. He was proud of her and sad that he'd missed it.

Sadder still over the notes he'd sent.

He leaned back against the steel fridge and closed his eyes. What had he been thinking? But that was the problem—he hadn't been thinking. He'd been *feeling* and letting all those stirred-up, messed-up, mixed-up emotions from meeting his long-lost brother rule over him.

He'd simply reacted. Matchstick fast, like he did in sports. When he went bungee jumping, he didn't let himself think. You don't give yourself any space to contemplate the decision. You just jump and free-fall. Same as snowboarding the black diamond back trails—just push off and attack the moguls with ruthless speed.

That kind of split-second fearlessness came in handy in his pursuit of adventure sports. But it could be the death knell for a budding relationship.

"Shit," he said, cursing at himself as he drank more of the caffeinated brew, then set the nearly drained mug on the counter. He'd already logged some time on the lake this morning, on top of last night's epic two-hour row club workout. The bookends to his midnight and dawn had worked—they'd kept him on the straight and narrow. He'd been tempted last night—the pull of the one sure way to wash away his woes had been potent. But he'd stayed strong, so at least he had that victory.

Now all he wanted was to see Elle and make sense of what had gone down. But it was too early, so he grabbed his keys and sunglasses, left his house, and headed to visit the two people he knew would be up at this hour on a weekend—his dad's two best friends, Sanders and Donald. That was the cool thing about older dudes. They could be counted on to be wide-awake at dawn.

He drove over to the Golden Nugget and found them where they always were on a Saturday morning. Sanders usually joined Donald at his table for a few final rounds with his favorite dealer before Donald's overnight shift ended. They'd cap that off with eggs and bacon, then meet their wives for coffee.

Donald dealt cards at the Golden Nugget and had for years, and Sanders was a mechanic at the limo company where Colin's dad had worked. Colin had known them growing up, before and after his dad's death. Sanders was a salt-and-pepper haired fellow with a bad back from working on cars his whole life, while Donald was a balding, skinny guy with an ever-present glint in his eyes that seemed to draw crowds to his tables whenever he worked.

At this hour on a Saturday, Sanders was the only one at Donald's table, so Colin caught them up on the latest news from the detective about the drug dealing, as well as yesterday's shocker.

"Is that not the craziest thing you've heard?" Colin said, as he finished the story and perused his cards.

Donald blew out a long stream of air, capping it with a low whistle. "If it's not the craziest, it's damn close. She was a real piece of work, that woman."

Colin huffed. "Yeah, that's for sure. Did my dad even know about the stuff she was up to?"

Sanders shook his head. "Hell no," he said emphatically. "He knew she was getting into some bad shit and running into trouble with money. But being pregnant? No way. He'd have told us for sure."

"He would?"

Sanders nodded as he studied his cards, exchanging one for a new card. "We were all pretty up front with each other. He told us some of what was going on at work. Like when there was some trouble at the company for a spell and he was trying to make heads and tails of it. Told us, too, what was happening at home with Dora and the fights they had about money, then stuff about you guys. Teaching Mike to drive and Shan to play pool. Hell, we all heard the story of that hickey you got," he said with a wink, darting out his index finger to tap Colin's neck as if he were twelve again.

Colin lifted his palm as if he were in a court taking an oath. "I solemnly swear it was an accidental scratch."

Donald nodded and adopted a too-serious look. "Yeah, that sixth-grader at your school dance had some sharp nails."

Colin chuckled, remembering when he'd made up that elaborate tale to avoid saying a girl had given him a hickey at a middle school dance. He'd been twelve and wildly embarrassed by the black and blue amoeba-shaped mark on his neck, so he'd concocted a crazy fable when his father had picked him up. His dad saw straight through it and teased him about it. Evidently his dad had told his best buddies, too. That warmed his heart.

He returned to less amusing topics. "What about the cheating, though? Did my dad know about Luke?"

"He was suspicious," Donald said as he doled out two more cards to Colin.

Colin arched an eyebrow. "He knew she was fooling around?"

"He didn't have any evidence, but a man just knows these things," Donald said, setting down the deck and parking his hands on the green felt of the table. "He could tell from her behavior. That's what he told us—that she'd been spending more time out of the house. More time unaccounted for. But you know, it was different back then. People didn't have cell phones and email, and didn't walk around with cameras, snapping pics of people having affairs. It was way easier for her to get away with it."

Colin's gut churned, and his shoulders tensed with simmering hate. He detested everything his mom had done to his dad. *Every single thing.* "Did he care? Was he bothered? Was he in love with her still?"

Sanders tipped his chin at Donald. "What do you think, Don? Did Thomas still love Dora?"

Donald ran his hand over his smooth head. "Ah, hell. How can I answer that? We weren't fond of your mom, kid. We didn't like her way before any of the real shit went down, because she was fucking around on him. So I don't want my dislike for her to cloud the answer. But I think he cared for her. And more than anything, he cared about you kids. You were the center of his world. The four of you— man, that's what he loved most. Being your dad. He was as good to Dora as anyone could be to a woman like that, and he cared about her because she was the mother of his children. He showed her respect. Because he loved you and your brothers and sister."

As Donald picked up the deck, Colin stared distantly at the sparse morning sprinkling of gamblers at slots and tables, blinking away the tears that threatened to well up. His father had been gone so long, and most days he honestly didn't think about him that much. Not for lack of love, but because time has a way of soothing the pain. The years made the hurt of missing him recede into the horizon.

But the time that passed would never take away the good things his father had passed on to him—love, respect, and truth. Colin might have spiraled after his dad's death, but he'd picked himself up since then. He'd apologized for his mistakes. He'd become a better man—the man his father had taught him to be.

That man needed to see one woman now.

* * *

The blanket fell to the floor.

Elle rustled herself from the couch, sitting up straight as she yawned. The light shone brightly through her living room window. She glanced around, getting her bearings, then she spotted a note on the coffee table. From her mom, it was written on a yellow piece of stationery with a cartoonish fox in the corner. *"Hey sweetie, I picked up Alex this morning. You were sound asleep. I'll take him for the day. Get your rest, my love."*

She grabbed her phone to check the time. It was after nine. She'd been conked out since before midnight. Those pills must have worked brilliantly. She hadn't even heard anyone leave. She never slept this long. She wiggled her thumb gingerly, and it didn't hurt anymore.

She wished she could say the same about her heart. She'd need super-duper strength pills to numb the sting of the barrage of notes from Colin. He felt so deceived by her. She understood why, and she'd tried to prepare herself for this moment, but there was no true way to be ready for a reaction to something that huge.

She'd just have to take her lumps like a big girl and move on from him. He clearly wanted nothing to do with her.

As she placed her phone on the table, a memory boomeranged front and center. An odd Facebook comment from last night. Something strangely…menacing. She clicked on her app and scanned the post on the team's wall. But whatever she'd been remembering was now gone. The post only included comments from her derby teammates, fans, and friends.

Weird. She shrugged, figuring the pain pill had made her a little loopy.

She padded to the bathroom, brushed her teeth, and took a quick shower. When she was through, she pulled on a pair of shorts and a T-shirt, headed to the kitchen, and punched in the 90s channel on her satellite radio. She hummed along to a Pearl Jam tune as she hunted for eggs and bread in the fridge.

The music was interrupted by a knock on the door.

With one hand gripping the open fridge door, she made a wish. She couldn't help it. She hoped against hope that it would be Colin. A foolish, ridiculous wish.

After all his notes, there was no way he'd be here this morning. She'd need to rid him from her mind. After breakfast, she'd tackle the *Forget Colin* project.

She headed to the front door, peered through the peephole, and squeaked when she saw that dark hair, that sandpaper stubble, and those yummy lips. *That man.*

She burst into a grin.

Wait.

Prickles of worry tripped across her skin. What if he was still pissed? What if he'd come here to tell her he never wanted to see her again? And what the hell? Had that dumb pill made her forget that he'd been kind of mean to her?

She inhaled deeply, letting the air fill her chest, and gathered her strength. Whether he was mad or not, whether she was hurt or not, she needed to say her piece. She opened the door, ready to finally explain that she'd been bound by her ethics not to say a word.

He was faster. He locked eyes with her. "Hey, so I'm an asshole, and I'm so fucking sorry."

The grin returned to her face, and she shook her head. "No, you're not," she said quickly, needing to reassure him. "Not at all. But do you want to come in?"

He nodded and walked inside. She shut the door behind him, and they stood in her tiny entryway. He wore cargo shorts and a blue T-shirt that revealed his strong biceps without being showy. A part of her wanted to run her hands along his arms, but that was not what this visit was about. There were things to be said. So many things. And though she was happy to see him, her heart still hurt from his messages, and from the weight of the secrets she'd had to keep.

"Colin," she said, starting with her own mea culpa. "You have to know how sorry I am. If there were a way I could have told you, I would have. I desperately wanted to. It was so hard for me not to say anything. I hated keeping it from you. But I couldn't do that to Marcus."

"I know. I swear, I know," he said, relief and frustration in his voice as he dragged one hand through his hair. "And I should have known better. I was so blindsided, and then a million times more shocked to learn you had been help-ing him. But instead of sitting down and talking to you to try to understand the situation, I just lashed out." He stopped to take a quiet breath. "And that's not the kind of person I want to be. My ex did that to me, and I don't want to be that guy. That guy who sends those messages."

"Then don't be that guy," she said matter-of-factly. She understood that he'd been knocked to his knees by news he couldn't have prepared for, but she also wasn't going to be on the receiving end of his anger. "Be the guy who gives me a chance to explain and work it out. And be the guy who treats me with respect even if you're upset."

"I will. I promise I will," he said, his voice a plea for for-giveness. "That's not how I want to treat you. I was just so stunned by everything that I stopped thinking." He rocked lightly on his heels as Eddie Vedder sang on the stereo in the kitchen. "It was all so out of the blue. There I was, talk-

ing to Ryan about how he's planning to propose to Sophie
—"

A full dose of glee raced through her veins. "He's going
to propose?"

He smiled. "See? There I go again, just saying what's on
my mind. Don't tell her, okay?"

She rubbed her hands together. "Ooh. Another secret.
But this one is the good kind to keep."

"So he's telling me about the trip, and his plans, and his
dog is jumping in the car, and, Elle..." He stopped to look
her in the eyes, letting the enormity of the moment register. "My fucking half-brother appears, takes off a cape, and
says 'Ta da!' It was beyond surreal. And he talked for a long
time, and then he told me you'd been advising him. And
boom." He smashed one palm against the other. "It was
like hitting a wall. I just didn't know what to think, and I
snapped back. I was too honest. Too direct. I should have
filtered myself and taken some time to process this news.
Instead, I processed it with you. Over a text message. And I
just typed everything that came to mind, rather than talk
to you." He downshifted to a gentler tone, meeting her
eyes and doing what she'd asked. "So talk to me."

At last, she was free of the burden of the secret. "I just
want you to try to understand that I didn't want to keep
this secret from you. But he asked for my confidence before he told me he was your brother, and I was torn apart
knowing that. But it would have been so wrong for me to
tell you." She reached for him, running her fingers gently
across the tanned skin of his arm, wanting contact.

"Wrong? Elle, that's not what I—" Then he stopped and
gestured to her thumb with the splint on it. "What happened?"

She shrugged it off. "Nothing. I crashed during the match."

He reached for her hand, brought it to his lips and brushed a kiss onto the small splint. Her heart fluttered. Maybe this wasn't the end of them.

"Are you okay?"

"I'm fine. Everyone is making a big deal of it. It was just a dislocated thumb, and evidently it's relocated now," she said with a small smirk as she wiggled her thumb. "It's not like I broke a tibia crashing off a sheer rock wall or something. But it did hurt like hell yesterday. They even gave me some pain meds." She gestured to the bottle on the coffee table. He followed her gaze, and she wondered if he was tempted. Perhaps she should have tucked them away. But then, as she searched his eyes looking for a sign of longing, she was glad to find none.

"Did they help you?" he asked, his tone one of concern for her.

She nodded. "I feel much better."

"Can I still hold your hand, though?" he asked, lifting his hand to hers then gently sliding his fingers through, lacing them together. Her heart danced a crazy jig. So much for that momentary panic. Now, the organ in her chest was engaged in a full-blown tango of joy.

"Yes," she whispered.

He stepped closer, tenderly clasping her hand. "I'm sorry I said all those things. I didn't mean it when I said I don't know how I feel about you. Maybe for a few seconds, or a few minutes, I didn't know which way was up or down. But then when I thought about it, I knew exactly how I felt about you."

"And how do you feel?"

CHAPTER TWENTY-THREE

This was the real risk. *Close your eyes, step off the cliff. No clue if there's anything to break the fall, but do it anyway.*

"How I feel is this." He took a breath before he spoke. "That I wish I'd been there yesterday to help you up when you crashed," he said, wrapping his other hand around her trim waist. She fit so well in his arms. "That I should have gone and talked to you. That I wanted to spend the afternoon with you and your son."

Her heart tripped when he mentioned Alex.

He continued, "And I know I need to make it up to him that I didn't show up, as much as I need to make it up to you. Because the two of you are a package deal. You matter so much to me, and I want to do right by your kid."

"You will do right by him. You already are," she said, her voice breaking as she inched closer, melting into him.

"I want so much more than what it's been. I can't pretend I just want *this*," he said, raking his eyes over her from head to toe. "I do want your body. I do want to have you all night long. But I want the rest of you, too." He let go of her waist and placed his palm on her chest, above her breasts. Such a temptation, but he was stronger than it. He was guided by the truth of his feelings for her, and the depth of them, too. "I'm falling for you."

Instantly she grasped his hand, tugging it even closer to her chest. "I'm falling for you, too, Colin. I was going to tell you the other night at your house," she said, words tumbling free in a mad rush. "I don't want these lines between us anymore. I want to see what we can become. I told Alex that I'm dating you, and I want to have you in my life as more than just the man I sneak away to see."

He nuzzled her neck, layering kisses on her skin, his heart beating hard and fast. "I want that so much, Elle. I want all of you."

"You can have all of me," she whispered then pressed her lips to his ear, making him shudder and turning him on. "Preferably now."

Colin needed no more invitation than that. Scooping her up, he carried her through the living room and down the hall, finding her bedroom easily. He'd never been inside her house before, and if he didn't have only one thing on his mind, he might have taken the time to notice fully the pictures on her wall, or the blinds in her bedroom, or maybe even the various shades in the sea of pillows on her bed. But nope. He was zeroed in on a mission—get as close as possible to her.

In seconds he'd stripped her down to next to nothing, tossing her shorts and tank on the floor. She scooted back on her bed, wearing only a pair of pink cotton panties and her tattoos.

She froze and held up her index finger. "Wait."

He raised an eyebrow in a question.

"Close your eyes," she told him.

He shrugged happily, figuring whatever was coming next would be worth the surprise. A drawer opened behind him with a squeak, then he counted the seconds as she moved around. Nineteen long ones later, the mattress dipped lightly and she told him to open his eyes.

Holy fucking fantasy.

The socks.

The roller skating socks. They were white with purple stripes at the knees, and they were so fucking hot. His dick was operating at a ninety-degree angle now.

"You are going to get fucked so good right now. In so many ways," he growled as he crawled up on the bed, running his hands up her legs, from the socks to her knees, to those gorgeous thighs, which led to his favorite place in the universe. He kneeled over her, bending his face to her center. Kissing her belly. Her hips. Inhaling her. Fuck, her scent drove him wild. He pressed his lips roughly against the waistband of her panties, then tugged at them with his teeth.

She laughed lightly, but her laughter was swallowed up as he yanked them to her knees, and her hips shot up.

"Colin," she whispered, surprise in her tone. But excitement, too, judging from the sexy little murmur she made.

Once he had the underwear to her ankles, he tugged them off.

"Just like I've always wanted," he said, meeting her eyes. Hers were full of lust—a lust that matched his. "You in just these."

"That's what I like—being your fantasy."

"Fulfilling my fantasy," he corrected, then he wrapped his hands around each sock-covered ankle and lifted up her knees. "Fuck," he said, in utter appreciation of the sight in front of him. "Just look at how fucking hot you are. I can barely take it. You're killing me with hotness," he said as he stared at her pussy. The absolutely divine, fucking gorgeous pussy that he wanted to worship. He loved the taste of her, the feel of her, and the heat of her. He loved traveling the path of her body back to that treasure. His cock throbbed insistently against his shorts as he nibbled his way up her legs. Bit the back of her knee above the socks. Kissed the inside of her thigh. Nipped that enticing, tantalizing spot where her legs curved into her slick folds. He ran his tongue along her wetness and she rose up, arching into him.

"My new addiction. I'm high on you," he whispered, before he buried his face between her legs until she was panting, screaming, and writhing. She flung her hands into his hair, grabbing him and pulling him as close as he could be. He was smothered in her, and he loved it. He could spend the day camped out there. Just tasting her, and kissing her, and savoring her. Slipping a finger inside, he drew her clit into his lips and sucked hard. She squirmed and moaned loudly. Soon she was frantically fucking his finger, so he added another, then pressed his thumb against her ass.

Like. Magic.

Like a secret *X* that marked the spot on his woman.

It turned her into a primal creature. As he rubbed his thumb against that forbidden spot, his sweet, feisty, fiery, complicated, lovely Elle became a two-minute timer of hot, dirty desire. She'd gone from zero to sixty in mere seconds, and her noises grew wild. Her hips rocked into his mouth as she wrapped her sock-covered legs so damn tightly around his head.

He was everywhere in her. Hands, lips, tongue, fingers.

Thrusting inside her. Fucking her in so many ways. Lust slammed into him from every corner of the world as his beautiful woman came undone in his mouth, her sweetness on his lips, her pleasure flooding his tongue. Her heady taste was all over him as she cried out his name like the chorus of a classic rock anthem.

After she came down from her orgasmic high, he went into the bathroom to wash his hands then returned to her. He shucked off his clothes and moved alongside her, her back to his front, yanking her alongside his erection. "I want to flip you over onto your hands and knees and fuck you on all fours with you dressed like that," he said, his voice hot and smoky with desire. She shivered against him. "I want to bend you over the side of the bed and just take you in nothing but your knee-highs." He pressed against her tailbone. She answered with a sexy purr. "But this poor little dislocated and relocated thumb of yours is making me think of other ways I can have you, since I can't put you on your hands and knees like I want," he said in her ear, in a dirty growl.

"Mmm…what other ways?"

"Where are your toys? Nightstand drawer?"

Her hazel eyes lit up as she shifted in his arms to face him. The gold flecks in them sparkled with a naughty glint. "Yes. What do you want to use on me?"

"Let's see what my options are," he said, then slid open the drawer. Holy shit. It was like a fiesta of sex toys. "I think they might be mating in there."

She laughed. "One can only hope."

The drawer was a shrine to battery-operated friendships. Elle owned everything from pearl-filled, ten-speed rabbits, to finger vibrators, to waterproof dolphin-style massagers.

But in the midst of all that purple and red and silver silicone, he spotted a slender pink vibrator with a small remote attached. It wasn't wide like the others, nor did it have the little fluttery wings for clit stimulation.

Which meant…

"Elle Mariano," he said as he grabbed it and arched an eyebrow. "I had no idea you were so advanced in your solo play."

She quirked her lips. "Now you know."

"Do you like this toy?"

She shrugged, a happy, woozy look still in her eyes. "I bought it one night when I went on a Joy Delivered online shopping spree. Never used it."

"What inspired you to buy it?" he asked, as he grabbed the lube in the drawer.

"Something I was reading," she said sheepishly.

"Ah, something dirty?"

"But of course."

"*Butt* indeed," he said, returning to her ass and squeezing it. Moving to a cross-legged position on the bed, he offered her a hand and tugged her lithe, naked body onto his. Damn, she was sexy as fuck straddling him in that hot as sin outfit—socks and nothing else. "Climb on top, my Skater Girl."

"Are you going to use that on me?"

"Considering how fast and hard you came with my finger in your ass, then yes, I am going to use this," he said, as he bent his head to her neck. "Unless you don't want me to."

She lifted her face and cupped his cheeks. "The woman in the story loved it," she whispered.

A bolt of lust tore through him. "You will, too."

* * *

He reached for her wrists and looped them around his neck carefully, making sure her thumb wasn't hurting. She didn't feel any pain. She felt only possibility—the alluring possibility of pleasure beyond her wildest fantasies.

She'd had so many fantasies about this man.

Trying new things with him. Testing boundaries. Playing, without pushing past her comfort zone. She wasn't sure how far she'd ever want to go in the backdoor department, but this kind of starter pleasure with the man she was hot for? She was ready.

And, oh hell, so was he. His cock was a thing of beauty —hard, hot, and heavy in her hand as she lowered herself onto him. Sensations rolled through her body. That delicious stretching. The intense depth. The way he moved. His eyes were dark, and she swore she could see all his desire written in them. His potent lust for her. She was sure two people had never wanted each other more—certain, too, that make-up sex had never been so good.

He laced his hands behind her waist, fiddling with the toy. The buzzing began, and the sound sent goose bumps across her flesh. He pressed the tip of the toy against her rear. It was better than good. It was mind-blowingly sexy. It was thrillingly dirty as it vibrated. He'd already lubed it up, so the tip slid easily inside.

"Rock into me," he urged as she rode him, rising up and down on his dick. He pushed the toy farther into her rear, and she tensed, tightening around it. Stilling herself, she drew a breath at the twin sensations shooting through her body. Together, they were heaven. This was the opposite of how she'd felt yesterday, when pain had torn through her on the floor of the rink. This was different, too, from the

Percocet. That pill had washed away the world around her, reducing it to a cool haze.

Here on her bed, straddling Colin as he shoved his cock deeper into her and played with her ass, she experienced every single wildly addictive wonderful feeling.

"So this is one of your fantasies?" he asked as he pressed a button on the remote.

She squirmed as pleasure raced through her. "Now, it is," she said on a pant.

"Any time you want to reenact something, I'm your man."

"You are," she said. *You are my man.*

Those words echoed in her mind, and she shut her eyes, clamping her mouth closed or else she'd say more.

She'd say too much. She'd serve up all that she felt for him. That she was falling harder than she'd ever imagined. That she was crazy for him. That she couldn't imagine how terrible she'd feel if she'd lost him.

But she hadn't lost him. Here he was in her home. Fucking her. Taking her. Owning her. Giving her more pleasure than she'd ever experienced, more passion than she'd ever known. Exploring their potential between the sheets. In some ways, trusting him with her body was helping her trust him outside the bedroom, too.

He layered kisses on her neck as he drove into her with his cock and the toy, pleasure rippling through her from all directions. Soon, she had no notion of where or how or why she felt like this—like bliss. All she knew was that every single cell in her body was comprised of ecstasy, because he'd done it again. He'd fucked her to the edge of reason. He'd ushered her to the far reaches of erotic joy, and she was breaking apart like a rainstorm, a gorgeous, brilliant summer rainstorm, as she came with no signs of stopping. Her climax had no end in sight. It washed over her, it pulled her under, and it consumed her.

Her whole body was a fucking orgasm. There was nothing else but this endless rush of pleasure blasting through her and taking her captive.

She moaned and groaned and cried out, and she couldn't stop because nothing had ever felt so good. "Oh God, oh my God, oh holy fucking…" And then her words became nonsense, just the echo of the intensity raging in her body.

Soon he tossed her on her back, wrapped her legs around his waist, and fucked her until his own oblivion smashed into him.

CHAPTER TWENTY-FOUR

Elle dangled her feet in the stream as the water gurgled between her toes. No socks on now. She was barefoot, and her Converse sneakers were next to her on the path.

The sun beat down hellishly, but tall trees with lush green branches shielded them from the bright rays, and a soft breeze circled. They'd hiked on one of Colin's favorite trails, which wound its way along a small creek.

"Did that mega intense hike get you all ready for your triathlon?" she teased, nudging him with her elbow as they perched on a rock at the edge of the water.

"Absolutely. Did you know the Badass Triathlon now includes a mile-long nature stroll?"

She pumped a fist. "Excellent. Sounds like my kind of race."

He draped an arm around her shoulders. "Kind of ironic, too, that you're the one with the splint and yet you worry about me doing crazy shit."

She turned to him, dropped her hand to his leg, and squeezed his strong thigh. "I do worry about you, Colin," she said, meeting his gaze.

He flashed a small smile. "I like that you worry about me."

"I worried about you yesterday, too. I was worried how you were going to take the news from Marcus," she said softly. "How was it?"

A bird chirped in a nearby branch, and Colin gazed at the rocks on the other side of the creek as he told her about meeting his half-brother, from the utter shock, to the sparks of humor he said he saw in Marcus, to how Michael and Shan had reacted when he'd told them—which was in much the same way he had. "Honestly, I didn't know how Michael would take it, since there's no love lost with him and our mom. I was worried he would want to have nothing to do with Marcus."

"But he didn't react that way?"

Colin shook his head. "Oh, he was surprised as hell, and had a few choice words to say about Dora Prince. But he's *always* looked out for the younger ones, and I guess Marcus is part of that now. But the whole thing is this big reminder of my mother, and how I barely even know who she is. She's like this strange, evil magician presiding over all of us from behind bars. Or maybe a master puppeteer, and she pulls all these strings whenever she wants," he said, holding up his hands to demonstrate an evil mastermind, adding in a cackle.

"She didn't pull this one," Elle pointed out. "Marcus came to you on his own."

He huffed. "I know, but she played her part by never saying a word for years." He shook his head in disgust. "How do you keep a kid a secret? Why? I don't get her. I don't know what language she speaks, if she's even human.

I seriously don't understand how I'm connected to her. I hate that I've ever had anything in common with her."

He turned to her, the sunlight streaming through the branches and illuminating the deep frustration etched on his handsome face. She ran a hand gently through his hair. "I don't know her at all, but I hardly think it does you any good to beat yourself up over whether you're similar to her. You're such a good person, Colin. You're one of the best people I've ever known."

He cupped her cheek. "Thank you," he said. But he didn't seem to hold on to her words because his tone turned dark again as he let go of her face and clenched his fist. "Most of the time, I've dealt with the stupid decisions I made as a kid, but sometimes I *hate* that I had friends with brothers in the Royal Sinners. I can't believe I even associated with them that way."

"And you didn't wind up in it. You didn't venture down that path."

"I was such a fuck-up as a teenager," he said, gritting his teeth.

"Please. It's not like I have some perfect record as a teen. I got knocked up."

"Yeah. But something good came of that. Your kid."

"True. But still, I was pregnant when I graduated high school. Of course I don't regret it, but my point is, you shouldn't let the past gnaw at you either. You are your present, and what I see in front of me is pretty great." A light breeze swirled the water by their feet as he smiled—a soft, tender smile. "Hate is a hard thing to hold on to," she added. "It can eat away at you."

He nodded a few times, as if he was letting her remark soak in. "Do you think that's happening to me?"

"Any time we harbor that sort of hate, it can't do any good. And it's all directed at her, but I think you're mad at yourself too, Colin," she said softly, placing her hand on his arm, tracing his tattoos that she loved. His skin was warm from the sun.

"Why?"

"Because you've struggled with some of the same things your mother struggled with," she said, stopping to pause before she said the next thing, "I think that's one of the reasons you have so much hate for her."

He scoffed. "Not because she, you know, killed my dad?"

"Obviously that is the biggest part of it. And in no way am I advocating you forgive that," she said firmly, holding her hands up in a gesture of surrender.

"Good. Because I won't and I don't."

"Nor should you. But you hate that you have this one small thing in common with her. Perhaps, the person you need to forgive is yourself." She softened her voice as she said the thing that she knew would be hardest for him to hear. "Maybe to do that, you need to see her."

He sat ramrod straight, as if he'd been jolted with high-voltage electricity. "Are you kidding me?"

She shook her head. "No. I'm not. I'm just putting it out there. This is the social worker in me. But I think you beat yourself up because you used, and she used. And maybe seeing her once will help you to let go of the hate you feel toward her. Because it's really a part of yourself that you're mad at."

He didn't say anything at first, just ran his hand over his chin and exhaled hard as he stared at the stream. A small bead of worry wormed through her, and she hoped she hadn't crossed a line with her suggestion, but she didn't want to take it back, either. She truly wanted him to consider it. "I think seeing her would be less about her and more about you. Almost as a way of making that last amends to yourself," she said, tapping his chest lightly. "To forgive yourself."

He looked at her, the corner of his lips curving. "You're too smart for my own good. So I'll tell you what. I don't know that I want to see her, but I'll think about it."

"Good." Warmth spread through her at the possibility. She did what she did for a living in order to make a difference, and she wanted to be able to do that for the man she was falling for, too.

"Now I have a question for you," he said. "Is this from experience? Did you hate Sam?"

She answered immediately. "No. I felt sorry for him. I was sad for him. I felt completely helpless. But I had to let go of all those feelings. He wasn't a good dad. He wasn't a good man, and there was nothing I could do to change him. I had to stop fighting all the battles with him. I couldn't make him a better father. I couldn't make him stop using."

He nodded sagely. "You can't make anyone hit bottom. They have to find it on their own. And man, am I ever glad I found mine. Even if it took collapsing in a race to do it," he said with a wry note in his voice. "But hey, I've come far since then. Hell, I wasn't even tempted when I saw those pills at your house today."

She was glad to hear that, but still, she planned to throw them out tonight. She didn't want to risk it.

* * *

Forgiveness was granted in all of a minute by the four-teen-year-old.

"He's your brother?" Alex's jaw dropped, and then he asked Colin for every last detail.

Colin gladly shared the story with Elle's son over pizza at Gigi's Pizzeria that night. Alex shook his head in amazement in between bites of cheese pie and drinks of soda. Organic pizza for Colin, of course.

When he was done, Alex said, "I guess I can let it slide, this time, that you missed my mom's match. That's a good enough reason. Even though there's no next time. She's out for the season."

"You know what that means?" Colin said, as the waitress cleared the table. "When the Fishnet Brigade wins big, we need to plan an awesome celebration for her and all she did to get the team there."

"Totally."

Elle didn't say much. She simply smiled, and nothing could have made Colin happier than seeing her relaxed and comfortable at dinner with him and the most important person in the world to her. She'd come so far. They'd made it past so much already. He'd never expected to knock down her walls so soon—or at all. But it had happened, and here he was, making his way to the other side with her.

When the check came, Elle reached for it, but he grabbed it sooner and paid. As they left the pizzeria, Colin tossed out a question to Alex. "Ever been to the Zombie Apocalypse store?"

"No," he said, his eyes wide and curious. "What's that?"

"Exactly what it sounds like. It's over in Chinatown. It's a small shop where you can work on your skills in preparation to do battle with the undead. It's tongue-in-cheek, lots of novelty items, but it's all good fun."

"Mom, can we go?" Alex asked, looking like a dog asking for a bone.

"Only if we can go now," Elle answered.

The three of them spent the next hour in the odd little store, where Alex plied the store manager for tips on how to stay ahead of the brain-eaters.

It was as perfect a night as a night could be, and Colin wanted to remember it as the start of this whole new chapter with the woman he adored.

* * *

After Alex crashed into bed, Elle grabbed the bottle of pills from her living room table so she could toss them in the trash. On the way to the kitchen, she peered through the orange case. Hmm. She could have sworn there was half of a pill in there from last night. But it was missing now. Twisting open the bottle, she reached inside and counted each one.

The half was gone.

Her stomach plummeted then twisted itself into knots. She winced and looked away from, then back at, the pill container.

No.

She told herself not to panic. He didn't take it. He simply couldn't have. She cycled back to last night, and bits and pieces of her own hazy memory played before her eyes. She'd reached for that other half, right? She couldn't remember taking it. But clearly she must have.

Colin wasn't Sam.

History wasn't repeating itself.

This wasn't déjà vu.

Besides, Colin had distinctly told her he wasn't even tempted, so she refused to let her mind wander that way. Trust was a choice, and she was making this one. It was the right choice. No question about it.

Closing her eyes, she breathed in deeply, letting the air settle. No reason to worry. No reason to doubt.

After she got ready for bed, she sent Colin a good night text.

Elle: Had such a great day with you.

His reply landed in seconds.

Colin: Let's do it again soon. All of it.

She closed out of the text app when a new message appeared. But it wasn't from Colin. It was from an unknown number.

Hey, pretty lady. Don't you be messing around with that new guy. WJ.

CHAPTER TWENTY-FIVE

Ryan turned off the engine in his truck, hopped out, and headed inside the convenience store off the highway. He grabbed a bottle of water, walked to the counter, then nodded to the cashier.

His brother.

"That'll be $1.21."

"No family discount?" he joked.

Marcus smiled and shook his head. "Sorry, man."

The convenience store was empty, so Ryan rested his hip against the counter, opened the bottle, and took a gulp. He tapped the plastic. "Can I treat you to a water? It's hot as hell outside."

"Sure."

He returned to the cold shelves, grabbed another bottle, paid for it, too, then handed it to the guy who he used to think was stalking his family. Now he was getting to know the kid. They weren't instant buddies, and Ryan hadn't signed the two of them up for Kumbaya-with-your-long-lost-bro classes. But Ryan *did* want to get to know Marcus, so he was trying to do it in a natural way. He'd taken him to lunch yesterday, the day after they'd met, and Marcus had told him he worked here at this store, saving money for community college, and that he was living with friends.

Which made Ryan wonder if the kid was on the outs with his dad.

His dad was another reason Ryan was here today.

"Listen, Marcus," he said, as a car pulled up to a gas pump in the lot. "I want to see your dad. I need to talk to Luke because I really want to get some info about the affair and about the pregnancy, and see if it played into why my mom killed my dad." Those words—they tasted like dry stones on his tongue. For so long he'd believed his mom might be innocent, but he'd been coming to terms and to peace with her guilt. Still, he was determined to help solve the case, and do everything he could to help find the other men involved.

Or at least to learn what had motivated his mother. The better he understood that, the greater the chance the cops had of nailing the other guys. T.J. and Kenny Nelson hadn't been found yet, and John had said he was still gathering evidence. By all accounts those two had left a trail of destruction behind them over the years, and Ryan's chest burned with rage over the fact that two killers—as far as he was concerned, they were killers—were walking free.

If it were up to Ryan, he'd have knocked on Luke's door already, banged hard with his fist, and demanded some fucking answers from the man who'd screwed his mother behind his father's back then hid the kid he had with her. But he couldn't do that now. It wouldn't be fair to Marcus.

"You want to talk to him?" Marcus repeated.

"I want to see what he knows. But to do that," Ryan said, gesturing from the kid back to himself, "I'd have to let him know I know about you."

Marcus shook his head. Adamantly. "No. Please no."

Ryan tilted his head, his radar going off, detecting fear in Marcus's eyes. "Why? He told you about your mom. You said it wasn't a secret."

"I know. But he doesn't know I talked to you guys."

"Are you going to tell him?"

"He would freak."

"Are you sure?" Ryan was asking for himself, but for Marcus, too. He didn't want to see this kid heading down the path of secrets like Ryan had done.

"I just don't think he'd be happy about it. He was worried for so long, and I didn't tell him I was going to meet you guys. I haven't seen him much since I moved out."

"Why not?"

Marcus shoved a hand through his hair. "We don't always agree. That's all I can say. If he knows I'm talking to you, then he's going to worry about Stefano's friends. About Kenny and T.J. He's going to think they'll come after my sisters and my mom."

"But is that a real threat? If it is, maybe we need to deal with it, rather than ignore it," Ryan said in a calm voice. "I can help you with that, you know. That's the business I'm in."

Marcus leaned forward and placed his palms on the counter. "See, I have no idea. All I know is he's terrified of Stefano's friends. I heard him talk to my stepmom when I was younger, telling her those guys threatened him—that if he said anything they'd go after him. He's made them out to be the bogeyman. Hell, the other day some dude with a goatee came in here chomping on potato chips and bitching about not having an iPhone, and for a split second, I started thinking he was one of them."

"Because he didn't have an iPhone?" Ryan asked, knitting his brow.

"No," Marcus said, shaking his head. "Because he was… I don't know. He just seemed the type of guy who'd stir shit up. That's all."

"Fine, I hear you. He set off your radar, and you gotta listen to that. But you really should talk to the detective. Are you going to?"

"I will. Soon. I was supposed to, but had to cancel because I got called into work, and then my car was in the shop. I know I need to see him."

"Are you worried your dad doesn't want you to talk to him?"

"I don't know," Marcus said, barely audible.

Ryan had no choice but to relent. He didn't know Luke Carlton well enough to understand how he affected Marcus. But he'd have to work with this wrinkle, not against it.

"Hey, do you want to come over for dinner sometime?" he asked, his voice dry and crackly. It was an awkward request, and he wasn't honestly sure what to do with it. But Sophie had insisted he ask, so he was doing it.

Marcus's eyes lit up. "That'd be cool."

"I'll make sure to invite the whole crew. Michael, Shan, Brent. We can have Colin and Elle, and Alex, too. If you'd like."

"I would," he said with a smile.

He had the sense that Marcus had been missing something his whole life, and it wasn't his biological mother. It was a connection to the rest of his family. That was easy enough for Ryan to give. He left as a new customer walked in to pay for gas.

* * *

After the customer left, Marcus dropped his forehead to the register. His heart beat furiously as if he'd been sprinting. His hands were clammy. That was what talking about his dad did to him.

Freaked him the fuck out. Damn near set off an anxiety attack.

He couldn't tell his dad that he'd found the Sloans. He just couldn't take the chance yet. He'd already taken a big enough risk meeting them. But knowing they existed had gnawed at him for years, and he'd longed to know them, especially since he'd never been close with his father.

He didn't agree with the decisions his father had made. At the same time though, his father had raised him and taken care of him. He'd been a decent enough dad.

His phone buzzed and he looked up. His stepmom had texted. *How did you do on your math test? Any results yet? Fingers crossed.*

His heartbeat turned more regular as he wrote back. *Got 'em earlier today. Aced it!*

An emoticon-filled reply landed on his screen. *Sundaes at Baskin Robbins to celebrate with the girls?*

He replied with a yes, reminding himself that he had to think of her and his sisters. It had been one thing for him to reach out to his family on his mother's side, but it would be entirely another for him to try to arrange some sort of a reintroduction of Ryan to his father.

Nope. Couldn't do it. Couldn't go there. His dad didn't want to revisit the past. Besides, there were too many people who wanted a piece of his dad, like Stefano's friends. His father had taught him to fear them. To keep quiet. They were rogue, uncontrollable men.

The bells rang and he raised his face. A hot blonde wearing tight shorts wandered in. She bought a cherry Slushee and started drinking it as he rang her up. Her pretty lips on the straw made him stop thinking about his family for now.

CHAPTER TWENTY-SIX

"Good thing we don't have a dog. Or a cat," Alex said as he pulled up a stool to settle in at the kitchen counter on Monday morning. He shot her a *gotcha* stare.

Elle quirked up her eyebrows as she served him eggs for his first-day-of-school breakfast. "Why is that a good thing? Because you'd have pet hair on your new T-shirt?"

He shook his head. "Nope. Because if we did, Fido would be all *happy* right now." Alex plunked half a pill on the Formica, and her heart leapt like a ballet dancer.

She wanted to kiss the damn pill. "Oh, thank God," she said, exhaling in relief.

"That we don't have a pet who nearly ate your Percocet?"

She smiled so broadly she couldn't contain it. She trembled with relief. "Yes. Exactly. Where did you find it?"

He pointed at the couch. "In between the couch cushions."

She flashed back to Friday night when she'd hurt her thumb. She'd reached for the bottle to take the second half-pill, but she must have dropped it right before she fell asleep. She grabbed the pill from the counter, tossed it in the sink, and ran water over it, washing it down the drain. Though she'd already chosen to believe Colin hadn't pilfered it, seeing evidence that he was on a steady path was a relief.

A huge one.

Now if only she could figure out who had texted her. She had no clue, so after she took Alex to school, while waiting in her car until she saw him walk through the front doors and safely inside, she called Colin and told him about "WJ's" creepy text from Saturday night.

"Come to my office. Let me see the text."

Twenty minutes later he was studying the message at his desk. *Hey, pretty lady. Don't you be messing around with that new guy. WJ.*

"It doesn't even have my name on it. Is there any chance it was just an error? Maybe it was meant for someone else?" she suggested, as she clasped the hope that she wasn't the target of some strange stalker, calling her a pretty lady and warning her to stay away from her new man.

"That would be great if it was just a mistake," he said, but his tone was completely pragmatic and she could tell he didn't think "oops, that was meant for someone else" was a likely scenario.

Nor did she. "Except I got a strange Facebook comment, too," she said, then told him about the hazy memory from the other night, including how odd the name was on the post. "It was gone as quickly as it was posted."

"Who was it from?"

"I can't remember. I was loopy on pain meds. But it wasn't a real name. It was like some weirdly menacing roller derby name, but for a guy."

He nodded and listened intently, her phone in his hand. He'd shifted into all-business Colin, and she sensed this was the newest challenge he was about to take on. He opened a browser window on his computer, and tapped the number into a reverse phone search. It showed up as *unavailable.* "Pretty sure this text came from a burner phone. If I looked up your number, it would show the wireless carrier it's registered to. A burner phone isn't registered, so it's hard to trace. Let me see what I can do, though." He set down the phone, cupped her cheeks, and met her gaze once more. "I promise, Elle. I'll fix this for you."

She didn't know how he could, but she loved that he wanted to. Loved, too, that he pulled her close and brushed his lips on her forehead. Loved that he wanted to take care of her. No one had taken care of her in years. She wrapped her arms around him and breathed him in—his clean, freshly showered, morning scent. She stayed like that for several minutes, there at his office, curled up with him. This was where she wanted to be when times were good, and this was where she wanted to be when times were tough.

The next day, he stopped by the center to tell her he'd tried to apply an IP tracer, then a prototype for a new phone security app, then even a silly app that let users spoof friends with anonymous text messages. None revealed the sender's info.

"Do you think it's about us?" she asked him, worry in her tone. That was all she could figure. That someone was trying to stop her from seeing him. "Do you think it's from your ex? That woman you said sent you angry messages?"

He shook his head. "No. I don't think so. I haven't heard from her in a year. That's so over it's beyond over."

"Who do you think is sending these to me?"

"I don't know. But I'm not going to stop until I find out."

* * *

All the fucking technology in the world at his fingertips and no one could trace a goddamn burner phone?

"Tell me, Larsen. Tell me when you get a pitch for a company that has that tech, and we're getting in on the seed funding round," he said, frustration thick in his voice as he sifted through app stores, past pitches from scrappy startups and app makers, and all the presentations he'd ever heard on new technology, with Larsen by his side, hunting, too. The two of them were parked on the couch by his coffee table, furiously searching for any startup, any technology they'd ever been pitched that could help their cause.

Were the drug dealers who used them really so far ahead that they'd found the one fail-safe method of covering their tracks?

"I'm on it," Larsen said with a crisp nod. "My ears are peeled. Or is that eyes?"

"Eyes are peeled. Ears are open," Colin said, tapping his temple, then his ears. "But none of it's working. My brothers don't even have tools to do this, and that's the business they're in. Security."

"Isn't that the point though? Not to go all Internet privacy on you, but isn't that why burner phones exist? Because people feel like they have no privacy. Facebook won't even tell you who sends you creepy messages because of privacy guidelines."

He sat up straight. "What did you just say?" The cogs whirred in Colin's head.

"Facebook won't even tell you who sends you creepy messages because of privacy guidelines?" Larsen repeated tentatively, furrowing his brow.

An idea hit him—it was out of left field, but sometimes the best ideas were born there. He latched onto something Detective John Winston had said.

The gang culture, oddly enough, loves social media. They post pictures of themselves online, on Instagram and Facebook, holding wads of bills from their drugs, or showing off phones they stole.

"You're brilliant," Colin said to Larsen, then flipped open his laptop, logged into Facebook, and started hunting. There were many ways to solve a problem. You could tackle it point by point, or you could go wide and surround the problem.

He'd had no success tracing the number, so rather than go from number to name, he'd have to amass a list of possible names and see what matched. He rolled up the cuffs on his white shirt—*nothing ventured, nothing gained*—and spent the next few hours digging into Facebook and Instagram for images of the Royal Sinners.

Don't mess with the Royal Sinners.

That was what they said about themselves.

Those were the words used in Elle's messages.

Don't you be messing around...

Whoever WJ was, he had effectively identified himself as a gang member in the text. Gang members had nicknames—*weirdly menacing ones*. WJ wanted to own his intimidation, and Colin was determined to find him.

Colin had something these gang guys didn't have.

Ingenuity. Resourcefulness. And one hell of a brain. He knew how to use his head to solve a problem. As he hunted, he unearthed a braggart's den. He found a treasure trove of images, just as John had said he would. Young guys holding wads of cash. Guys aiming guns at the camera. Others pointing to the ink on their arms. *Protect Our Own.*

He captured screenshots. He saved images. He took notes. He checked geotags on Instagram. He studied the pins on the back of images.

He did it again the next day.

And the next.

And the next.

He didn't have an answer, or a name, or a number. But he had a database now. Soon, WJ would tag something. That was what these guys did. Then he'd zero in on him.

* * *

Two Elles.

Over the next few days she returned to her split self. Only this time she was Happy-Go-Lucky Elle, and she was Sleeping-With-One-Eye-Open Elle.

Her schedule was packed with work, and school pickups, and the start of Alex's first history project of the year, and cooking dinner for her son. It was stuffed with Colin playing a few rounds of *State of Decay* with him, and then basketball with Rex, Tyler, Marcus, and Alex at the center. Tomorrow was jam-packed, too—during the day she had a board meeting with the center's directors over the remodeling progress, and at night Ryan was proposing to Sophie. He'd planned a surprise family celebration for Sophie afterward.

Life was almost too good to be true.

Almost.

Because there, in the background, slinking over her shoulder was her phone stalker. *WJ*.

She hadn't said a word about it to her son. He didn't need to know. It was his first week of school, and she wanted him to be able to focus on being a freshman. But she needed desperately to talk to someone.

"It's been three days since the text message. Maybe it's all over," she said to her sister as she visited with her at the Skyway rink on Thursday evening.

"Let's hope so. Did you get a new cell phone like I told you to?"

"What's the point?" she asked as Camille straightened up napkins and straws at the snack counter. "My number is on the center's website. Anyone can get it."

Camille gave her a pointed look. "Maybe it shouldn't be so easy to reach you."

She drummed her nails against the counter. "I want the boys to be able to reach me. That's the point of doing what I do. To be accessible. To be a resource for them. I can't shut myself off from the world."

"Just be careful. Because someone clearly doesn't like your boyfriend if they're sending you messages not to mess around with him."

Elle sighed heavily and twisted her hair into a makeshift ponytail. "I know. It just makes no sense."

"Maybe it's an angry ex of his. Someone who's pissed you have your claws in him?" Camille suggested, reminding Elle about Colin's ex who lashed out when he broke up with her.

"I don't think so. Why would she sign it WJ?"

Camille shrugged. "Who knows? Maybe WJ stands for Whack Job."

Elle cracked up, the first good laugh she'd had in days.

Twenty minutes later, she picked up Alex from Janine's house. He'd been working on a history project with Janine's son. In the past she'd have let Alex take public transportation home, but there was no way she was letting him on the city bus with WJ hanging over her. No way, no how, not going to happen.

She chatted briefly with Janine on the porch then headed to the car, waving good-bye. "Good luck this weekend. I'll be there cheering you on, though it'll pain me not to skate," Elle said.

"It'll pain me more not to have my favorite blocker," Janine said with a pout.

"Are you going to come with me to the final match this weekend?" Elle asked Alex once they were inside the car.

"Can I stay home and hang out by myself?"

She flinched at the idea, gripping the steering wheel. "No. I want you to come with me."

"But why? You're not even skating. I just want to hang at home. Play Xbox and stuff."

"We'll have fun. We'll get pizza at the rink," she said through pursed lips. She didn't tell him the truth—that she could barely stomach letting him out of her sight.

He kicked his foot against the floor of the passenger seat.

"Alex, don't do that," she said, as she changed lanes.

"I just don't feel like going. First you won't let me take the bus, and you always let me take it last year. You're treating me like a baby. Now I have to go to a game you're not even skating in. Can't I just chill? What if Rex and Tyler come over?"

But before she could say no one more time, her phone buzzed in the console.

"Want me to see if that's Colin?" Alex asked, grabbing the phone.

"I'll look at it later," she said hastily, as the truck in front of her slowed. She didn't want Alex seeing any messages from Colin, though they hadn't exchanged many dirty ones lately. Still, her phone was private. It was hers.

"*Mom.*"

She hadn't heard that tone in years.

His voice was laced with fear.

She snapped her gaze to him, and her son was staring at the screen, jaw agape.

Pure, primal terror burst through her, like a dam breaking. "What is it?"

But she knew.

It could only be one thing.

"Who sent you this?" he asked, his voice thin as a thread, cold as winter.

She yanked the wheel right and pulled into the lot at a Burger King. Slamming the car into park, she grabbed the phone from him.

The hairs on her neck rose.

Pretty ladies should be smarter about who they get INVOLVED with.

The phone slid from her hand, clattering to the console.

"What is this?" Alex asked again.

She inhaled deeply then did her best to channel a calmness she didn't even come close to feeling. "I've been getting some strange messages."

He shook his head adamantly then stabbed his finger against the screen. "This isn't strange, Mom. It's fucking creepy. It's stalkerish. Who is sending you these?"

"I don't know," she said, her hold on a cool, collected tone faltering.

"Someone who doesn't want you to be with Colin." His voice rose with every word.

She bit her lip and managed a small nod. "It seems that way."

His eyes widened as big as the moon. "Mom! I like Colin. He's a cool guy. But seriously, this is freaking me out."

It was freaking her out, too. More than she could ever have imagined. But she couldn't let on. She had to stay strong for Alex. She had to be titanium.

"Colin is working on it," she said, taking her time with each word. "He's working on figuring it out, and we'll make it stop."

"'*We*?" he asked, arching an angry eyebrow. "Who's 'we'? You and Colin? Or you and me? Or you and—"

"I've got this. I've got this under control. You don't need to worry about it."

"Just like when you had things under control with Dad?"

She held up her index finger. "That is not fair. And this is not the same."

"You're right," he said, spitting out the words. "It's not the same. Because he's not Dad. He's just a guy."

"*Alex*," she said, but she let her voice trail off because he was right. Colin was just a guy. Alex was her flesh and blood.

He stopped talking, crossed his arms, and slumped down in the seat.

"Let me get you home and make you dinner," she said, as calmly as she possibly could.

She stuffed her phone into her purse in the backseat, as if that would erase the message. But the text was still there, staring at her, breathing hot fumes on her like it had a pulse, a heartbeat. Like a shadow that lurked by her side. Colin had thought a Royal Sinner was sending these to her, and she was sure now that he was right. Sure, too, that someone in the Royal Sinners didn't want Colin in her life.

Seemed her son felt the same way.

* * *

He didn't talk to her at dinner. All he said was "thanks." He got up from the table, finished his homework, showered, and went to bed.

"Night."

Barely a word.

Just like *that* year.

The year he didn't talk.

The year he was nearly destroyed by his father's death.

She sank down on her couch and ran her hand over the back of her neck. Her sparrows. Her guide to finding her way home. This was her home, here in this apartment, with her son, who she loved madly, fiercely, to the ends of the earth and back again. *He* was her home, and she'd helped him find his way back to her after he'd lost his father. She'd do it again, and again, and again. She reached for a framed picture of him on the coffee table—his fourth grade school photo, where he wore a goofy, toothy grin. A small smile surfaced as she ran her finger over it. A tear threatened her eyes, but she refused to allow it to appear. She would not wallow. She would not weaken.

She had one goal in life and it was to take care of her son, no matter what.

Colin had told her he had some leads and was tracking them down, and she was grateful for that. Damn grateful. But as she set down the photo, she *knew.*

Knew it was time to hit the brakes.

Ironic, because she thought it would be the past with pills and the drinking that were her deal breakers. But she'd gotten over the addiction issue faster than she'd imagined she would. This new threat, though? She didn't know for certain if the texts were because of her involvement with Colin. But they sure seemed to be tied to his past. Not the addiction, the history he'd proven time and time again that he'd moved beyond. His *other* past.

The one he had zero control over.

Through no fault of his own, that past had resurfaced to the present. The past where a gangland shooter killed his father, and the present where a member of that same street gang was harassing her. All because she was in love with him.

Holy shit.

In love.

She was in love with him.

That was going to make it so much harder to do the right thing.

CHAPTER TWENTY-SEVEN

He wished he could be there with her. Holding her 'til she fell asleep. Kissing her forehead as her eyelids fluttered closed. Brushing loose strands of hair away from her face.

Instead, from the wooden swing on the back deck of his house, Colin zoomed in on the screenshot Elle had sent him a few hours ago. The one of her newest text. A night breeze tripped through the trees as he studied the message. He stared so long he let his vision go blurry. The message turned hazy around the edges of the words, and the letters seemed to float off the screen.

Ladies. Smarter. Pretty.

Then one word, in all caps, slammed into him.

INVOLVED.

He tapped in the community center's web address into a search bar. Quickly he found Elle's bio, where it said she prided herself on being *involved* with the local community.

In his head, he replayed the messages.

Be careful who you get involved with.

Hey, pretty lady. Don't you be messing around with that new guy. WJ.

Pretty ladies should be smarter about who they get IN-VOLVED with.

The blurry haze evaporated. The clouds burned away, and the sky was clear. Colin had figured a gang member was somehow targeting her, because she was involved with a man whose family had been torn to pieces by a gang. Someone like Kenny or T.J. Nelson, who didn't want the case reopened. Someone who was trying to intimidate Colin's family through the woman in his life.

But that theory didn't entirely add up.

He called Ryan. His brother answered on the first ring. "What's up? It's late. You okay?"

"Yeah. You answered quickly. What are you up to?"

"Sophie and I just finished a game of pool," he said, and if there was ever code for fucking, that was it. But now was not the time for razzing his brother.

"You told me something the other day, about visiting Marcus at the convenience store," Colin said, reminding Ryan of a conversation they'd had earlier in the week. It hadn't seemed like much at the time, but now he was examining every possible connection. "The kid mentioned a guy who'd been there?"

"Yeah. He got some weird vibe from him. Thought he reeked of Royal Sinners. Said he had a goatee and was bitching about not having an iPhone."

"And that made him think he was a Sinner?"

"More like Marcus had a gut reaction to him. And he said his dad has always been worried about those guys coming after them."

Colin snapped his fingers. That was it. Instinct told him the warnings Elle had received weren't about Colin—but they might very well be about Marcus.

Elle wasn't only involved with Colin. Elle was involved with the local community. Elle was involved in helping the kids at the center. Elle had been deeply involved with helping Marcus. And Marcus's father had been worried about gang members targeting his family. Were they targeting Marcus through Elle?

In the morning, he called Marcus and asked him for help.

"Tell me everything about the guy who came by your store the other day," Colin said, and his young brother described the guy in detail, right down to his hands.

* * *

After Colin finished a training swim at lunch, his phone buzzed as he left the gym. He'd set up an alert for any new photos from the Instagram and Facebook profiles he'd check-marked as likely belonging to the Royal Sinners. The account that had pinged was called *Don't Mess With*, and it often featured snapshots of stolen goods.

As he walked across the parking lot to his car, he scrolled through the new set of photos in the feed.

Boatloads of iPhones.

In some of the pictures, a guy pointed at his stash, his fingers in the shape of guns. The guy's face wasn't in any of the pictures, but Colin punched the air when he read the caption.

Looks like Wicked Jack is gonna make a cool couple of Gs on this haul. Burner phones are the shizz, but iPhones are the biz. $$$$$

"Wicked Jack," Colin said out loud. "WJ."

Anger rolled through him, and he slammed the door on his car. Who the fuck was this guy harassing his Elle because of Marcus? What did Marcus have to do with the Royal Sinners? Was it because he was in the Protectors? He couldn't imagine gang members caring that much about a guardian angels–style group of volunteers, especially teenagers. The Royal Sinners trafficked in guns and drugs and stolen goods, so why would a group of unarmed vigilantes bother them? And why would they care that Elle was talking to Marcus?

Outrage filled his chest, but he forced himself to let it go, and set to work.

The thing about gang guys was they didn't always realize that some types of technology were highly traceable. They might have mastered the burner phone and made its anonymity their ally. But Instagram? That social media service was like a dog with a microchip.

Every picture had a location attached to it unless you turned off the geotagging feature, and not everyone knew to do that. Or chose to turn it off—because street gangs tagged. They left their mark. They bragged.

Colin wanted to kiss the original investors in Instagram and thank them for the geotagging technology that made it possible for braggarts to be found. In a few minutes, he had a longitude and latitude. As he looked at the picture one more time, something else clicked.

"Wicked Jack's" fingernail was black and blue.

It matched the description of Marcus's convenience store visitor.

* * *

Her nerves were frayed and worn thin. They were nails bitten to the quick. As she dressed for Ryan and Sophie's proposal celebration, slipping into a dress and fastening a necklace, her stomach dived. Twenty million times. She ran a brush through her long hair, tugging, pulling, and yanking. Punishing it. She tossed the hairbrush in a basket on the bathroom floor, left her apartment, and took her son to her mother's house. "I'll pick you up later."

He shrugged. "Okay."

There it was again. The dead voice. The empty tone.

She wrapped her arms around him and gave him a hug. "You always come first. You know that, don't you?"

He managed to quirk his lips up in a small smile, then she said good-bye. Even if he didn't believe her now, she'd prove it to him.

* * *

The second the call came from Marcus, Colin pounced on it.

"Talk to me," he said, then glanced at the time on his wrist. He needed to leave the office any second to make it to Ryan's event.

"I went in early for my shift, and I found the video from the other week," Marcus said. "I just played it on the work computer in the back office and shot a video of it with my cell. You should have it any minute. I emailed it."

"Let me see if it's here." He switched to his email program on his laptop, clicked on the new message, and hit play. The video was black and white, and the conversation was barely audible.

"Do you know who he is? You think this is the guy who's sending harassing notes to Elle?" Marcus asked.

"I don't know for sure," Colin said, then zoomed in on the guy's hands. Lo and fucking behold, there it was. The messed-up fingernail. A chill ran down his spine. "It has to be the same guy. The comments about the phone in his Instagram, then this stubbed fingernail, then the location. I just don't know his name." He crooked his head against the phone as he grabbed a screenshot and dropped it into a reverse image search. "But I'm going to call the detective after I plug this into a—"

His heart stopped beating. His blood froze. That last name. It echoed in his nightmares.

"You still there?" Marcus asked.

"Yes," he whispered, his voice a hiss.

"What is it? Who is it? What did you find out?"

The photo had taken him to a Facebook page for Jerry Stefano's teenage son. The photos matched the ones he'd found on Instagram.

"Lee Stefano. The shooter's son. And it looks like he's following in his father's footsteps. He calls himself Wicked Jack, and he's in the Royal Sinners."

CHAPTER TWENTY-EIGHT

Sophie's hand was adorned with the most gorgeous diamond Elle had ever seen. Brilliant and vintage cut, it was one hundred percent Sophie. Elle held her friend's left hand and couldn't stop oohing and ahhing at the beautiful bling. Nor could Shannon.

The women and the men gathered around the blue plush lounge chairs in one of the bars at New York-New York, having just surprised Sophie with the proposal celebration that Ryan had put together for her. Elle focused on the diamond and on Sophie's happiness, letting it distract her from the inevitable turn her own life was taking.

This was antithesis of what she had to do later this evening, but for now, Elle wanted to soak in the romance. She wanted to savor all her friend's happiness. Sniff it like a fine perfume she could enjoy but never own for herself.

"Tell us everything. Did he actually take out the ring at the top of the roller coaster, too?" Elle asked.

Sophie shook her head, her pretty platinum blonde curls bouncing. She looked windswept, and radiant, too. Not to mention like a total knockout in her pinup girl dress with a peach pattern on it. "As soon as we reached the top, the very second when the car just sort of hovers there on the track and you're about to scream your lungs out, he shouted 'Sophie, will you marry me?'"

Shannon clasped her hand on her mouth then dropped it just as quickly. "Oh my God, that is so perfect."

"And what did you say?" Elle asked, making a rolling gesture with her hands, eager for Sophie to tell the rest of the tale. A Bruce Springsteen tune played in the background at the bar, while the men toasted to Ryan. Colin, Michael, and Sophie's brother John—one of the most handsome detectives Elle had ever seen, with his dark blond hair and blue eyes—were all there. "Well, obviously you said yes," Elle quickly supplied. "But how? Tell us, tell us."

"I shouted *yes*! It was that simple," Sophie said and her joy was infectious. Elle beamed as she listened. She couldn't stop smiling. Not even the specter of the rest of her evening could cast a pall on this moment.

Ryan leaned in, draped an arm around Sophie, and raised his finger in the air. "Actually, to be precise, she said 'Oh my God, yes, yes, yes.'"

Sophie swatted him on the elbow. "*Ryan Sloan.*"

"*Sophie Sloan*," he countered.

He tugged her in for a kiss, and even though Elle's chest ached with sadness, she clapped loudly and cheered them on. She couldn't help it. This kind of bliss needed to be celebrated, even if a relationship like that was too risky for her. Even though love was biting her in the ass.

Oh, wait.

That was Colin grasping her rear. He brushed his lips to her ear. "You look beautiful tonight," he whispered. "And

I'll be right back. I need to talk to John. But I have good news."

She flashed him a smile. "Can't wait," she said, her eyes following him briefly as he walked into the casino with Sophie's brother. But truth be told, she could wait, because she desperately needed the second-hand high she was getting from Sophie's tale. The only good news would be that her stalker was arrested, and she doubted that was the case, so she opted to exist in this bubble of happiness for a few more minutes.

"Tell us the rest," Elle demanded when Sophie and Ryan managed to pry their lips off each other.

"I need every single detail of how my brother finally got down on one knee," Shannon added.

Sophie laced her fingers together and continued. "As soon as the cars stopped and everyone got off the roller-coaster, the attendant handed Ryan the box. Ryan didn't want to have it on the ride, obviously, since it goes upside down. He stepped off the car, reached for my hand, dropped down on one knee, flipped open the box, and said..." Sophie stopped to clasp her hand on her heart. "'You are the love of my life. And I have never wanted anything more than I want to marry you and spend the rest of my life with you.'"

Elle shrieked. She couldn't help it. It was so perfect. Her heart skipped around the room. It traipsed and pranced, and sang *tra la la*. She grabbed both of Sophie's hands. "That is the most romantic thing I've ever heard."

A tear of happiness slid down her cheek. Followed by another. Only this one was laced with sadness, because she couldn't have that kind of romance right now.

Maybe not ever.

* * *

The sound of shrieking distracted him momentarily. As he and John threaded their way through the slot machines, he glanced back at the bar and spotted Elle holding Sophie's hands and beaming. Man, was there anything better than a proposal to send the woman you were crazy for into romantic overdrive? He couldn't wait to have a minute alone with her tonight. They hadn't been together all week, and he wanted to feel her in his arms. To hold her, touch her, taste her. To tell her how he felt, tell her he wasn't just falling.

He'd fallen.

But this had to be done first.

The problem wasn't fully solved yet.

That was where John came in.

They continued past the Willy Wonka slots, where the chocolatier presided over Oompa Loompas, and reached a quiet hallway near the restrooms.

"I've got some info for you," Colin said, then told him everything about the texts, the convenience store visitor, the Instagram pictures and the name. "Is Stefano's son part of the case? Why would he have something against Marcus and be trying to get to him through Elle?"

John nodded a few times, seeming to process the news. He blew out a long stream of air. "Lee Stefano *is* one of the reasons there is an investigation. When he started falling into the gang activities, we were tipped off about what Lee was up to, and started looking into the possibility that his father had accomplices in the Sinners. He might have a bone to pick with Marcus."

"But Lee's dad is in prison, so what would he have against Marcus or Elle?"

"That's what we're working on. My belief is that Kenny Nelson and T.J. Nelson were supposed to look out for Lee Stefano and keep him out of trouble. They did for a while, but then they stopped keeping him away from the gang and brought him into it instead. He's one of them now, and I'm willing to bet that Lee is doing his part to look out for the men he thinks of now as his brothers—Kenny and T.J."

Colin knit his brow. "How is he looking out for them? Especially since they're on the run."

"That's exactly why Lee's looking out for them. So we don't get to them. This is Lee protecting them, and they don't like that Marcus is talking to you. I have some leads I'm chasing down, but my gut is telling me that these guys figure the more Marcus talks to your family, the more they're at risk."

"Do you think Marcus knows something?"

John paused and clenched his jaw, his eyes hardening. "I have my suspicions."

"Jesus Christ," Colin muttered in utter frustration. "This is like a fucking onion. Peel off one layer and there's another one underneath."

"Believe you me, I know. But we're getting closer to the key suspects, and now it looks like Lee Stefano just put a sign on his back that says *arrest me for grand larceny.* After all, iPhones aren't cheap," he said with a wry grin. "And on that note, I need to cut out of here and get on with paying a visit to a certain longitude and latitude."

* * *

He couldn't wait to tell Elle, to let her know that the end was in sight. They had a name, and the name was in the hands of the cops, and the cops were doing their job. She was going to be safe. Safe with him.

When he returned to the bar, he reached for her hand, pulled her up, and led her into a quiet corner. He grabbed a small booth and told her every detail. She cycled through surprise, shock, and fear.

He threaded his fingers through hers, trying to reassure her. "But John's on his way to make an arrest."

She parted her lips to speak then simply said "good" in a voice that was devoid of emotion. He wanted to reach back in time and recapture some of that magic she seemed to feel moments ago. Maybe it had all disappeared. Abra-cadabra. Now you see it, now you don't.

"Elle, this is a good thing, isn't it?"

She shook her head then she nodded, as if she couldn't decide. "It is good. It's wonderful. It's everything I hoped for. But he's not in handcuffs yet, and we don't know if he'll be at his home when John goes there to arrest him. We don't know what will happen," she said, fiddling with her necklace. "All I know is my son is freaked out, and he's barely talking again. I can't take this chance right now. He is my son. He is my world."

"Oh."

His heart cratered. It fell from the sky and crashed hard at his feet, in pieces.

"I want to," she said, squeezing his hand. "You have to know how much I want to be with you."

He nodded. He didn't doubt it for a second. "I under-stand," he said, though the words cut his throat.

She let go of his hand and ran her fingers through his hair. Fuck, he would miss this. He would miss her touch. He would miss all of her.

"I think we just need to cool it for a bit, until things settle down." She kept her chin up but the trembling in her shoulders gave her away. "This is temporary."

But temporary had never felt so miserable.

All that joy, all that happiness, all that possibility unwound into a heap on the floor of the bar at New York-New York. He'd always known Elle was his Everest. He'd always suspected he'd never have her the way he had hoped. But he'd been wrong about why. He wasn't losing her—whether temporarily or permanently—because of his bad choices. Instead it was due to the choices of others. Choices he couldn't control. He had no notion what was next for them, or how long this separation would last. Maybe a day, maybe a year.

But there was one choice he could control. He brushed the back of his fingers against her cheek and gazed into her hazel eyes. In them he saw everything he'd ever wanted. Love, peace, acceptance, understanding, and so much passion.

"There's something I need to tell you," he began. "I told you I'd always be honest with you. And I don't want you to think that will stop even if we can't be together right now."

"I don't want you to stop being honest with me. What is it? Tell me."

He drew a breath and then said the easiest words in the world. "I'm madly in love with you."

The smile that he'd seen earlier, when she'd been listening to Sophie, reappeared for a moment. "I'm so in love with you, too," she said, her voice bare. "That's why this is so hard. I hate cooling things off when it feels like they're just starting."

Elle rarely used the word *hate*. He didn't want to end this night on that note. He wanted her to feel hope, even if they were heading their separate ways. He wrapped an arm around her, pulling her as close as could be in the corner booth. "They're going to arrest him. This is going to end. I don't want you to be scared. I told you I'd find whoever was doing it. So just know as you go to sleep tonight that even though I'm not the guy in blue knocking on a door and putting someone under arrest, that I will take care of you." He pressed a soft kiss to her forehead, and a sweet, sad sigh fluttered from her lips. "And your son."

Her throat hitched on those last three words, and she met his gaze. Her eyes said everything—those were the words that mattered most. "Thank you," she whispered.

There were a million more things he could say, and yet there was nothing more to talk about. He had to tell her good night. He ran his thumb over her bottom lip then pressed his mouth to hers. Brushing his lips over hers. Tasting her. Savoring everything about the way they came together.

Wanting to linger tonight in their last kiss.

And he did, for a too-brief moment.

Until it ended, and he walked her to the lobby, hailed a cab, and sent her home.

CHAPTER TWENTY-NINE

Michael eyed his brother and in a nanosecond guessed what Colin had been up to. "You look like you just booked a room for a quick lay."

"Whoa." Colin held up his hands.

"Am I right or am I right?" Michael asked as he knocked back a beer at the blackjack table. Ryan had taken off with his bride-to-be, Shannon had hopped on the back of Brent's bike and headed home with her husband, and the detective had gone off to do whatever detectives did. Solve cases, hopefully. Arrest bad guys. Deal with the shit on the streets.

"You're wrong. Wish you were right," Colin said. Michael's youngest brother—wait, make that second-to-youngest-brother—settled in next to him for another round of cards as the clock ticked closer to midnight.

"What's the story?"

Colin sighed. "It's a long one."

"Looks like you got all night, buddy," Michael said, then pushed some chips into the center of the green felt.

"Hit me," he said to the dealer, who doled out another card.

"There was a girl. There was a guy. There was some trouble," Colin said, summing it up.

Michael raised his beer and quirked up his lips. "Tell me about it."

"What about you?"

He waved a hand dismissively. "You know me," he said, keeping it vague because his romantic life was…well, it was just fine and fantastic, except for that little problem of Annalise.

"You're still hung up on her, aren't you?"

Michael scoffed, dismissing the idea that he was mooning over a girl. "Who?"

Colin cracked up and pointed at him. "That's a good one. That's the best. How long did you practice to make that 'who' sound convincing?"

"I have no idea what you're talking about," Michael said as the dealer laid down an eight of hearts. His hand busted. The house scooped up all the chips.

"You know exactly what I'm talking about. You should just look her up. Find her."

"Yeah? That's your advice? This from the guy who's having his own woman trouble?"

Colin nodded vigorously. "You'll always wonder 'what if.' Better to try than to keep asking. Better to find your what-if woman than to wonder if she's asking the same questions."

It must be obvious she'd been on his mind, even though he hadn't seen her in years. Not since he'd bumped into her at the airport in France, and they'd had an hour together on a layover. He didn't think he'd hear from her again, and then she'd reached out to him last week.

He pushed her out of his mind as his brother-in-law's friend Mindy walked toward them—he'd invited the cute blonde to join him for cards. He wanted to talk to her about something he'd heard the other day when he'd visited his dad's old friends. Something about trouble at his dad's company from way back when, and some details he recalled his father sharing with him at the time. He wanted to see if it added up to anything. Plus, he liked spending time with Mindy. She was a straight shooter, and he liked that in a woman. Liked the way she looked, too, in that little skirt she wore. She waved when she spotted him, and he tipped his chin and patted the stool next to him.

"What about you? How are we going to get you out of the girl trouble you're in?" he asked his brother before Mindy arrived.

Colin sighed heavily. "That is the million-dollar question, and I don't know that I have the answer. About the only one who might is John Winston."

Then Mindy joined them, giving him a quick hug, and doing the same for Colin. Time to set thoughts of other women aside.

* * *

When Colin woke up at dawn, the sun streaming through the open window in his house, he didn't embark on his usual Saturday morning routine. The mountains called to him, but he ignored them. The lake wanted his company, but it would survive without him today. No gym, no workout, and no quiet contemplation.

There was one thing he had to do, so he lobbed a call to his youngest sibling and suggested a road trip.

Marcus was game. "I'll be ready in twenty minutes."

Colin suspected this was why Marcus had wanted to get to know his siblings. Not necessarily for a trip like this, but to be *invited*. To be included.

Two hours and one hundred miles later, they were drinking Slushees and arguing over whether rock music was better than hip-hop. Marcus kept trying to take control of the radio, tuning in to stations Colin didn't want to listen to. Colin gave Marcus a hard time because that was in the how-to-be-a-brother handbook, and the hazing made the kid laugh.

At the next gas station, they added Doritos to the haul. Colin ripped open the bag. "I think this might make my system go into shock. It's the first true junk food I've had in ages."

Marcus scoffed. "Dude. You drink soda all the time. Your body's not a temple twenty-four-seven."

"Touché. I just can't give up the hard stuff, I guess. Me and Diet Coke—we're like this," he said, twisting his index and middle finger together. "Diet Coke has gotten me through many moments of temptation."

"Then you need to keep worshiping the almighty beverage," he said.

They returned to his car and plowed through Doritos, Peanut M&Ms, and more Diet Coke as they drove.

By one p.m., they pulled into the lot at Hawthorne. Colin froze momentarily at the gate as he showed his ID. It was as if all his systems simply stopped functioning for a few seconds. Not because he was nervous. Not because he was scared.

He didn't feel either of those emotions.

Instead, astonishment gripped him.

He was amazed that the woman who had given birth to him had lived eighteen years behind this fence, past that barbed wire, beyond the concrete walls.

Ryan had told him that today was a visiting day, but Dora Prince wasn't expecting them. Colin wasn't here for her, though, or for the investigation. He didn't come to question her, or obtain evidence. He had nothing to ask her. That wasn't his job. That wasn't his role.

He was here for the healing.

As much as he'd tried to dismiss Elle's suggestion, it had hovered at the front of his brain for the last week. To keep moving forward in his life, whether with Elle or without her, he had another step to take.

Recovery was a daily practice. It didn't end. He would always be unfinished, but this was part of coming to peace with his unfinished self.

Before they entered the visiting room he turned to Marcus and said, "Bet you didn't think you'd be here with me visiting our mom today, did you?"

Marcus shook his head. "Nope. But is it weird to say I'm glad we're here?"

Colin managed a small smile. "It's not. Let's go see her."

"Let's do it," Marcus echoed as they entered the cold, concrete visiting room.

A minute later, a woman in orange walked through the door, a corrections officer at her side.

Colin felt nothing and he felt everything.

She was the woman who'd raised him for thirteen years, and she was the woman he'd hated for eighteen years. She was the murderer and the mother. She was everything he never wanted to be, and then he'd become like her in ways he never wanted.

She was a prisoner, and she was a human being. One who still felt emotions, because oceans poured from her eyes, and they were tears of joy, as if all she'd ever wanted was to see her kids.

Despite all his efforts to remain stoic, a lump rose in his throat.

"My babies," she said, crossing the distance in a nanosecond and wrapping her two youngest kids in the strangest hug Colin had ever experienced. That was no small feat for her to hug two men, considering both towered over her tiny frame. "My babies, my babies, my babies," she sobbed.

She couldn't stop weeping, or saying their names.

Eventually, the corrections officer made her let go. The front of Colin's shirt was wet from her tears.

"Colin," she said with a crazed kind of joy as she looked at him. Then, she shifted her gaze. "Marcus."

"Hi," Marcus said, and his voice seemed horribly dry as he added, "Mom."

Colin couldn't bring himself to call her that. But he had something else to say to her. He clapped Marcus on the shoulder and met his mother's eyes.

"You don't have to worry about Marcus anymore, because he has brothers and a sister who will look out for him. He has a good family on the outside. And I want you to know we're going to do everything we can for him. He's part of us." He swallowed, and raised his chin up high, girding himself for the hardest part of the visit. For the reason he drove to the prison for the first time in years.

A piece of his heart had been metal, an alloy of shame and guilt. With words like a scalpel, he cut it from his body. "Because I'm a good man," he said, letting go of the hate, letting it crumble to the ground. It couldn't weigh him down any longer. "I had a good father, and you have good kids. All of them."

Then, because it was the compassionate thing to do, he sat down with her and spent the next hour listening to her talk.

On the ride home, he and Marcus stopped for a burger, then John Winston called to give him the news he'd been waiting for.

CHAPTER THIRTY

Elle's heart still raced furiously. That had been a hell of a game of laser tag. It was made all the better by Colin's news.

She hung up and turned to her son as they walked toward the rental counter to return the laser tag equipment. "My text message stalker was arrested this morning."

Alex punched the air. "Yes! That is awesome."

"The cops got him on grand larceny. He stole two dozen iPhones."

Alex scoffed. "Androids are way better phones. Better games on them," he said, and Elle smiled because her son hadn't spiraled. He hadn't returned to the silent boy he was before. In fact, his temporary sullenness had ended last night when she arrived home—before she'd even told him she'd broken it off with Colin. She was glad that he'd come around *before* this news because it meant he was stronger than he'd been before—that he was finding the internal resources to deal with the highs and lows of life.

"Anyway, he's in jail now. Colin just talked to the detective who has been working on his father's case," she said, before they reached the counter.

Alex stopped in his tracks. "You said in the car the other day, when you were talking about the messages, that Colin was 'working on it.' What did you mean?" he asked, his voice softer now. He hadn't let her explain the other day; he hadn't wanted to listen. He wanted to now.

"He took it upon himself to find out who the guy was. He studied the texts, and he researched a number of possibilities as to who was sending them, and he used every tool at his disposal. Instagram, Facebook, and then good old-fashioned elbow grease. He pulled together clues from things people had said, from pictures he had seen, and when Lee Stefano posted again, Colin was ready, and he was able to track him down and give the info to the police."

Alex whistled in admiration. "That's impressive. That's some serious detective work."

She smiled, a burst of pride surging inside her over what Colin had done. "Yes. Yes it is." She shifted gears. She needed to talk to her son, to let him know that they were going to have to learn to roll with the punches and not always retreat. "I made a decision to stop seeing him when this got too complicated. I made a choice because you're my top priority and you always will be. But I also want you to know that I won't always be able to step back. In this case, it was a choice I *could* make. But there will be other times when we have to go into the fire. When we have to face it and walk through it and be strong. I know you have it in you," she said, wrapping her hand around his arm and squeezing.

He nodded solemnly. "I can handle it. I'm sorry I flipped out."

"There's no need to be sorry. You did nothing wrong. But I want you to know, too, that whatever challenges come our way, we'll tackle them together."

"Hmmm," Alex mused as they headed to the arcade gallery.

"Hmmm what?"

"That's pretty cool," Alex said, like an admission. His voice was deeper now; it had officially changed.

She furrowed her brow. "What's cool?"

"That Colin did that for you. That he didn't stop until he'd solved the problem. Dad was never like that. He didn't solve problems. He only caused them."

She looped an arm around him, her heart lighting up. "Colin didn't just do it for me. Or for us. He did it because it was the right thing to do. He's that kind of a guy."

"You miss him, don't you?"

She gave him a noogie. "You're too observant for your own good." She pointed to the motorcycle game. "Let's go kick some ass on the road."

* * *

John Winston removed his shades when he spotted the young man waiting at a picnic table in the park. Though it was a Sunday morning, the park was quiet, and the picnic tables were far enough away from the playground for a private conversation. Marcus had said he didn't want to meet at his apartment or at the store where he worked, and not anyplace where someone might see him. John had chosen a park thirty minutes outside of Vegas.

The teen sat on the table itself, head down, tapping away on his phone. When John reached him, he noticed the kid was swiping pages in a book.

"Thanks for meeting me," John said.

"Thanks for meeting me here."

John took a seat next to him on top of the green slatted wood of the table.

"So you arrested Lee Stefano yesterday?"

John nodded. "My guys found him Saturday morning at his place. Same place that was tagged in the photos," he said. It was almost as if the thief wanted to be taken in. Or more likely, that he wanted his "Sinner Stripes," as they were called. Stefano's son wanted to be able to say he served time, like his dad. Now that John had him in custody, he was hoping Lee would talk. Would tell him more about T.J. and Kenny. Tell him where to find them. John Winston wanted nothing more than to see those two men behind bars for the rest of their lives, and Stefano's son might very well be the linchpin to making that happen. Lee's mother was the one who'd tipped off the cops in the first place about the role T.J. and Kenny had played in the murder of Thomas Paige two decades ago.

That was their first accessory to murder.

Didn't seem to have been their last.

John's blood boiled over the evidence he'd amassed linking those two men to other crimes, and more unsolved murders. By all accounts, T.J. Nelson had embraced his job as the broker of Stefano's hits, working with other gunmen over the years that followed, taking his role as the planner and plotter to a new level. He was the man pulling the strings on hits for the Sinners, and Kenny was his right-hand guy. John was determined to find them, especially since he'd learned that T.J. had had words with Thomas Paige several weeks before the man was killed. John was talking to other witnesses later today who knew more about that encounter, and he fiercely hoped he'd be able to link all the details together and track down the Nelson cousins.

They were tough to nab. Harder to find. They'd earned some kind of protection from their brothers in the gang. Some of that protection had come in the form of Lee Stefano trying to keep Marcus quiet by intimidating the social worker he'd been confiding in. John wasn't one hundred percent sure why those men wanted Marcus's mouth zipped, but he had a few good leads. Marcus was untouchable; they'd never hurt him. But they needed him to keep their secrets quiet, so they'd tried to shut him down.

John, however, needed Marcus to talk. He believed that Marcus knew more than he'd told him when they met a week ago.

"Is Lee going to leave Elle alone now?" Marcus asked.

Maybe the threat to someone he cared about would push him into talking finally. "Yes, we've got him. And I think we can get him to give up some info on Kenny and T.J."

"What about my stepmom, though? Will they leave her alone?"

John arched an eyebrow. This was news to him. "Someone sending her harassing messages, too?"

Marcus nodded, his young eyes etched with worry. "I saw her a few days ago, at Baskin Robbins with my little sisters. I overheard her talking on the phone. I think she's worried that those guys are going after her."

"To make sure your dad stays quiet about all that he knows about the murder of Thomas Paige?" John asked, hoping Marcus would finally give him an answer.

Ever since John had uncovered the details of Dora Prince's drug trade—that the woman was a dealer, Stefano was her supplier, and she sold to the Nelson cousins and many, many others—he was sure that her ex-lover had intel about the business she'd been in. Luke claimed he met Dora at Narcotics Anonymous, but John wasn't convinced that's how the affair began. Nor did he buy that Luke's hands were clean. Because as John saw it, Dora Prince planned the murder of her husband to get his life insurance money so she could run away with her kids and her lover.

Luke had to know *something* about the murder. Especially given the leads John was chasing down about him.

And if someone was trying to shake down Marcus's stepmom now, well, that only bolstered John's belief that Luke was keeping quiet.

Just like his son was.

But the son was here. Marcus was trying. He just needed to feel safe.

"I can protect you," John said calmly. "I can protect her. That's what I do."

Marcus hung his head, exhaled, then lifted his face and met John's eyes. He started talking, and holy hell-of-a-secret, this was the mother lode. This was the golden goose of information.

CHAPTER THIRTY-ONE

"Are you sure? Absolutely sure?" Colin asked as he loaded his climbing gear into the trunk of his car, his phone pressed to his ear.

"One hundred percent."

"You know for certain this is what she wants now? That she's ready?" he asked, as Rex tossed his carabiners and ropes in next. He'd joined Colin today, to make his first climb.

"Yes. Trust me."

"I do. But this is a big deal. I want to know this is definitely what she wants."

"Aren't you the guy who takes risks all the time?"

"At work, yes. At play, yes. Right now, though? I want to know this is a sure thing if you're asking me to show up for her," he said as he locked the trunk.

"You make her happy. I want her to be happy. It's that simple."

"See you later then," he said, then ended the call.

Rex shoved his shoulder. "Hello? You said yes, didn't you? You better have."

Colin narrowed his eyes. "Did you know he was calling me?"

"No, but I heard your end of the conversation. It didn't take any of my new math skills to figure it out." Rex walked around to the passenger side, grabbed the door handle, and yanked it open.

Colin got into the driver's side and turned on the engine. He was quiet, contemplating the phone call that had come out of the blue.

"You gonna go see her now?" Rex asked, picking up the thread.

Colin glanced at the time on the dashboard. "She'll only be there for a little longer."

Rex held his arms out grandly. "Then you better step on it, man. Because you need to make a big-ass entrance."

Colin scoffed. "I don't think so."

Rex nodded. "Oh, trust me on this. You might know math and outdoor shit, but I know women. They love all that grandiose stuff."

"Do they now?" Colin asked with a wry smile as they headed back to town.

"Absolutely. What does she like? What are her favorite things?"

Things he couldn't give her right now.

Tattoos. Neck kisses. Multiple orgasms.

Wait. He could definitely give her those. Hell, he could give her enough of those to keep her toes curled all night long.

"Mob movies. Roller-skating. Laughing. Time with her family. Giving back," he said, detailing what he knew of the woman he loved.

Rex counted off on his fingers. "Take her to a Holly-wood movie set. Buy her a roller rink. Tell her a dirty joke," he began, and Colin cracked up as Rex continued working through his list.

But then, he had an idea.

* * *

She longed to be the one sending Janine racing around the curve. She craved the rush of the wheels, the speed of the chase, the vibrations of the music in her bones. Instead, she cupped her hands over her mouth and shouted her encouragement from the half-wall at the edge of the rink.

"C'mon!"

"Block her!"

"Go, Cool Hand Bette!"

She screamed and cheered the loudest from the side-lines, rooting on the Fishnet Brigade. The league championship was in their grasp. Just a few more points. Just a few more minutes.

"Bet you twenty bucks they win, even without their best player."

That voice. It sent goose bumps over her skin. It lit up her chest. All her lady parts tingled.

She turned around. Her heart skipped, and her skin sizzled. She was fighting a losing battle if she even tried to pretend she wasn't ready to fling herself at him, or climb him like a tree. Especially with him here at the roller rink, wearing shorts and a T-shirt, his tanned, inked arms on display, his dark eyes sparkling like he had a secret.

"I bet they win, too," she said, and her heart beat fiercely against her ribs.

"You know," he said, taking his time with the words as he inched closer, "if they do, we should celebrate."

Celebrate.

Heat raced through her body. Sparks roared through her. A celebration with Colin Sloan was code for the most mind-blowing sex of her life. But it was also code for so much more. It was how they'd spent their night together at the Venetian, and that evening had sent them hurtling down this twisting, turning path to lust, longing, and love.

Wait.

She pressed her foot on the figurative brakes. She couldn't leap back into his arms just because he showed up. They'd agreed to take a break. She'd retreated because of her son. He was her top priority and would be until he left her home. But she didn't have to shelter him, either. She couldn't shield him from all the dangers of the world by shutting out love. She could, however, teach him about taking a chance. Taking the *right* chance, with the right person. Seizing the opportunity.

She'd cooled things off with Colin because of her need to protect her kid. The threat had never been about Colin though. It had been because of her work, because of what she did, because she was *involved*. That wasn't going to change. The one thing she could adjust was her approach.

Including her approach to Alex. She needed to tell him she was going to take this chance.

She held up her finger. "I just need to find—"

A hand touched on her arm—her son's hand. "I thought you were playing pool with your buddies," she said, gesturing to the pool table at the rink.

"I was, but I wanted to let you know I called Colin and asked him to come down."

"You did?"

He nodded, and he looked proud of himself. "I'm sorry I freaked out the other day."

"It's okay to freak out sometimes. I was freaked out, too," she said, fighting to stay calm, even though every cell inside her buzzed with elation. Her son, her sweet, wonderful son, had made this reunion happen.

"But I don't want you to worry and think I'm gonna turn into a basket case," Alex said. "I'll probably freak out again over something else. But I'm also stronger than I was before. Because I have an awesome mom, and I want her to be happy."

Her son clasped her in a hug, and there was no point in fighting back the tears. She let them flow. She let them fall. She let herself feel everything.

"You're titanium," he said, just to her, and another surge of tears streaked down her cheeks. "And I'm glad you met someone you like."

"And I'm glad you realized you're strong inside. That you can handle things. That's what I was telling you at laser tag. You've come far, and I'm proud of you."

He broke the hug and tipped his head to his group of friends. "So, um, I'll stay at Aunt Camille's tonight, and you guys can…" He pointed from Colin to his mom, and she got his drift. She was glad he couldn't say it. She wanted him to be fourteen. To embrace all that it meant to be young. "Whatever. You know what I mean."

"I do," she said, a wild grin on her face.

He walked off to join his friends, and she returned her focus to the man who stood in front of her at the Skyway roller rink. The music blasted from the DJ booth, the crowds cheered, and the soundtrack of arcade games and pool, of sodas fizzing, and of skates whipping around the oval, surrounded them.

"Hi," she said.

"Hi. I went to prison yesterday."

She arched an eyebrow, not computing at first. Then it hit her. "You did?"

He nodded. "Yes. This woman told me she thought it would be a good idea."

"Did she?" she asked, playing along now. "Sounds like a smart lady."

He nodded as he grasped her hips in his hands, curling his fingers into her. "She's amazing. And she always knows exactly what I need. She pushes me in ways I need to be pushed, and she lets me give to her in ways I want to give."

"How do you like to give?" she asked as his fingers traveled up her waist, his touch setting her on fire.

He inched closer, molding his body to hers. "I like to give her pleasure. I like to give her love. I want to give her reason to trust that I'm the kind of man she can lean on."

She laced her hands in his hair. "Oh, Colin. I know that. You are the best man I've ever known," she said, and her heart was full nearly to bursting with a piercing, rich kind of joy. But somewhere in the back of her mind, her worries still lived and they needed to be voiced. They were different, though, than what she first thought they'd be.

"I missed you like crazy. It was only a few days, but I don't care. The way I feel about you isn't rational; it isn't logical. But it's so real. And it's so true," she said, dropping her hands to his chest and gripping the fabric of his shirt. "And I need you to know that I'm going to do everything I can to balance it all. You, and Alex, and being a mom, and work. And not get scared."

She stopped talking as his lips quirked up, and he simply smiled, just as if he was madly in love with her. "It's okay," he said. "You don't have to have it all figured out. You don't have to be fearless all the time. Just be with me."

"I want to be with you. I want to be fearlessly in love with you." She tugged him to her, not caring that her team was circling the rink behind her, barely thinking about the crowds around them, only feeling this immeasurable closeness with this man. "And I am."

He groaned and brought his lips to her neck. Instantly, a flurry of delicious tingles flared over her skin. "I can't resist kissing you. Pretty soon I'm not going to be able to resist fucking you," he whispered.

It was her turn to moan. To murmur. To let him know she wanted his resistance broken down...but not quite yet.

She pressed her hand to his chest. "We should have the place to ourselves in about an hour, if you'd like."

"If I'd like?" he asked, wiggling his eyebrows. "If I'd like what? Tell me, Elle. What are you asking?"

She shot him a sexy grin. "To celebrate. Celebrate with me."

He dipped his hand into the pocket of his shorts. "If you wear these, I will."

He dangled a long pair of socks in front of her. They were red with *V*s of illustrated birds on them. "Holy shit," she said and grabbed them. "Where did you get them?"

"My soon-to-be-sister-in-law knows how to find *anything* on the Strip. So she found a store for me that sells all kinds of socks."

She clutched them to her chest. "To some women, giving her socks would be like giving her a vacuum cleaner. I, however, am not one of those women."

He quirked up his lips and ran his finger along the outside of her thigh. "And I am one of those men for whom socks are a crazy turn-on."

CHAPTER THIRTY-TWO

The disco lights swirled in crazy-eight circles, and Elle raced around the rink, hot as fuck in her tight T-shirt, short skirt, and red socks. Bon Jovi blasted out of the sound system.

"Catch me if you can."

Oh hell. There was no way he was backing down from that challenge. He pushed harder and faster on his wheels, and soon enough he caught up with her, grabbing her waist and pulling her to the side of the rink.

Breathless, she laughed in his arms as "You Give Love a Bad Name" echoed around them.

"Hey, you're not even supposed to be skating for another week," he admonished her.

"No," she said, correcting him as she shook her head. "The doctor said *no contact sports.* Skating itself is fine."

"*Contact sports,*" he said, cupping her ass in his hands. "Seems you already violated that doctor's order a few times."

"Not enough though. Let's violate it again."

They had the rink to themselves. Camille had given Elle the key, and they were all alone, the game over and everyone cleared out.

Even though he'd never fucked her wearing skates before, he was confident he could pull it off because he was an athlete, a risk-taker, and a man madly in love with the woman he wanted. But maybe they'd move off the slick hardwood and onto the carpeted floor.

He threaded his fingers through her hair and kissed her —a hot, wet kiss that had her shuddering in his arms and rocking her hips into him in no time. She moaned as he deepened the kiss until their mouths tangled together and became nothing but a fevered, hungry prelude to hard sex.

He needed that. Needed to reclaim her. To take her. To own her. To feel her body move in tandem with his. He craved that kind of sex as a sign that this reconnection would last. He believed it in his heart, and now wanted to experience it in his bones.

He spun her around, a task made easier with her on skates. "Hands on the railing, Skater Girl," he growled, and she bent over in a perfectly glorious *L*. He inhaled sharply at the sight of her giving herself to him. She glanced back at him, licking her lips as he hiked up her skirt, then unzipped his shorts and pushed down his briefs.

"I missed all of you, including your cock," she purred. She was his dirty-mouthed woman. His filthy talker, and God, he loved all of her—dirty words, strong body, witty mind and gorgeous heart. "Take off your panties, and show me how much you missed me. I want to see how wet you are."

With one hand, she tugged down her pink panties to her knees, then she lifted her ass in the air and wiggled. His breath stopped as he stared at her beautiful body, ready for him. He grabbed her hips and sank into his heaven.

Then he picked up speed and fucked her by the railing as rockers sang anthems about love gone wrong. But there was no love gone wrong here. It was only right, only true, only real.

Soon she neared the edge, and called out his name as the disco ball cast silvery lights on the floor. Before he could join her on the other side of bliss, she said, "I want to turn around. I want to look at you."

"Then be prepared for me to give you another orgasm."

They switched to a new position as he lifted her onto the railing at the edge of the rink. She looped her arms around his neck. "I always knew," she whispered as he thrust into her.

"Always knew what?"

She grasped him tighter, pulled him closer, and tilted her chin. Her hazel eyes were full of so much love that he wasn't sure he could last much longer.

"That I'd find my way back to you," she said, and exhilaration tore through him. It sped through his body in a mad rush of savage ecstasy. He wanted her to find him always. He wanted to be her home.

"I'll always be here."

She was the only kind of intoxication he wanted anymore. He planned to stay hooked on her for all time.

She was the risk. She was the reward.

They came together once more.

* * *

Later she poured a lemonade from the tap at the snack stand.

"One virgin for you, sir," she said and slid a red and white paper cup across the Formica. "Since that's the only virgin you're getting."

He laughed and took a drink, then he set it down and laced his fingers through hers. "Hey. You think the bartender would go home with me tonight? I'll bring you back here to get your car tomorrow morning."

That sounded good to her, so she said yes as Foreigner's "Feels Like the First Time" played faintly in the background. As the chorus repeated, it hit her. Tonight would be her first night with him. She'd never stayed over. She wanted all these firsts with him, and all the lasts, too. She wanted this man with a fierceness she hadn't expected, and she was giving herself permission to feel it. To finally let herself have him. All of him, in all of her life.

"But do I have to get up at the crack of dawn when you go rock climbing or whatever crazy thing you have planned for tomorrow morning?"

"Only if you want to."

She did want to. She wanted to make good on a wish she'd made. She wanted to turn a one-time maybe into a full-on yes.

The next morning, she asked him to take her kayaking.

Maybe some days you'll want to kayak and some days you won't, and whatever you want is fine by me.

The look in his dark eyes said that it was more than fine. That it was pure magic to share what he loved. And it became pure fun, too, when he taught her how to paddle in a kayak built for two. She didn't flip over, she didn't drown, and she didn't slice her head on a rock at the edge of the lake.

After they pulled the kayak out of the water, she sank down on the edge of the lake, enjoying the clear blue sky of an early morning on the outskirts of Vegas. He draped an arm around her, and she expected a kiss to come next—maybe even a kiss that would turn into outdoor sex on a kayak.

Instead, his voice was intensely serious. "Elle, do you want me to quit?"

"Quit?" she asked quizzically. "Quit what?"

"Doing the adventure sports? Not kayaking, but the ones you worry about more. The rock climbing, hang gliding, mountain bike riding, and the skiing?"

"Wait. You hang glide, too?" That was news to her.

He smiled widely. "No. I want to try it, though. But I know the sports worry you. I'll give it up for you."

Her eyes widened with shock, and her heart beat wildly as she soaked in the knowledge that he would give up something he loved madly for her. "You'd do that for me?"

He nodded, no questions asked. "I would. I don't want to cause any more stress in your life. I don't want you to live with that kind of fear."

Happiness rained down on her. Bliss spread from her chest to the tips of her fingers. The fact that he'd offered thrilled her. It delighted her to the ends of the earth and back. But she shook her head. "No. I don't want you to quit. I want you to go for it. I want to cheer you on. I want to be the first person you see when you cross the finish line at your triathlon later this month."

He exhaled deeply and smiled like she'd given him the greatest gift in the world—permission to do what he loved without fear. She'd still worry about him, but it wasn't her place to hold him back. She ran her hand over his hip.

Though he was clothed, she liked tracing the outline of his phoenix tattoo. For new beginnings. Like this one. "In fact, I was going to ask if you'd be interested in starting a climbing or kayaking group for the boys at the center. They never get to go, and I bet some would like to."

He arched an eyebrow. "I already took Rex yesterday. He loved it."

She nudged his elbow. "See? You don't have to give up something you love to be with me."

"I'm glad I don't have to, but I would," he said, running his hand through her hair then pulling her in for a quick kiss. "And I can't wait to cross the finish line and see you."

"I'll always be there."

EPILOGUE

Hot. Sweaty. Exhausted. Aching.

And elated.

Add in thrilled as the finish line came into view that hot Saturday afternoon in August, and he saw where Elle waved and cheered him on. He was overjoyed as he put one foot in front of the other, ceaselessly running until he nearly collapsed in her arms.

Nearly. But didn't.

He finished this one the way he wanted to, and even though every muscle screamed, and his throat cried out for water, he was flying high. So high, he lifted her up in his arms. She wrapped her legs around his waist and kissed him.

"You did it!"

"I did it."

There was no medal. There was no prize. There was no ranking. There was only this—the satisfaction of a job well done and the love of a good woman.

That was everything, and he wanted to share it with his family the next day. The crew joined him for a celebratory dinner at his house—Brent and Shannon, Ryan and Sophie, Elle and Alex, Michael and his grandparents, as well as Marcus, Rex, and Tyler. The boys seemed to travel in a pack, and Colin was glad that Marcus had such good friends—friends who were also good guys.

Marcus had more than that. He had his new family, too, and he'd been spending more time here at Colin's house, crashing from time to time at night when he had class the next morning, since his school was nearby. But he hadn't been himself for the last few weeks. Not since they'd visited their mom in Hawthorne. He'd seemed remote, nervous even, spending more time clutching his phone as if he were waiting for a dreaded call to arrive.

Colin had asked a few times about his mood, and if he wanted to talk. Marcus always shook his head and said no. Colin tried again that evening after everyone left and the two of them were straightening up in the kitchen.

"What's going on? College harder than you thought?"

"No. It's fine," Marcus said as he loaded a plate in the dishwasher.

"Is it work?"

His phone rang. With the speed of a cheetah, Marcus whipped his cell from his back pocket. He glanced at the screen and answered immediately. Colin didn't even see the name or the number.

"Hey."

A pause. Colin tried to tune in to the conversation, though he knew he shouldn't. Still, he was damn curious, especially since the caller sounded a hell of a lot like Detective John Winston.

"Holy shit. That's fucking amazing," Marcus said, and the sullenness vanished. It was replaced by something that looked and sounded like jubilation. Marcus ran a hand through his hair and exhaled like he'd been holding ten thousand breaths. "Tonight? You arrested him tonight?"

Colin straightened, set down the dishtowel, and mouthed *who?* Anticipation barreled through him as he zeroed in on Marcus.

"Yes. I can talk. I'm at Colin's house." Marcus covered the phone and said, "Can John come over?"

"Um. Yeah. Obviously," he said, then made a rolling gesture with his hands. *Hurry up and tell me.*

When Marcus hung up, Colin parked his hands on his hips. "What's going on? Who was arrested?"

"Kenny Nelson."

Colin punched the air. "Yes. Fuck yes!"

"The cops have him in custody now," Marcus added, and he'd become the very embodiment of relief. Then his expression shifted once more. "But it's not over. T.J. Nelson is still at large."

"They'll find him, too," Colin said as excitement consumed him. This was huge. This was a big break, and he couldn't wait to tell his brothers and sister and grandmother...

Wait.

"Why did John call you? Why is he coming over here?" Colin asked, curiosity taking over. Something didn't add up. Some piece was missing.

The sullen Marcus briefly resurfaced, but he let go of it in seconds, pushing past it. "I've been helping the detective for two weeks now. Helping him with the case."

"How?"

Marcus squeezed his eyes shut then opened them. "My father."

Colin tensed all over. "What about him?"

"He was involved."

His jaw dropped. His blood chilled. "How? How was he involved?"

Marcus swallowed then words rained forth. "There are things I know about my dad. He *is* a piano teacher. But he's much more. So are the Royal Sinners. They're a street gang, but they're powerful. They have friends in high places. And my dad is one of them. He's so far inside that hardly anyone knows who he really is, or that he's starting to lose control of some of his men. Like Kenny and T.J."

"Your dad works with them?"

"My father is the head of the Royal Sinners."

THE END

Stay tuned for the final novel in the Sinful Nights series— SINFUL LOVE! Michael Sloan's love story will take your breath away in the stunning conclusion to the Sloan family saga! SINFUL LOVE releases in March 2016 and can be preordered now!

Want to be the first to hear about new releases, pre-orders and newsletter only special deals? Then, please sign up for my newsletter. It's fun!

laurenblakely.com/newsletter

COMING SOON!

After Sinful Love, I have many more books for you! Here's a sneak peek at other new releases in 2016! Big Rock, Mister Orgasm and The Sapphire Affair!

BIG ROCK

A sexy, dirty standalone novel coming in 2016

It's not just the motion of the ocean, ladies. It's definitely the SIZE of the boat too.

And I've got both firing on all cylinders. In fact, I have ALL the right assets. Looks, brains, my own money, and a big cock.

You might think I'm an asshole. I sound like one, don't I? I'm hot as sin, rich as heaven, smart as hell and hung like a horse.

Guess what? You haven't heard my story before. Sure, I might be a playboy, like the NY gossip rags call me. But I'm the playboy who's actually a great guy. Which makes me one of a kind.

The only trouble is, my dad needs me to cool it for a bit. With conservative investors in town wanting to buy his flagship Fifth Avenue jewelry store, he needs me not only to zip it up, but to look the part of the committed guy. Fine. I can do this for Dad. After all, I've got him to thank for the family jewels. So I ask my best friend and business partner to be my fiancée for the next week. Charlotte's up for it. She has her own reasons for saying yes to wearing this big rock.

And pretty soon all this playing pretend in public leads to no pretending whatsoever in the bedroom, because she just can't fake the kind of toe-curling, window-shattering orgasmic cries she makes as I take her to new heights between the sheets.

But I can't seem to fake that I might be feeling something real for her.

What the fuck have I gotten myself into with this...big rock?

To be notified when Big Rock becomes available, **please sign up for my newsletter: laurenblakely.com/newsletter**

MISTER ORGASM

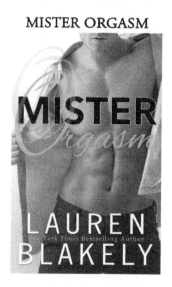

Just call me Mr. Orgasm. No, really. I insist.

Orgasms are my specialty. Delivering them. Administering them. Giving them in multiples. Then doing it again for an encore. I'm like the superhero of pleasure.

But before anyone gets all up in a lather about my "manwhore ways," remember this. You probably didn't even look at me years ago. You likely didn't give me the time of day when I was the quiet geek bent over his notebook drawing cartoons about a caped crusader bestowing orgasmic pleasure to womankind.

Now, that I'm creator of the hottest animated TV show in the world — The Adventures of Mr. Orgasm — everything has changed. The women have lined up. The checks roll in. And the life I'm living is gooooooood — looks, talent, and a masterful dong have gotten me far.

There's only one thing in my way — the woman I took home last night has turned out to be my new boss.

Oops.

Looks like the Adventures of Mr. Orgasm have only just begun...

To be notified when MISTER ORGASM becomes available, **please sign up for my newsletter: laurenblakely.com/newsletter**

THE SAPPHIRE AFFAIR

The Sapphire Affair is a two-book series about a sexy, high-end bounty hunter hired to find stolen jewels, and the only thing in his way is a gorgeous and adventurous woman who's after them too...

Both books should be available for preorder soon! Get ready for a sexy, witty, suspenseful, contemporary romance with shades of mystery and crime — Seductive Nights meets the Thomas Crowne Affair.

To be notified when The Sapphire Affair becomes available, **please sign up for my newsletter: laurenblakely.com/newsletter**

Check out my contemporary romance novels!

The New York Times and USA Today
Bestselling Seductive Nights series including
Night After Night, After This Night,
and *One More Night*

And the two standalone romance novels,
Nights With Him and *Forbidden Nights*, both
New York Times and USA Today Bestsellers!

Sweet Sinful Nights and *Sinful Desire*,
the first two books in the New York Times
Bestselling high-heat romantic suspense
series that spins off from Seductive Nights!

Playing With Her Heart, a USA Today
bestseller, and a sexy Seductive Nights spin-off
standalone! (Davis and Jill's romance)

21 Stolen Kisses, the USA Today
Bestselling forbidden new adult romance!

Caught Up In Us, a New York Times and
USA Today Bestseller! (Kat and Bryan's romance!)

Pretending He's Mine, a Barnes & Noble and
iBooks Bestseller! (Reeve & Sutton's romance)

Trophy Husband, a New York Times and
USA Today Bestseller! (Chris & McKenna's romance)

Far Too Tempting, an Amazon
romance bestseller! (Matthew and Jane's romance)

Stars in Their Eyes, an iBooks bestseller!
(William and Jess' romance)

My USA Today bestselling
No Regrets series that includes

The Thrill of It
(Meet Harley and Trey)

and its sequel

Every Second With You

My New York Times and USA Today
Bestselling Fighting Fire series that includes

Burn For Me
(Smith and Jamie's romance!)

Melt for Him
(Megan and Becker's romance!)

and *Consumed by You*
(Travis and Cara's romance!)

ACKNOWLEDGEMENTS

Thank you so much to all the fabulous people who played a role in this book getting in your hands. I am immensely grateful to Sarah Hansen, Steph Bowers, Jesse Gordon, Kara Hildebrand, Kelley Jefferson, KP Simmon, Jen McCoy, Kim Bias, Helen Williams, and Lauren McKellar, among many others. Thank you to the amazing bloggers and reviewers who spread the word and share their love, to the readers who make everything possible, to my author friends who keep me sane, and to my family who I love dearly. Thank you to my dogs! Love, hugs and kisses to all of you. You are beautiful.

CPSIA information can be obtained at www.ICGtesting.com
Printed in the USA
BVOW06s0126071215

429550BV00013B/167/P

CONTACT

I love hearing from readers! You can find me on Twitter at LaurenBlakely3, or Facebook at LaurenBlakelyBooks, or online at LaurenBlakely.com. You can also email me at laurenblakelybooks@gmail.com.